Judy Finnigan is a bestselling author, television presenter and columnist. In 2004, Judy's name became synonymous with discovering and sharing great fiction, through the Richard and Judy Book Club, where authors including Kate Mosse, Rosamund Lupton and Victoria Hislop were championed and brought to the attention of millions of readers. Her first novel, *Eloise*, was a *Sunday Times* Top Ten bestseller in both hardback and paperback.

Judy Finnigan

I Do Not Sleep

sphere

SPHERE

First published in Great Britain in 2015 by Sphere
This paperback edition published in 2015 by Sphere

3 5 7 9 10 8 6 4 2

A CIP catalogue record for this book
is available from the British Library.

ISBN 978-0-7515-4865-5

Typeset in Bembo by M Rules
Printed and bound in Great Britain by
Clays Ltd, St Ives plc

Papers used by Sphere are from well-managed forests
and other responsible sources.

MIX
Paper from
responsible sources
FSC® C104740

Sphere
An imprint of
Little, Brown Book Group
Carmelite House
50 Victoria Embankment
London EC4Y 0DZ

An Hachette UK Company
www.hachette.co.uk

www.littlebrown.co.uk

For my much-loved children:

Tom, Dan, Jack and Chloe

And also for our latest family addition:

Darling little

Ivy

Do not stand at my grave and weep;
I am not there. I do not sleep.
I am a thousand winds that blow.
I am the diamond glints on snow ...
Do not stand at my grave and cry;
I am not there. I did not die.

MARY ELIZABETH FRYE,

1932, BALTIMORE, USA.

The Island

The Island of St Michael of Lammana has been lashed by vicious seas since prehistoric times, and only eighteen feet below the windswept surface legend says there is a complex network of ancient caves. There are scores of them, and they are evidently man-made, dating from the very early Etruscan period, two and a half thousand years ago. To this day the ancient lore holds sway, and the caves guard their dark secrets undisturbed. Who knows what lies beneath the stunted woods and rocks that litter this inhospitable and unwelcoming little sanctuary? Because, however unlikely, a sanctuary it was for eleventh-century Christians. They believed the island was holy and built a chapel there around the year AD 1085. A cell of Benedictine monks, affiliated to Glastonbury Abbey, dwelt continuously on Lammana, sometimes numbering only two because living there was almost impossible, so harsh was the environment. The frequent storms were unpredictable, ripping across the tiny island (only a mile in circumference) and if you were out on one of the many treacherous footpaths when the gales were unleashed, you were in grave danger of being swept onto the rocks below. And the tides were turbulent. Many were the drownings around Lammana; not least those of the fishermen who bravely plied their trade, battling through cruel and monstrous storm-tossed waves, desperate, terrified but driven by the need to put food in their children's mouths, before, defeated, they perished, their boats run aground on the sandbar lying hidden beneath the sea.

So, for the most part, Lammana was unreachable except in the rarest, fairest weather. The rest of the time people stayed away, safe in Looe, despite the siren call that sighed softly across the water when conditions were clement, the sun shone, and (viewed across the short distance which separates the island from Hannafore) the magic mysterious vista of this most ancient place was at its most seductive. Some could not resist its charmed spell. Often they did not return; and the legend of Lammana was born. *Stay away, stay away*, the wind whispered. *Do not come here, traveller. You are not welcome. This sanctuary is a chimera. You may think you see a glimpse of paradise, but paradise is lost, and you shall surely risk the inferno if you attempt to regain it here.*

Prologue

May, Cornwall, 2009

Molly walked along the coastal path, head down, oblivious to the beauty of the day, the singing surf, the call of the gulls, the sheep dotting the coarse green grass. She always kept her head down on this walk, determined not to feel any pleasure in her surroundings, as if she were afraid of being moved by the loveliness of this place. She had armoured herself against enjoyment; there was no longer any of that to be had in her soul, and should any momentary surge of joy caused by the brisk salty beauty of the footpath touch her heart, she regarded it as a betrayal. Besides, it made her cry, and she'd done enough of that for a lifetime.

No, this pilgrimage was not a pleasure, it was a grim necessity. She did it every day; it was an hour's walk along the coastal path to get from her rented cottage in Polperro down to Talland Bay and then on along to Looe, until she reached the spot. Only then would she lift her head, only then when she knew what she would see: the island. This was the whole point of her journey; this view had become the whole point of her life.

She stood, every day, never sitting down on the nearby grass. She never brought a drink, or anything to eat. She just stared steadily at the wooded green contours of the island, so close to the mainland yet so remote and secret, cut off for weeks at a time by roaring seas, treacherous riptides, and the terrifying sandbar between the foreshore and Looe Harbour, where so many fishing boats had come to grief.

People watched her, of course. Tourists passed with questioning looks. The locals who walked the path had stopped trying to approach her. Instead they shrugged and whispered in the shops in Looe.

'That poor woman,' they said. 'It's terrible what happened; she seems to be losing her mind.'

And she stood, watching, motionless except for her hands. They never stopped moving, winding themselves incessantly through the folds of a thick woollen scarf. Joey's favourite, left behind in the cottage. Red, vibrant, the colour of life.

And afterwards, the punctured colour of death.

Chapter One

Five Years Later

Adam glanced over at me as he overtook a battered old Transit van on the A38. We'd passed Exeter, which meant there was less than an hour to go to get to Treworgey. He smiled hopefully at me, willing me to feel happy, or at least positive. I saw his look, did my best to smile back. At least we weren't going to Polperro. At least we were staying slightly inland, at a farmhouse in the Looe Valley, with beautiful views; we knew the place well, having stayed at the old homestead many times when the children were small. I remembered Joey and Daniel, careering down the slope beside the house on their skateboards; how Danny had broken his arm riding his bike round a treacherous bend in the lane, which the family ever after called Broken Arm Corner; how Adam took him to Derriford Hospital in Plymouth; and how ridiculously proud Danny had been when they arrived back at Treworgey with his arm in plaster and a sling. I really did allow myself to smile as I thought of Danny's self-important face and his little brother's woebegone look as he realised his sibling had trumped him in the stakes of parental concern.

That was then.

Way back then, when Danny's silly little accident had seemed so dramatic. Before the clouds collapsed and obscured the ocean, shrouding it in fog; before the seas swelled into the monstrous wall that engulfed my youngest child, swallowed him down into the oh-so-familiar story of Cornish tragedy, the accident from which there was no way back. Ever. No plaster, no sling could cure this. There was no body, even. Nothing left to mourn except an absence, a space; a gap that would never be filled.

Adam looked in his mirror. 'They're right behind us,' he told me with a reassuring grin. This time, I gave my husband a look of genuine relief, because in the black Peugeot which followed our Volvo Estate was all that remained of our little family: Danny, Lola, and, most precious of all, Edie, my shining light, the only purely good and wonderful thing that had happened to me since Joey's disappearance. I still used that word because I found it almost impossible to think of him as dead. Adam and I had had a blazing row about it two months ago when he told me he'd booked our old cottage for the summer.

'How could you?' I'd asked. 'How could you try to make me go to Cornwall on HOLIDAY, for Christ's sake? I can't believe you've done this. Wild horses wouldn't drag me down there, ever again.'

Adam had put his hands on my shoulders and looked me steadily in the eyes. 'I've done it for us, Molly – and for Danny. He wants to come with us; he says it's unhealthy for us all to pretend that Cornwall doesn't exist. Before Joey died . . . ' I flinched. Adam felt the tremor, but his voice stayed firm. 'Before Joey died, we went to Cornwall as a family every single summer.

Danny misses it, and he wants to take Edie there, let her play on the beach.'

'There's nothing to stop Danny going back. Without us.'

'Yes there is. You.'

'What are you talking about?'

'Danny won't go back to Cornwall without you. Don't you see? He needs your permission. He told me he was terrified of hurting you by taking Lola and the baby down by themselves. And so I thought about it. Believe me, Molly, I thought about it for a long time. I was frightened of telling you, I knew you'd be upset, but in the end I made a decision. And that was to risk your anger and book it anyway. It's not as if it's in Polperro, where Joey ... died. You don't have to get up and look at the harbour every day. We'll be at Coombe, which is sheltered and which we always loved so much. Where the boys were happy.' His voice softened. 'Do you remember how they used to try and round up the sheep? The farmer got furious, and we had to buy him a beer to placate him. And remember how Joey used to ride the family pig? And how they both adored the horses?'

Of course I remembered. Didn't Adam understand how agonising those memories were? I started crying, the happy memories blending with my ache for Joey. Adam folded me into his arms. 'Don't, darling. Don't. Look, I think Danny's right. We have to do this for him. Danny misses him desperately too. But now he's married, he has a baby. He needs to move on, live his life. And, Molly, so do we. We have a grandchild now, hopefully the first of several.' I smiled at this. 'We have a future; we have a long life to look forward to. And this is the first step. If it doesn't work, if you really are terribly unhappy there, we'll come back home and I promise you I won't ever ask you to go back to Cornwall again. But never going back there won't bring Joey back. And we'll be sacrificing so many happy memories if we don't ever go there again; it's special, you know that. Cornwall is part of our family history, a precious place for us. It will always be in our hearts. We have to reclaim that happiness, because it's real, it's what happened. Molly, you simply have to accept what's happened to Joey. For all our sakes, you can't be in denial any longer.'

In denial. He was right. I was. And I still wasn't ready to let Joey go. But Adam was persuasive; he'd convinced me, and against my better judgement I found myself speeding down the A38.

Chapter Two

As Adam drove, I remembered the night a year ago, when my granddaughter Edie was born. How Danny wept in my arms. 'God knows I'm happy, Mum, I'm so happy, but I just wish Joe were here to see the baby. My little brother ... he would have loved her so much.' I had comforted him, had tried to tell him not to feel guilty and accept that this new life was a miracle, her birth an occasion of great joy, that she was sent to heal us. And I truly meant it; I did feel deeply delighted, as if life had given us, our family, another chance.

Adam swung left into the driveway at Coombe at the

last minute. The lovely old greystone house is hidden from the lane, and after so many years – thirteen now – since we were last there he had forgotten its exact location. But when he saw the open gate with the handwritten sign reading *Mr and Mrs Gabriel and Family*, he swung the car, followed by Danny and Lola, into the picturesque courtyard in front of the house – where we were immediately astonished, as always, by the perennial lushness of the white climbing roses encircling the porch.

I took a deep breath. *This is going to be hard*, I thought, my mind immediately enslaved by pictures of Danny and Joey as toddlers, feeding the ducks in the pond behind the house, squabbling outside in the embers of evening about who should have the first bath before bed.

But then Danny opened the Peugeot's door and lifted Edie out of her car seat. Lola followed with a huge smile. 'Molly, this is so perfect,' she said. 'I've never seen such a pretty house.'

And I looked again at Coombe, and saw it as I had that first year we all came down on impulse, when Joey was only two and Danny five. I remembered my motherly misgivings, my fear that the longed-for perfect seaside holiday with our little sons would be spoiled by domestic glitches. No view, perhaps, or a shabby house and garden.

There was no need to worry. The place was impeccably kept back then, and it looked exactly the same now. And despite my reluctance about returning, my anxiety about my missing son, the fear that Joey's memory would haunt my days here in our old family paradise, I sighed with pleasure. Coombe was after all unsullied, a peaceful, lovely house, awaiting our return with quiet welcoming warmth. There was nothing strange about it – nothing dark, threatening or spooky.

I breathed again, and went to take Edie from my son. 'Look, Edie,' I whispered. 'It's fine. We're home. You'll come to love this place so much.'

Adam took the keys from the plant pot in which they were always left, opened the porch door, stepped across the grey slate floor leading to the hall, and, hesitantly, we all followed him.

We quickly settled in. There was a cosy wood fire in the sitting room, all set and ready to light, which we immediately did. Best of all, the owners had left a home-cooked three-course meal in the fridge. Chicken-liver pâté, freshly baked brown bread rolls, a delicious fish pie and apple crumble with cream. All we had to do was heat it up. It was so welcome, so unexpected, and so appreciated after our seven-hour drive down from Manchester, although now I remembered it had always been one of the great selling points of these lovely cottages at Treworgey: a daily delivery service of wholesome good food. All you had to do was call the farm kitchen in the morning. The owners of this little village of picturesquely restored holiday cottages were that thoughtful.

We ate the delicious supper, Edie barely awake but still cheerful in her high chair. She loved mealtimes; loved the sociability of eating with adults, playing with her food, offering it to us with grave infant generosity, teasing us by snatching it away again, chuckling with pleasure when she eventually gave in and let us chomp on her mashed potato and toast fingers.

She was in her tiny element, surrounded by grown-ups who obviously adored her; and so, suddenly, was I, briefly transported to a place where I actually forgot my grief. It was extraordinary, the hold Edie's presence had on me. I was entranced by her gummy smile, now punctuated with two tiny white teeth at the bottom. During that first evening at Coombe, I was completely focused on this miraculous baby, so much so that when I occasionally drifted back up to the surface to face who I actually was, a bereaved mother who had never even seen her missing son's body, I felt quite shocked. What was happening to me? Had I stopped being a mother, and become so besotted with my granddaughter that my pleasure in her had almost wiped out the grief of my terrible loss?

No. That was ridiculous. I was still locked in a fight to find Joey. His body was missing. The little boat he had been piloting had washed up ashore, with no clues about my boy's fate, how he could have vanished off the face of this earth, even given the treacherous seas of Cornwall. So five years on I was still bleeding. God knows I'd tried to carry on living. I was still working at a girls' school in Manchester, still trying to take pride in the pupils' achievements. I suppose some of our friends thought I had recovered. But I hadn't. I'd just been putting it off. Surviving, trying to keep my marriage intact.

But I always knew there would be a reckoning. I always knew I would have to come back and find him. And now Adam had forced my hand by bringing us all down here. He had meant it to heal me. But as I sat surrounded by my family, I knew this was my chance. I needed to know. I would find Joey; I would discover what had happened to my son. And I knew, without a shadow of a doubt, that somehow Edie would help me.

Chapter Three

I had taken a punt on this pretty little hamlet many years ago after seeing an enticing ad in *The Sunday Times*. We and our boys had loved it, cocooned as it was in the gentle Looe Valley, close to beautiful beaches and also to Polperro and the Land of Legend, a small but enchanting attraction depicting ancient Cornish myths, which had fascinated and terrified our sons in equal measure.

Although we were always happy at Coombe, as the boys grew older we began to rent cottages in Polperro instead. They were mad about boats and wanted to stay closer to the harbour. Adam had taken them on a sailing proficiency course, and in their teenage years we hardly saw them as they spent whole days at sea with friends who, like them, came back to Cornwall summer after summer. Their reunions were joyful, and while they often spent their evenings illicitly drinking 'smuggled' beer and cider on the little beach, we whiled away our time with the other parents, thoroughly enjoying wine and barbecues at each other's holiday cottages. We were a group of like-minded people from all over the country, mostly professionals, teachers like Adam and me, lawyers and doctors, all liberal enough to ignore the fact that our kids, who although well into their teens were still technically underage, were getting slightly tipsy with beer we had bought for them and left casually in the kitchen for them to 'sneak' out to their harbourside camp fires. The children never let us down, though. None of them ever got thoroughly sloshed. Our kids knew we were watching beady-eyed from our warren-like houses, clustered closely together round the harbour.

We were all devoted to Polperro. Other couples, our contemporaries, may have preferred to get together in the Algarve, Spain or Brittany, but we and our little summer circle stayed loyal to Cornwall.

Then, I had loved the place so much. I had felt our family history, small as it was, belonged here. I'd believed our lives would gain meaning here, and – ridiculous as it sounds, since none of us was Cornish-born – that somehow, our destiny would unfold in this mystical place. And of course that had proved all too true for my Joey. His destiny was here, all right. Vanished in our little paradise. And here I was again, so many years on, without the slightest clue about what had happened to my darling boy.

Chapter Four

I tried with all my being, all my soul, not to dream that first night at the cottage. I prayed that hideous thoughts would stay away; and for once someone listened. I had refused to believe in any kind of God since my son disappeared. There were no answers from Him in the desperate weeks and months before we gave up hope, not of finding him alive but at least of retrieving his body, something of Joey to wrap warmly in cashmere and lay gently inside a casket; a casket in which to place his favourite old cuddly toys, a casket to lie before the altar in Talland church, a tangible body to pray for and weep over. 'Hand it over to God,' said a well-meaning vicar friend when my grief became too much to bear. And I'd tried, but nothing came of it. Just silence. No news. Only the sympathetic words of the Coroner who told us that bodies often disappeared at sea and they were not always, as I had supposed, washed up ashore, even as close to land as Joey's empty boat had been found.

He didn't elaborate, but the dark voice inside my head found its own narrative. *Yes,* it intoned bitterly. *Nothing left, of course. He'll have been eaten; he'll have been devoured by marine life.* The monsters of the deep.

Adam and I didn't discuss it. Our thoughts about what was left of Joey remained for each of us our secret. Horrible images. Private nightmares, not to be discussed in daylight, for fear we should go mad.

So I had no faith in prayer, and yet that first night at Coombe the entity that guides our dreams thankfully spared me.

The first few days of our summer holiday passed pleasantly enough. I still couldn't face Polperro, but there were lots of other pretty coves to take Edie to. My favourite was Talland beach, small and unthreatening, with its cosy little café, softly lapping waves and hordes of tiny children digging in the sand, building lopsided towers out of pebbles and bits of shale. Yes, I had to look at the sea, and it was the same sea that had claimed Joey, but here during these soft summer days the water looked so gentle that I couldn't equate it with the tempestuous tides that capsized Joey in a sudden April squall more than five years before. Apparently it had blown in out of nowhere, Joey's friend Ben had told me. It wasn't that my son, skilled sailor that he was, had taken a foolish risk and set sail in bad weather. The sea was calm as a millpond when Joey left the harbour. Half an hour later the wind whipped up and the waves grew fierce and choppy.

And yet . . . it wasn't a violent storm, Ben said, just a bit of a blow. He hadn't been worried about Joey at all until he didn't return in time for the pub lunch they were supposed to meet up for at the Blue Peter. He confided his concern to a fisherman he met in the pub. The fisherman took Ben at once to find the harbourmaster, who immediately ordered a search. Late in the afternoon Joey's boat was spotted, wrecked on rocks down the coast near Looe. Joey, of course, was not on board. Joey was nowhere to be found.

As I played on Talland beach with Edie, who was valiantly trying to fill her little seaside bucket with pebbles, I tried not to think of that dreadful day at the start of the Easter holidays, when Ben had called me as I sipped wine in the garden at home in Manchester. Oh, foolish, stupid woman. Just to think of myself sitting there without a care in the world, waiting for Adam to get home, planning a barbecue, made me feel sick.

Ben had stayed on in Polperro while we rushed down in a panic that night. We moved into the same cottage he and Joey were renting. As day after day passed with no news, I took to sleeping in Joey's bed, his sweater on my pillow, his red scarf wrapped around my shoulders. The local doctor gave me pills, but it was Joey's scent that enveloped and calmed me on the rare occasions when I managed to drift off. On those nights, inhaling his robust young man's smell, I felt he was joining me in my dreams. I could hear his voice calling to me, urgent, pitiful, above the sound of crashing surf and howling wind. Oh, how desolate it made me feel.

Now, years later, sitting on the rocks with Edie and

Adam, as Danny and Lola, child-free for a few blessed minutes, strolled arm in arm along the beach, I made a decision. I needed to see Ben. Yes, we'd talked about that day many times but I wanted him here with me in Cornwall. I felt a desperate need to go through it all again.

I knew Adam would be unhappy. He saw this break as an opportunity to move on, not to get stuck again in the past. But there was no help for it. He had brought me here, and now I needed to ask more questions. Ben seemed the only person who could possibly answer them. If we went over that Easter day again, now, with the immediate panic of Joey's disappearance long past, with the questionable benefit of five years' mourning behind me, maybe Ben would tell me something he might have mentioned before, when I was too dis-traught to listen properly. The more I thought about what I knew about that day, the more I realised what a blur it had all been.

I began to feel excited, as Edie chortled over some sandy shells I stopped her trying to eat. There must have been something, I thought. Something Ben might have noticed; maybe Joey had told Ben exactly why he wanted to take the boat out alone that morning. Usually they sailed together. Why had Joey decided he wanted to make this trip on his own? I decided to call Ben at once and ask him to come and stay with us at Coombe.

Except I couldn't get a signal at Talland, and even back at the cottage I would have to use the landline. No keeping it secret then. I would have to tell Adam. I braced myself.

Chapter Five

Edie began a swift crawl along the beach, evidently heading towards a small boy who was building a sand-castle with his dad. I lunged forward and grabbed her just before she ploughed into his lovingly crafted hand-iwork. The boy looked at her with annoyance and disdain. Edie, bless her, gave him an enormous grin and held out a grimy shell. He took it and placed it on the turret of his castle. Edie promptly swiped it back, demolishing a large section of the tower into the moat his dad had just finished digging. I smiled apologetically, and shrugged: *what can you do?* But the dad scowled. *Not*

a nice man, I thought, as I scooped Edie up and took her back to our beach towel. Adam was watching with amusement. 'What a plonker,' he said. 'Honestly, I'll never understand territorial wankers like that.' He looked so chilled that I decided now was the moment to broach my idea about Ben.

'Adam,' I began hesitantly. 'How would you feel if I asked Ben Thomas down to stay with us for a bit?'

He looked puzzled. 'Ben?' he asked. 'Why on earth . . . ?'

I looked at him, and at once he understood. 'No,' he said immediately. 'No, no, no, no, no. Not under any circumstances. That would be all wrong, completely wrong for us right now.'

'It wouldn't be wrong for me,' I said quietly. 'In fact, I really need to see him.'

Adam looked at me carefully. 'When did this come on?' he asked.

'Just now,' I said honestly. 'But I think it's been in my subconscious ever since we got here.'

Adam sighed. 'I suppose I should have thought of this. I guess it was inevitable.'

'Yes,' I murmured. 'Once I came here I was bound to

start thinking about it all again. Bound to start asking questions.'

'But, Molly, Ben's already answered all our questions. He's told us everything he knows about Joey and ... that day.'

'I know. But I was in such a mess I didn't listen to him properly.'

Adam looked grim. 'Well, I did,' he said. 'And I can assure you he knows absolutely nothing more about Joey's last day than we do. Molly, love, it's all over. I brought you here because I wanted you finally to accept that.'

'Well, what if I can't?' I asked sadly. 'What if getting me here just stirred it all up again? You must have known it was a risk.'

'I thought that Edie ... I thought your focus would be on her.'

'Adam, I love Edie with all my heart, but she's not going to make me forget about Joey.'

'No, of course not. I just hoped we could have a new start.'

I looked at my husband, my heart swelling with sadness and despair. 'You don't understand. There can't be a new start for me until I know what happened to Joey. I know you meant well, but did you really think you could bring me back to Cornwall with Danny and Edie and somehow I would waltz into a new future? How can I possibly come down here, sit on a few beaches with the baby, and somehow forget my son vanished here? Or worse?'

Adam shook his head and looked down at the sand. 'I thought you were ready for this. I'm sorry.'

I took a deep breath, steadied my voice and said, 'Look, Adam, I don't want us to quarrel. I know you meant this holiday for the best. And you were right, certainly for Danny, who means the world to me. And maybe it still could be the right thing for all of us; help to lay things to rest. But I'm not ready yet. There are still questions I need to ask. I won't ever have any peace until I'm sure.'

'Oh, Molly. How can you NOT be sure? It's five years now. He's gone, love. You know that.'

I sank down onto the sand to cuddle Edie, who was looking anxious at this unaccustomed tension between her grandparents. 'I know he's gone. I just need to know where.'

And as Edie began to wail, I held her and looked out to sea, the sea that took my boy. *I want him back; and while I'm here I'll do everything in my power, move heaven and earth, to find him.*

Chapter Six

2004–2009

'Mum, can I talk to you?'

Joey was uneasy, and I was busy. It was September 2004. The school year had just begun, and my life was engulfed in study plans and meetings. We had a new Head. I liked her but she had different ideas, naturally, from her predecessor. We, her teaching staff, had to absorb the new atmosphere as well as dealing with the normal chaos of starting school up again after the long summer holidays. Adam, who taught at the city's prestigious boys' grammar school – an enormously influential establishment which, like my own girls' high school, was held in huge respect by the most prominent and powerful people in Manchester and by education-alists throughout the country – was equally preoccupied. Our sons both went to Adam's school, and so the whole family was deeply entrenched in educa-tion; possibly not always to the boys' advantage. We were, I suspect, a tiny bit neurotic about their academic progress. We expected them to do well, as if it were our right. Fortunately, they were both bright and did OK. They weren't geniuses, but kept their heads above water and were expected to get good A-levels and go to uni-versity. And they were well behaved. Thank the Lord, they didn't shame us before our colleagues.

I like to think we didn't put too much pressure on them. I like to think we were a happy family, normal, with lots of interests outside school, emphasising that achievement and good grades weren't everything. But who knows? Certainly the question Joey asked me that golden September afternoon threw me com-pletely.

'Can Ben come and live with us?' Joey asked without

preamble. I must have looked shocked, because he suddenly became nervous. 'Please, Mum? I wouldn't ask except he really needs a proper home.'

I gulped. 'What do you mean, Joey? Live with us, here? What about his mum? What's happened?' But I knew, of course. This had been brewing for a long while.

Oh, Ben. Such a lovely little boy, and yet his early promise had seemed to wither on the vine. Every time Joey told me about his friend's unhappy home life, I wondered how we could help him. And yet it was never simple. By the time Joey asked his anxious question Ben was sixteen, living with his neurotic, divorced mother. It was already too late to assimilate this troublesome child into an ordinary home. He was, even then, beyond the pale. He was into drugs. Brilliantly clever, exceptionally intellectually gifted; but frankly not someone you could introduce into a normal household without causing domestic waves as threatening as a tsunami. So what could I say to Joey?

'What about his mum?' I repeated.

Joey looked impatient. 'She's chucking him out. Says she can't manage him any more. And his dad won't have him either. He's remarried, and his new wife can't stand Ben. Mind you, it's mutual.' Now my son was upset. When he looked at me I saw his eyes were glistening. 'But, Mum, he's only my age. I don't see how he can live on his own in some crummy little flat.'

Neither did I. I told Joey I'd talk to Adam when he got home. Of course I knew exactly what he'd say. And he didn't surprise me.

'Molly, are you out of your mind? Of course Ben can't live here. I'm hugely fond of him, and he has enormous potential, but he's a mess.'

'I know, but that's his parents' fault, not his. And we've known him since he was four.'

'Yes, and I'm more than willing to keep a close eye on him at school, although he's not in any of my classes. I do watch out for him, always have. But I won't have him living in this house. He has massive problems, Molly. If he moved in here we'd be asking for trouble. And it's not fair on Danny and Joe.'

I didn't put up much of a fight. Adam was right. Poor Ben. As it turned out, he seemed to manage in the little flat his parents found for him. He saw his dad sometimes, hardly ever his mother, who had been diagnosed as bipolar and said she simply couldn't cope with him. Outwardly, Ben didn't seem to care.

He was a frequent visitor to our house, and both Joey and Danny were enormously fond of him. Did I think his druggie lifestyle affected our two boys? Naturally I worried about it, and so did Adam. But whatever our sons got up to, they never caused us serious concern. Obviously we were on the lookout for problems, but they seemed to have a charmed life. Their schoolwork thrived, they were happy and steady at home. I was constantly wary of Ben and his chaotic life, of course I was, but Danny and Joey seemed impregnable; sturdy high achievers, our boys were, set well on course for university and a prosperous life.

Adam and I both felt for Ben. We wanted to help him, opened up our house and our lives to him within reason. A couple of years passed without incident, and we were happy and relieved when first Danny and then Joey passed their A-levels with distinction. Mind you, so, against all the odds, did Ben.

He had been Joey's best friend since they met at nursery in Manchester. Together they had spent their primary years at Beaver Road school in Didsbury, gathering cohorts of other little lads around them, all of whom often came back to our house to play. We lived in an Edwardian cul-de-sac with a park at the end of the street, and I used to love those days after school when they all descended for Ribena and biscuits. Being a teacher myself, it was relatively easy for me to be home early for them a couple of days a week, if I traded time with my colleagues. Danny, too, went to Beaver Road, and when he and his friends also flocked to our place after school, it was bedlam, but gloriously so. Our beautiful road, Old Broadway, was built by a White Russian émigré at the very beginning of the twentieth century. Each house was different, some detached, others, like ours, semis, but they were all spacious and full of character.

And Ben? The flat his businessman father bought him made him very popular. His friends – including Joey, as he later confessed – spent many hours there with him, probably smoking weed. Ben's parents gave him money instead of love, but despite that he did well at school – very well. He got into Manchester University to read English and Drama. So did Joey. I had expected my son to want to move away from home for Uni, like Danny who was studying Psychology at Leeds. But Joey was a home bird. He loved Manchester, although he moved into a Hall of Residence in his first year rather than stay at home. That was fine by me since his digs were only a mile or so away from us, which meant, as a mum, I had the best of both worlds. An independent son who did his own laundry in Hall, but who still came home regular as clockwork to see his old mum and dad and, however hungover, usually turned up for Sunday lunch each week.

And a lot of the time Ben came with him. They were fast friends. Ben seemed somehow to have sorted himself out; he looked well and happy and was always good company. As for Joey, I couldn't wish for a better son. He was healthy, good-looking, full of verve and high spirits. Adam and I would grin at each other when the boys left us after a convivial meal, and raise a glass.

'Hey, Moll. Here's to us. We must have done something right.' And we would clink glasses and thank God for our lovely, happy family.

At the end of his first year at university, Joey and I had a heart-to-heart. My son told me Ben's drug days were over. 'I mean, Mum, you know, he does a bit of weed every now and then. But so does everyone else.'

I tried to look unconcerned. 'Everyone?' I asked. 'Including you?'

He grinned. 'Well, yeah, but don't worry, Mum. I'm not a druggie and neither's Danny. I think we imbibed responsible behaviour with our mothers' milk.'

'That would be me you're talking about,' I said smiling. 'And I'm glad to hear it. But hasn't it been difficult for you while Ben was so wild?'

'No, not really. I mean,' he said, a little embarrassed, 'like I said, we have experimented a bit, Danny and me, at parties, that sort of thing. Everyone does. But we were never really tempted to go on with it. I mean, Ben used to go too far. Class A stuff, cocaine, what have you. We saw he was on a knife-edge and it scared us. He could have destroyed himself. He didn't have the right parents. We did. And anyway, Ben's so bright. He's got big ambitions. He wants to be a film director. He's really talented. You should see the stuff he makes at Uni. The film department think he's amazing. He gets a lot of positive support, which means he's finally found the strength to sober up.'

'Really?' I asked. 'He's stopped using, for good?'

'Yes, Mum. I promise. He really has.'

And so by the time the boys started their second year at university, Ben was not only clean but flying high. He was full of plans for the future, charming, healthier and happier than I'd ever seen him.

Autumn Term began in October 2008. The following April, when Ben and Joey were just twenty, they went on holiday together. An Easter break, boys only, in Polperro. Where they could both indulge in the hobby they loved most. Sailing. The hobby that took my son away from me, seemingly for ever.

Yes, I lost Joey that day, and I had failed to keep in contact with his best friend. I simply couldn't bear to talk to Ben afterwards. The thought that he had seen Joey, been with him for those last days when I was going about my normal existence in Manchester, happy, totally unprepared for the cataclysmic shock about to devastate my life, meant that my throat closed up in horror when I thought about calling him. In some irrational way, I blamed Ben for being with my son when I was not. As if I might have prevented his disappearance. I knew I was being unfair, but there it was. Now, five years later, back at the scene of so many happy family holidays, I thought maybe it was time to change that.

Chapter Seven

Present Day

We got back to Coombe in the late afternoon. Edie was sleepy and went down for a nap in her cot straight-away. I could have done with a lie-down myself, but I was still wrestling with my plan to call Ben. Because of Adam's reluctance, I decided to put it off for a while. Besides, if I seriously intended to ask Ben to stay here with us on our holiday, I had to talk to Danny and Lola. I knew my elder son thought everything was going fine. He was loving Cornwall with his wife and their gorgeous little girl, and he thought I was too. Danny was congratulating himself; his coup to get me down here, his appeal to Adam, had worked. Here we all were, having a lovely time. The future lay hazy, rosy and bright on the horizon. And – guess what? Mum seemed to be having a ball down here, on the beach with her grandchild.

I could imagine Danny whispering to Lola, when they were in bed at night, that it had all been a great success. 'I knew this would be OK,' he would say to his wife. 'I knew I just had to get Mum down here with Edie and she would fall in love with the place again.' He would smile as he said it and settle down to sleep. Lola would stroke his cheek and murmur soft agreement. But Lola was not deceived. She was, after all, a mother. She knew, more than Danny, more even than Adam, what was going on in my head. She had no illusions that this holiday was for me just a ritual of acceptance. How could it be? It involved remembering the disappearance of my child.

Lola knew that. And she had loved Joey. I thought my daughter-in-law might be my ally.

*

After supper that night, we watched some television. I was restless, and knew I wouldn't sleep. Danny and Lola went up to bed early, knowing they'd be woken by Edie before the night was through. Adam went upstairs to read; I told him I wouldn't be long. I wanted a walk around the garden before I came to bed.

And so, holding a gin and tonic, I stepped outside into the moonlight. The grass was silver, the leaves on the soft-lit trees glittered like diamonds. It was so quiet. The gentle breath of a breeze sighed around me, swaying, holding me steady. And as the clouds drifted softly over the garden the night revealed herself in a sensuous dance. Slowly, minute by minute, she tantalisingly showed me the darkness, as if I watched a curtain pulled teasingly apart by ghostly fingers, quietly, gradually, so as not to alarm me. But as each drape was drawn tenderly aside, I saw more. One by one, tiny glinting fragments opened up the magic moonscape, and there it was, the whole fantastical landscape, stamped on my heart like an impossible fairytale postcard.

And Cornwall suddenly burst upon me.

For all the jolly days we'd had on the beach since

we'd arrived, the spirit of this magic place had not yet touched me. I had been out of its reach for years.

Now in the silver, shadowed garden, the essence of Cornwall at last stretched out its arms, its limbs, wrapping itself around me so tightly I could barely breathe. Tendrils of sea mist seeped into my head, swirled around my brain. I was back, claimed once more by the strange, mythical home which had sung seductively in my soul until the day I lost my son.

I'd re-entered this mystic realm, I'd returned, and now all things were possible. I felt I could touch Joey. He was here, next to me. I could feel him, smell him, almost see him. I could certainly hear him.

And what I heard was a long, soughing sigh. What I heard, or thought I heard, was one word:

'Mother.'

Could this be happening? I listened with every nerve I had, every sensory receptor in my body trembling with fear and pain. Was he trying to reach me? Please God, make it be so.

And his voice came again. Plaintive, pleading, dying, sighing on the breeze. 'Find me. Find me.'

He sounded so sad. I cried out: 'Joey. Where are you?

Tell me. Help me. Please, Joey. I'm coming, darling. I'll find you. Wait for me.'

I sank down onto a white stone bench. I sobbed, but I felt happier and more alive than I had in years. He had found me, my boy, at last. As I had prayed he would. He was here. Close, in Cornwall. I would find him even if it killed me.

And I knew this strange, haunted county had stirred again, as it does when the need is great. Cornwall had waited a long time, but until now I couldn't hear her. The remote landscape of the far West Country had failed to reach me while I mourned my loss in Manchester, the northern town where Joey was born. I had to come back here, to the place he went missing, to be wrapped tightly in its flowing spirit-haunted cloak. Who knew what was real in this land of legends?

That night, wrapped in Faerie, I dreamed about an island. I was puzzled. In my dream I knew where it was. I had been there, surely, in the past? What enchantment had guided me? Something had taken me there, had held me in its spell for many days. So why was the place so mysterious to me? The image of the island cocooned me in enormous grief. Where was it, and when had I seen it? I had to tune in to this new sensibility, the wave of thought that had suddenly presented itself. If I could, I would know the answer to Joey's fate. If I didn't, he would be forever lost to me. I had no choice. I had to listen to Cornwall's beckoning song. I had to let myself be haunted.

Chapter Eight

None of this made any sense in the morning. I had gone to bed, snuggled up to Adam and found comfort in the warmth of his body. But when I woke up I felt bereft, my stomach nauseated with what felt like a hangover. I knew this had nothing to do with alcohol. My brain was sick, scoured, scavenged. As Edie ate her breakfast porridge, I tried fiercely to concentrate on her, this gorgeously predictable little child pulling her usual wake-up faces, making her lovely tiny noises, communicating as always with the adults she knew would never disappoint her. The parents and grandparents who formed the boundaries of her happy baby life, the small circle of security she knew would never fail her.

But, much as I loved her, my mind was elsewhere, pinging off walls of doubt and uncertainty. What had happened in the garden last night? Somehow I had found Joey, I thought. Surely I had spoken to him? But I couldn't remember how, or what he'd said.

I had to get away from everyone. Danny and Lola were taking Edie to Polperro. Thank God they understood this was still a bridge too far for me. Adam was keen to see a vintage classic car rally at the Talland Bay Hotel. Lunch was included in the ticket price, and he evinced no surprise when I said I didn't want to go. Cars and me don't mix, and I think he was relieved that he wouldn't have to put up with my boredom as he swapped motoring tales with other enthusiasts.

As for me, to my astonishment I realised I had decided to visit Jamaica Inn, the old house on Bodmin Moor made famous by Daphne du Maurier's novel. I had no idea why. I had been to this over-populated tourist trap many years ago, and vowed never to go back. But when Adam asked me what I was going to do with myself, I found myself blurting my destination before the words even reached my brain. Adam was quizzical. 'Why on earth do you want to go there?' he asked. 'At this time of year it'll be heaving with coach parties. You'll hate it, Moll.'

He was right, but I knew I had to go anyway. It was as if, in the night, I'd received a voiceless command I couldn't ignore.

Danny said he'd drop Adam off at Talland Bay on the way to Polperro, leaving me the Volvo to drive to Bodmin. I sat behind the wheel, disconsolate at the thought of turning up at Jamaica Inn at the height of the tourist season. I didn't even like the place. But the insistent demand in my head told me that was where I had to go. Resentfully, visualising crowds of day-trippers, I set off.

Bodmin Moor is a forbidding place. Even on a sunny July day, the deeper you travel, the higher you climb, the more hostile the landscape becomes. There's a sense of utter timelessness up there among the craggy tors; mist creeping around the inky rock pools, the black silent rivers which for thousands of years have wound their way from their moorland genesis, through dark wooded banks until they find their release, joining the pounding seas thrashing the coastline. The purple heather, sorrel, ivy and the golden glint of celandine have been trodden underfoot for millennia. If you walk on the moors, you feel besieged by ancient spirits. How could you not?

I shivered as I continued my impetuous journey to Jamaica Inn. Why was I doing this? I only knew I felt compelled to get to this old hostelry, high up at Bolventor, a house of legend so chillingly remote that even the thought of travelling there at night makes your skin crawl.

But it was broad daylight, even though the sun had retreated, hiding shyly behind a looming cloud-bank. Within minutes the sky was grey, the ever-present mist gathering dankly, swirling round the trees, mobile and ominous as ghosts in a horror film.

I shook myself, stopped the car. I would go back to Coombe, I thought. I would light the fire, put on some music, read a good book. I would have a lunchtime glass of wine and banish all thoughts of spirits, spooks and supernatural encounters. I might even drive over to the Talland Bay Hotel and join Adam for lunch, braving the inevitable stories of heroic trips in classic cars. Anything to shake off the increasingly morbid thoughts that were beginning to immobilise me on my reluctant jaunt to Jamaica Inn.

But I was almost there. And, despite the predictable number of coaches in the car park, I drove the Volvo in and parked as far away from the tour buses as I could get. I stood beside the car, restlessly putting the keys into my handbag and wondering what on earth to do next. My inner voice seemed to have deserted me. The Inn forecourt was swarming with families, all heading into the pub in search of lunch. I wasn't at all hungry, and wandered aimlessly towards a small meadow to the side of the hotel. This was deserted, unsurprisingly, since the smutty grey cloud already threatened rain, and the untidy patch of ground I'd stepped onto held no attractions for children. I remembered there was a proper kids' playground with swings and slides behind the Inn, and felt grateful that, for the moment, I had this squelchy, slightly slovenly spot to myself.

Except I wasn't alone.

Chapter Nine

Jamaica Inn

Lore and legend surrounded Jamaica Inn, enveloping it in a miasmic cloak of mystery, full of ghoulish ghosts and murders, all of which meant the place did a roaring trade. I was sceptical of course; well, wouldn't any educated person think it was a load of old nonsense? A good tale to scare children with, and rope the punters in, but really just a spooky old Cornish yarn, the kind of stuff tourists loved to tell each other sitting next to a roaring fire in an ancient pub, holding a pint or a large glass of Merlot.

So what was I doing here, feeling idiotically 'drawn' to a place I knew, rationally, was a nest of fraudulent but profitable legends? The field I'd wandered into was no atmospheric Scaddick Hill Meadow. No haunting presence hovered over this unlovely spot.

In fact, there was nothing much to see in the grey light. Mud; scuffed grass. The churned-up holes and messy mounds that meant badgers dwelled here. My gaze swept restlessly over a prosaic vista that looked utterly unrewarding. Nothing mystical, nothing at all noteworthy here, certainly nothing to suggest why the insistent voice in my head had told me to come. There was a scruffy fence at the bottom of the meadow, neglected for years, its struts rotten and broken, a rickety property marker that would these days deter neither man nor beast from invading the deeply unattractive little plot it guarded.

I sighed. What a waste of time, I thought. How utterly stupid of me to listen to the nonsense in my head. I'd had some kind of nightmare, not the revelation or discovery I longed for, and I'd let it take me over, bring me to this desolate spot where I had hoped to find salvation, only to find all that awaited me was boredom and crushing disappointment.

Feeling foolish, I turned back towards the car park. And then I stopped in my tracks. I was an English teacher. Lines from classic plays and poems were never far from my head. And suddenly what leapt into my mind was one of the scariest passages I had ever taught to a breathless sixth form. It was Coleridge. From *The Rime of the Ancient Mariner*.

> Like one, that on a lonesome road
> Doth walk in fear and dread,
> And having once turned round walks on,
> And turns no more his head;
> Because he knows, a frightful fiend
> Doth close behind him tread . . .

As the words reeled in my head, I knew there was something behind me. Something that made my nerves quiver, my skin shrink and the hairs on the back of my neck stiffen with fright.

There had been something in the field after all. I had barely registered it, so commonplace was the sight in these parts. A decrepit old scarecrow leaned drunkenly against the sagging fence. Little was left of it; just a bent, rotting, half-collapsed effigy, loosely wrapped in tattered remnants of black cloth clinging stubbornly to desiccated twig-thin limbs.

I looked back nervously at the dilapidated fence. My vision blurred. Was it a scarecrow, or just an old black tarpaulin flapping in the wind?

I turned away again, my sight diminished by the fog floating now across the meadow, thickening as it drifted. My eyelids fluttered. A small wave of dark light, so suppressed, so charcoal grey that it was hardly visible, flitted across my brain. A swift shadowy impression, so indistinct it almost missed my retina, and yet there it was. A movement throbbing across a ruined useless boundary that may once have served some practical farming purpose, but was now merely an indication, a warning, that something wicked this way comes.

The scarecrow turned its head.

My heart almost stopped. I stood still though I wanted to run. Because I knew instantly that this terrifying vision was what had summoned me to the moor. Slowly, although it looked as if it could snap and shatter any moment, it began to move. It knew me. It had eyes:

small, glittering, intense. Malevolent. They were fixed on my face.

> Because he knows, a frightful fiend
> Doth close behind him tread ...

This was not what I had been searching for. It was not Joey. Joey was not a fiend, a demon. Whatever scrambled thoughts had curdled my brain, I knew this was not my son. But it was evil. And I had seen it before. Where? When? My mind couldn't grasp what was happening. And as my sense of horror deepened, I knew that whatever had happened to my son was dreadful beyond belief. I was being warned. My search for Joey would be dark and terrible, and my lovely summer holiday would be shrouded in fear.

I turned and ran back to the car, fumbling with the keys, my heart racing, desperate to feel Adam's arms around me.

Chapter Ten

As soon as I got off the moor the grey fog lifted and I drove back to Coombe in blazing sunshine. I shook my head as the hedgerows flashed by, dotted with banks of wildflowers, and breathed in the Cornish air through the open windows. With each breath I felt calmer. The mist and the scarecrow receded in my mind, and the impossible beauty of the landscape tranquilised my thoughts. By the time I got back to the old farmhouse, my heart had stopped thudding, and I was beginning to convince myself I had had some kind of hallucination brought on by my strange moonlight vision in the garden last night.

I walked in the door, and was confronted by a pathetic little domestic scene.

Edie had a bad cough, and her small head blazed with heat, her cheeks burning red, a feverish glaze in her eyes. Our chatty little girl was silent, gazing reproachfully at us, the grown-ups who were supposed to protect her from harm. Lola was reasonably calm, but Danny seemed distressed.

'We're taking her to the doctor's, Mum. There's a surgery in Looe.'

'Yes, of course,' I said. 'Many's the time I've been there with you or Joey. Don't worry. I'm sure it's just a summer bug.'

I waved them off from the porch, smiling to myself. New parents. Poor things, consumed with fear because their first-born had a cold. The smile disappeared when I thought of Joey. All those trips we took to see GPs when he was little. All those cough medicines and Calpol, our anxiety when he spat the medicine out. And of course he always got better. Until the day when all the doctors and all the Calpol in the world couldn't help him. The day he disappeared off the wild Cornish shore.

Adam came home, having got a taxi to bring him back from Talland Bay. I told him about Edie's trip to the doctor's and he chuckled.

'Brings it all back again, eh, Moll? Rushing off to see the doc with a poorly baby? She'll be fine.'

I smiled back at him.

He looked at me closely. 'Are you OK, love? You look pale. Did spooky old Jamaica Inn give you a fright?'

He laughed but stopped immediately as he saw the tension in my face. Putting his arms around me, he pulled me close. 'Molly, what's the matter?'

'Nothing. I've just got a headache from the drive, and I feel a bit sick. It was very misty up on Bodmin, and before I left it was turning into fog. I couldn't see more than a couple of yards in front of me,' I lied.

'Poor sweetie. You've always hated driving in fog. Why don't you go upstairs and lie down. I'll bring you some tea and a couple of panadol.'

I closed my eyes. Adam was so sweet. I let him rock me in his arms for a couple of minutes, then pulled away. 'Thanks, Adam. I think I will.'

I went upstairs for a siesta. But kind and loving as he

was, when Adam brought me the tea I found I couldn't talk to him about what I'd seen at Jamaica Inn. He would have thought I'd gone mad, and rightly so, I thought. That stupid old scarecrow was the result of a protracted infirmity of my brain, caused by a delusional nightmare the previous evening. There was no way I could justify my experience in that muddy old field. I had to forget about it. Sleep seemed the quickest route back to sanity.

Upstairs at Coombe, I felt enveloped in the cosiness of the bedroom. It really did feel like home, with every comfort provided – a huge four-poster bed, red and blue Persian rugs on the old oak wooden floor, chintz-covered armchairs dotted round in the wide window alcoves, soft floral curtains to protect against the night. It felt like an enormously generous environment, welcoming me with warmth and open arms. I sank into the soft mattress, pulling the duvet over me. I was still fully dressed apart from my shoes, but I didn't care. Sleep beckoned from every corner. Oblivion called me with a calm promise of escape; the only possible respite after a horrible, nasty day.

I woke to the sound of the telephone ringing

insistently downstairs. I could hear Adam's muffled voice as he picked up. Moments later, as I tried to surface after a dark and murky nap that had done nothing to restore my sense of well-being, Adam appeared at the end of the bed. Cautiously he whispered, 'Molly? Are you awake?'

'Yes. What's wrong?' Like every mother, and now more than ever, I always assumed unexpected telephone calls meant trouble. No longer would I make the mistake of taking a surprise call in a sunny garden and naively expecting nothing more than a happy little chat about the weather in Cornwall.

'It's OK, but Danny's panicking. The Looe doctor referred them to the hospital in Plymouth. He was worried about Edie's cough. Now the hospital says they want to keep the baby in overnight. They think she might have croup, and they're admitting her as a precaution. Danny and Lola are going to stay with her, but I think he needs to talk to you. You know, as his mum, just to calm him down.'

Worried, I sat up, drank some water from the glass on my bedside table and heaved the bedclothes aside. I picked up the handset from Adam's side of the bed.

Danny sounded flustered, but relieved to hear my voice. The doctors thought Edie was fine, he said, but her breathing was laboured and they wanted to monitor her overnight. Danny said he and Lola would stay with her, sleeping in campbeds by her side.

I tried to reassure him, though I felt a little shaken by this turn of events. 'Look, sweetie. She's in the safest possible place. She'll be fine; don't worry. Do you want me and Dad to come to the hospital to be with you and Lola?'

'No, Mum. I appreciate it, but there's no point. I'll ring you if there's a problem; otherwise stay put. You and Dad can have a night to yourselves.'

Now there was a novelty, I thought: Adam and me, on our own on a family holiday. That had never happened before. Cornwall meant the Gabriels en masse; demanding children ruled the roost when we were down here, whether they were tiny or grown-up.

I told Adam what Danny had said. 'Are you worried about the baby?' he asked, smoothing down my bedhead hair.

'Not really. The doctors think she's fine; they're just being ultra-careful. Danny's worried, but it's his first baby. They'll call if they need us.' I paused. 'Do you want to go out for dinner? Just the two of us?'

'God, Molly, that sounds like you're asking me out on a date.'

I felt a bit embarrassed, as if I'd asked a man I hardly knew to share the evening with me, and he was likely to turn me down. I know I flushed and looked at my feet. Adam grinned, walked towards me and tilted my chin.

'Honestly, Moll, you look like a schoolgirl. Yes, let's have dinner. It's been ages since we had a date night.'

Date night? I couldn't remember anything resembling such a romantic prospect between us for years. And yet, before Joey's disappearance, we went out together all the time. To the theatre, the cinema, dinner. Utter guilt-free enjoyment, followed by long, passionate interludes in bed. I could hardly remember those days now. Any kind of joy felt selfish after we lost Joey. As if I was forgetting him, betraying him by feeling any normal happiness.

'I'll ring the Talland Bay Hotel,' Adam said briskly.

'But you've just had lunch there,' I laughed. 'Don't you want to try somewhere else?'

'We haven't been there together for dinner for years.

And it's quite romantic, don't you think?' I blushed. Adam smiled. 'We'll have a good meal there, if they can fit us in.'

They could. I had a bath, took care dressing. I wore a long black dress embellished with silver beading around the neck, and a beautiful gauzy evening coat embroidered with black silk roses, their petals sparsely but elegantly dotted with Swarovski crystals. I don't know why I'd brought this outfit down with me. I hadn't worn it for ages, but then again I hadn't been on holiday, a proper carefree holiday, for six long years now.

The whole effect was somewhat over the top for dinner at a country hotel, but it made me feel glamorous. I hadn't dressed up for what felt like a lifetime.

I dried my hair, styled it with a hot brush. I was punctilious with my make-up. I hadn't bothered with all that for years, but putting on eyeliner, mascara and blusher gave me an odd thrill. As I finished with a rose-tinted lip gloss, I looked in the mirror and hardly recognised myself. I looked pretty and well; ten years younger than the wan grey ghost that normally haunted my home and school. I finished with a long spray of Jo Malone, and was ready to go.

Chapter Eleven

As I walked downstairs to face Adam, I felt self-conscious. I wondered if I'd gone too far with the dress and the make-up. But his face as I joined him in the living room showed me why making the effort was worthwhile. He looked mesmerised. I realised I had made no attempt at all to court his love for five long years. He had been uncomplaining and totally patient with this shadow of a wife; a life-partner who had taken her eye off the ball because her main focus was her youngest son. Once he had gone, this wife was not interested in the rest of her world. Not in her other son, and certainly not in her husband – a man who had suffered the loss just as much as she; a man who needed comfort she could not provide.

'You look lovely, Molly,' he said softly.

'Thanks. I feel a bit overdressed.'

'Oh, no. It's lovely. Perfect for me.'

'Well, that's what I hoped; to look good for you. I know it's been too long since I made the effort.'

He shook his head. 'That's OK, darling. I know ... well, I know how hard it's been.'

'For both of us, though,' I replied. 'Not just me. This ...' I looked bashfully down at my frock, a hint of cleavage peeping out for the first time in ages, 'this is to say to you that I want to try and make our marriage work, like it used to. I've been unapproachable, I know. I've neglected you, us, for too long.'

Adam looked at me with great seriousness. He took my hand and walked me to the porch, opened the front door and gestured to the gilded green garden beyond.

'Darling, this is Cornwall. It's still here, still sunlit, still beautiful, still ours. It's not the same, it won't ever be; our love for it will be forever tinged with sorrow. But, Molly, tragedy happens anywhere. Everywhere. This place will always be Joey's. And yours, and mine, and Danny's. And now Edie's and Lola's.'

He kissed me. I let myself lean into him. He smelled gorgeous, looked ridiculously handsome in his dark grey suit. I felt happy.

'I do feel different here, and I'm glad you made me come. But something's happening. It's not over yet.'

Adam smiled and led me to the car. 'I know that, sweetheart. But as far as I'm concerned, it's going in the right direction.'

We drove to Talland Bay through a golden evening. The sea, when we glimpsed it, held a promise of Avalon, King Arthur's magic kingdom, glittering and gorgeous, mysterious, just beyond our reach. When we got to the hotel, I felt that I had passed through some temporal barrier. I had definitely arrived somewhere else. A place of magic, where ordinary human grief momentarily held its breath.

As the soft green evening light began to fade, we sat in the hotel garden with our drinks. I felt strange, as if I were on the verge of something tumultuous and new. But, for now, we chatted inconsequentially about Edie, the hospital, and the beauty of the night. The sea was a subtle pewter blue, beckoning us, promising peace.

Adam sighed happily. 'This is beautiful, darling, isn't it? And Edie will be fine. It's only a bit of a cough. They'll be back tomorrow, right as rain.'

I acknowledged his contentment, happy to see his face relax. I had been so needy since I lost Joey. I had absorbed comfort from everyone who offered it, without finding any relief. I had had no idea how Adam was coping. I just accepted that the greater loss was mine, and judged all our dealings, all our progress through this raw new world, by how it impacted on me.

I had been completely selfish. I looked now at my life-partner, a man who had steeled himself against tragedy, against losing his younger son, without asking for any reassurance from me. He had shouldered the burden with a strength I had never realised. I did now.

But I felt unable to tell him that without breaking down. And I really didn't want to ruin this night. It felt special, unique even, because for once I was putting him first.

We moved inside to the wood-panelled dining room. There were flowers and candlelight, glinting shadows in the alcoves, and we began to enjoy our meal. It was delicious, and yet again I started to believe I was in a different reality. I was Molly Gabriel, here dining with her loving husband, successful teacher, mother of two strapping sons, grandmother of the most precious girl in the world. After two glasses of wine, I felt I was floating.

It seemed incredibly important to woo Adam, to flirt with him. I was coquettish, giddy, talking rubbish and yet he seemed to enjoy it. Poor man, of course he did. He'd got this long-lost creature back, his wife, a pretty woman who for once seemed enamoured of his company, who even, perhaps, held out the promise of a long and loving night in bed.

It didn't happen. I was expecting too much of us both. We had coffee, drove back to Coombe, poured a nightcap, chatted, watched the TV news. We both knew we were putting off the moment when we faced each other, naked and vulnerable. Finally we went to bed. And we hugged, cuddled. But neither of us could make the breakthrough to initiate sex. The whole thought seemed too crude, invasive, carnal. We felt tender towards each other, and I was grateful for that. We held each other with a warmth and softness I hadn't felt for years. And although we didn't make love, it felt as if we'd made each other a promise. We'd welcomed each other somehow. At least there was a possibility of happiness. Somewhere.

We fell asleep, wrapped in each other's arms. I was vaguely aware of the night beyond our windows.

And something seeped through the walls. I knew what it was: grief, loss. It wouldn't be denied. All the marital love in the world could not shut this out. Joey was still out there, unfound, unburied. And his spirit was insisting I had profound, unsettling work to do.

Chapter Twelve

I felt well, even relieved, the next morning. An early call from Danny had told me Edie seemed better, the doctors were pleased with her, and they were on their way home. Good news, but I was still aware that I had to talk properly to Adam. Never mind glossing over the atavistic fear that had gripped me at Jamaica Inn; if I really wanted us to be together again, united in seeking resolution after tragedy, I had to be honest with him. Yes, he might think I was mad. I had to take that risk. If he wanted to love me, he had to know me.

I got up to make tea. I would bring it up to him in

bed, and then suggest we went somewhere quiet for lunch. There, I would tell him about how I heard Joey in the night garden, and the terrifying apparition in the muddy field that had made me think I was losing my mind. But before I had a chance to talk to Adam, Danny and Lola came home.

It was late in the morning when they arrived, a subdued but obviously better Edie with them. Their relief was palpable, happy smiles on their faces as we all sat together round the kitchen table.

'They said she'll be fine, Mum,' said Danny.

'But honestly, I'm glad we took her to hospital, even though it turns out she's OK,' said Lola. 'They've given us antibiotics and a kind of vapouriser to help her breathing. The doctor said she was convinced she'd get better soon.'

'Of course she will. You were just doing your job as parents,' I said. 'You both look knackered, though.'

'We didn't get much sleep on the ward. It was so busy, and we were worried about the baby.'

'Why don't you both go upstairs for a rest?' I asked. 'You can leave Edie with us. We might take her out to lunch, if that's OK?'

'That would be wonderful,' smiled Lola. 'Are you sure you don't mind, Adam?'

'I was going to take Molly out anyway. Edie will be a delightful extra guest.'

So, off we went, Edie in her baby seat in the Volvo, still a bit peaky but bravely chuckling away as we drove. We decided to drive to Fowey, crossing over on the ferry from Bodinnick. We did some shopping at the fish shop, at Kittow's Butchers, and – I insisted – The Romantic Englishwoman. There I bought the baby a tiny stuffed rabbit that played Brahms' Lullaby when you pulled its tail. I could never resist this shop, full of the most charming little gifts, nightwear, quilts and candles. I always bought presents for the only two girls in my family here, deprived as I had been of giving feminine cadeaux within my predominantly masculine environment. I found a pretty cotton dressing gown for Lola, a summer print of delicate blue flowers.

Then we headed for lunch at Polkerris. It was a sunny day, and we ate outside at Sam's on the Beach. Afterwards, we would let Edie play on the sand, maybe even get her little toes wet in the small, calm, waltzing waves. And it began as the perfect afternoon I'd planned. A halcyon day to treasure, warm as toast, clear and bright as a pathway to heaven.

As our drinks arrived, I took a deep breath, and as Edie played happily with her new toy bunny rabbit, biting its ears and sucking its tail, I told Adam everything that had happened to me since the night before last. I told him about hearing Joey's voice in the moonlit garden. And I told him about the scarecrow at Jamaica Inn.

Adam listened, concern written all over his face as he tried very hard to take me seriously.

'OK, Molly. I do get that you are totally convinced something's happened to Joe that isn't just a tragic accident, and that you feel you have to find out the truth. And I could tell when you were so determined to go to that silly old so-called haunted pub that you were expecting something significant to happen. You were at fever-pitch; I'm not surprised you thought you saw some macabre vision.'

I resisted the urge to snap back at him. After all, he was right. I had felt compelled to drive to the Inn. It was irrational. My glimpse of that animated horror of a scarecrow was about as convincing as thinking the wicked old witches stirring their cauldron in Polperro's Land of Legend had suddenly come to life and stepped out of their glass case. Actually, it was a relief to be told I'd imagined it. Because I had, of course. Adam's brisk common sense felt like a welcome cold shower of reality. I smiled at him, glad that I had such a strong, sensible husband.

'I was feeling very highly strung,' I agreed. 'Coming back to Cornwall sort of pushed me into a nightmare. I went to Jamaica Inn precisely because it *is* supposed to be haunted; I suppose I subconsciously wanted to see something that would tell me I'm on the right track, that Joey needs me to find him. But, Adam, that's why I need to talk to Ben. If I can just find out everything that happened that day, it might bring me some peace.'

'Oh, Molly. I really don't think you should do that.'

'But why not?'

Adam briefly closed his eyes. When he opened them, he leaned forward, stared closely at me and took my hand.

'I don't think you understand what you'll be getting into if you rake all this up again with Ben. You remember how he used to be so into drugs? I do, and I'm worried that had something to do with what happened that day in Polperro. There are things he doesn't want to tell us. And I think with good reason. Joey's gone. We don't need to sully his memory by dragging up nasty stuff. We don't need to know. You, especially; you must stop digging. Believe me, it's for the best.'

'What are you talking about?' I asked, horrified. 'What things does Ben not want us to know? Drugs? Joey? You must be mad. I need to talk to Ben and I'm going to.'

Adam looked almost threateningly grim.

'Have you thought what seeing Ben again, talking about that day, will do to Danny? Do you even begin to realise what that will do to his peace of mind, his happiness, to rake all this up again?'

I was bewildered.

'Danny really thought this was all over,' said Adam. His tone became increasingly serious. 'He misses Joey enormously, of course he does, but he's young, Molly. His life has moved on and he wants us to acknowledge that a future is unfolding for him. I admire him, I really do. He's determined that his life with Lola and Edie will be fruitful, happy. He won't let his brother's tragic death blight their lives.'

My eyes filled with tears. I hated it when Adam said 'death'.

'I won't accept he's dead, Adam. There's no proof. He's just missing. But of course I want Danny to be happy. Of course I do.'

'Then, to be honest, Moll, you've got to let this go.'

Yes, I thought. *I suppose I must. I have to think of the future, of the happiness of my remaining son. Which means letting go of Joey. What's done is done. Joey is gone. Danny and Edie are the future.*

But as I tried to let that thought absorb me, tried so hard to let Joey sink into his watery grave, his voice came back to me. *Mother. Find me.* And I knew I had no choice.

I shook myself. I tried to pretend to Adam that I was fine, I understood his urgent plea not to phone Ben, not to dig any further. We finished our lunch and carried Edie the few steps down to the beach. I laughed, sang silly songs with her as she sat on the sand. But I had to talk to Ben, of course I did. My son's insistent call would not be denied.

Chapter Thirteen

That evening, I made up my mind. I would call Ben. Danny and Lola had gone upstairs, giving Edie a bath before putting her to bed. Adam had driven into Looe to buy groceries, kindling and wine. I picked up the phone, feeling sneaky. I resented the way I felt guilty, the fact that I had to make this call under the radar because everyone would be cross with me if they knew. *For Christ's sake*, I thought, annoyed, *I'm a grown-up, I know what I'm doing. I don't have to get everyone's permission to make a phone call.*

I had to steel myself to pick up the receiver and dial

the number I found for Ben in my diary. I had painstak-
ingly transferred his mobile number into each new
yearly aide-memoire, every single January since Joey
had disappeared. I felt I had to, that not to make a note
of Ben's whereabouts would somehow betray my son.
But I had never called Ben, never spoken to him, not
once since the inquest decided Joey had died in an accident at sea. And he had not attempted to contact me.
Perhaps, for him too, the whole episode had been too
cruel to revisit.

We both had a lot of explaining to do. I felt I owed
him an apology for my distance. As I dialled his number,
I felt sick with apprehension.

A woman picked up. She sounded young, but then of
course Ben was only twenty-five. I realised I didn't even
know where Ben lived now, let alone if he had a girlfriend. I'd assumed he'd stayed in Manchester; if Adam
or Danny knew where he was, neither had said a word
to me. But of course, they wouldn't. They had to tread
so carefully around my grief.

I asked for Ben. There was a brief hiatus. And then:

'Hello?' A young, hesitant, masculine voice. 'Who is
this?'

'Ben, it's me. Molly Gabriel. Joey's mum.'

There was a pause. Then an attempt at a hearty welcome.

'Molly. Mrs Gabriel. How amazing to hear from you, after all this time.'

'Yes. I'm sorry, Ben. I should have contacted you a long time ago. It's just ... well it's been difficult.'

A pause, and then, 'How ... how are you?'

'I'm fine; it's just ... I know it's been ages, but do you think we could meet? The strange thing is I'm in Cornwall – the first time I've been back since ... '

'Ahhh. I see. Where are you?'

'At Coombe in Treworgey. I suppose you remember it?'

'God, yes. So well. We had such brilliant times there.'

'We did.' I took a deep breath. I wanted to sound warm, not pleading. 'Ben, I need to see you.'

'Yes. OK. Could I ask why now, after all these years?'

'Being back here has flagged up so many memories.' I rubbed my eyes, impatient with the tears threatening to escape. 'There's still so much I don't understand about what happened to Joey. I so want to talk to you, to find out what really happened.'

'But, Mrs Gabriel . . . '

'Please call me Molly.'

'Molly, I told you everything about that day. I really did. I haven't got much to add.'

I remembered what Adam had said about Ben on Polkerris Beach: *There are things he doesn't want to tell us.* I had to convince the boy I wasn't threatening him.

'I accept that, Ben. I'm not suggesting you've held anything back. This is just for me. Look, I'll tell you that coming back to Cornwall wasn't my idea. But we did it for Danny.'

'Danny? How is he?'

My voice softened. 'He's well. Married now, and with a gorgeous baby girl. We're all here together. I suppose we're trying to reclaim Cornwall, to try and remember it before . . . Well, to get the joy back, the love we felt for the place before . . . '

'I understand that, and it's very brave. But very hard, I would think?'

'Enormously hard. And that's why I want to see you again, to talk and lay demons to rest.'

Another long pause.

'I'm not sure I can do that, Molly.'

'Yes you can, Ben. In fact, only you can.'

He sighed.

'All right. I'll come to Coombe. Is tomorrow afternoon OK?'

'What? How can you get down so fast from Manchester? I mean,' I said, confused and aware I was waffling, 'what about work? Won't you have to get time off to come down here?'

'Mrs Gabriel. Molly. I live in Cornwall now. In fact, I live in Polperro.'

That was a total shock. Astonishing, actually. My mind caved into all sorts of strange perceptions. Ben lived in Polperro? The village where my son had disappeared? Why on earth would a young man who had shared a terrible experience, had lost his best friend, want to live in the place where tragedy had happened?

I asked him, hesitantly, why he had moved down here. He took a while before answering.

'It's complicated, Molly. There's a lot to talk about. But it's not really to do with what happened to Joey.'

No? I didn't believe him. This was a coincidence too far. I was silent, and eventually he responded.

'Look, I fell in love with someone down here.

Someone Cornish, and we're together. So, after I finished Uni in Manchester, I came back down. I've been here for nearly four years now.'

Why did this seem like a betrayal? It wasn't, of course. Ben had an absolute right to live wherever he chose. So why did I feel I'd been kicked in the stomach? Why was I so instinctively hostile to the idea that the boy who had been the closest to my son's last moments on earth had chosen to live so near to the seas that had claimed his life?

I hid my dismay, of course. I also decided Ben could not possibly come to Coombe. So much to explain, and it would involve Adam and Danny. I wasn't ready for that.

'Could we meet somewhere else, Ben?' I asked tentatively. 'I mean, it will all be a bit of a shock for Danny. I'd like to talk things through first. I'm sorry, but this is all to do with me. I don't want to upset anyone else.'

There was a pause, and I realised that of course I was upsetting Ben. He must hate being reminded of all this. It was ruthless, but I had to insist. So when he suggested he could meet me at the Blue Peter in Polperro tomorrow at one p.m., I agreed immediately.

It was only when I'd put the phone down that I realised I had just made an appointment to see the last person who had seen Joey alive at the very place where he was supposed to meet my son on the day of his death.

Disappearance, I told myself desperately. *Not death. Not yet.*

Chapter Fourteen

Polperro

I told Adam the next day that I needed to go to Fowey. Kittow's was the only really top-class butcher in the region, and I wanted to buy a large joint of their fabulous lamb for Sunday lunch. Also they had a really good delicatessen, and I could find some excellent cheese.

Adam was indulgent. He knew I loved Fowey, and teased me that I obviously really wanted to go back to The Romantic Englishwoman to buy more toys and fripperies for Edie and Lola. 'And for me!' I said indignantly, playing my part to the hilt, and he laughed.

'Of course, sweetheart. I wouldn't expect anything else. But you don't mind if I don't come, do you? There's cricket on the telly. I know you hate it, so if you're going out I might as well ...'

My views on football and cricket were well known in this masculine family. To Adam's credit he wasn't a boorish sports fanatic, the kind of man who felt his membership of the human race depended on baying for his team to win. But if he got an opportunity to watch a match when I wasn't there to cramp his style, of course he took it. And today, that suited me just fine.

So he and Danny settled in front of the television. Lola said she was going to have a much-needed nap while Edie slept, and that if the baby woke while Daddy was watching TV, well, that was too bad. Daddy would have to look after his daughter even if it meant missing an innings win or defeat.

And so I drove to Polperro: the gateway to my son's horrible fate.

It's beautiful, Polperro; about as charming as a village can get. White cottages winking in the sun. Swishing little weirs and streams washing around the pretty houses, many of them built on stilts so the ever-present water burbling through the streets would not disturb the tranquil lives of those who had pledged their futures here. Beyond picturesque. Wholesome, delightful, the ultimate Cornish holiday destination. With pasties for sale, fresh fish, fudge.

When you're in it, walking through the lanes, past the quaint tourist shops selling little brass jack o'lanterns and models of a bare-legged Joan the Wad – Queen of the Cornish Piskies as she is billed, a lissom female lucky charm to help you win the lottery – it seems like a homage to bygone days of smuggling. But it's not. People live here. Polperro's a dense community, and like all small and close-living habitats, it's full of tales, gossip and rumour.

I left the Volvo in the enormous car park at the head of the village, and I thought back to happier days when we'd visited the little town. *It's a shame really, that car park*, Adam always said. So much at odds with the small-scale charm of the village, but the streets are so narrow that vehicles are forbidden; and yes, the car park is a bit off-putting in its size, but people have to make a living, and Polperro has to make a killing in the tourist season.

Every year, come Easter, the place is full, and it's vibrant. All spring and summer long holidaymakers flock here. I love watching the children, utterly bewitched by this Cornish fishing village's otherness, its complete differentness from the industrial towns they live in. It's stunning, Polperro. Like staying in an enormous doll's house, or Captain Hook's gigantic galleon. Utter magic if you're a kid from a big city: a place of enchantment, magic, and legend. And of course there's always Merlin's Kingdom; the ultimate childish treat; along with the Cornish fudge heaped in the sweetshop windows, Merlin is the icing on the cake.

Of course that's how I used to think of Polperro, totally captivated, along with my sons, by the village's filmic beauty. Not now, though. Now it was a different place, no longer full of swashbuckling pirates and green-capped benevolent elves, all bent on making your stay a time of wonder. For me, now, it was a place of sadness. And I had come here, for the first time in five years, to hear how my boy was never seen again after sailing from this very harbour. The harbour I now crossed to climb the rocky steps leading to the Blue Peter.

Chapter Fifteen

The Blue Peter

I was very nervous as I pushed open the old pub's dark blue door. I hadn't been here since we'd holidayed with the boys years before. Adam, Danny and Joey had loved the place. It was small, smoky and dark, a real fisherman's favourite, with a blazing log fire, a bar garlanded in evergreens threaded through with white fairy lights, wooden tables dotted around the charcoal slate floor and narrow windows looking onto the ancient harbour. When the tide was in, the local fishing boats, red, green, yellow and blue, bobbed gaily on the waves, as merry a nautical scene you could ever wish to see. But when, as now, it was low tide, the small vessels were grounded in mud. It was impossible to believe they could ever get out to sea.

Because of its size, the pub's L-shaped room always looked busy, but today at the height of the summer season it was absolutely heaving with locals and tourists. I peered around in the gloom, but Ben was nowhere to be seen. Hardly surprising, since tension had brought me here very early. I glanced at my watch. Only half past twelve.

I found a small table tucked into a recessed window and considered braving the packed bar to order a drink. I hate being a single woman in a busy pub, especially one as masculine as this. But just as I was screwing up my courage to squeeze through the crowd I heard someone shrieking my name.

'Molly! My God, it IS you, isn't it? I haven't seen you in years. Oh, good heavens, what a marvellous surprise!'

Alarmed, I turned to find the source of that loud, confident voice. And almost fell over with shock. Queenie. How extraordinary, although of course it wasn't, because Queenie had worked behind the bar at the Blue Peter for donkey's years. I'd forgotten; had never considered that I would bump into someone I knew. She bustled over, throwing her arms around me, a large friendly woman a decade or so older than me.

'Oh, Moll. How lovely to see you.' I was sincerely delighted to see her too. 'Is Adam here?' she asked.

'No, just me. How are you, Queenie?'

'Oh, you know me. Same as ever, mustn't grumble.' She looked at me keenly. 'I'll get you a drink. What is it? Still a G and T?'

'How can you remember that after all this time?' I asked.

'Because I'll never forget you telling me it's the most civilised drink in the world. Oh, Molly, you always were so elegant.'

I laughed. 'I don't think so, Queenie, but actually I'd love a gin and tonic.'

'G and T, ice and lemon, coming up. I'll have one myself as well.' And she swept back to the bar, ignoring all the other customers vying for her attention.

I watched her with affection. Queenie's given name was Elizabeth, but one day, long before we began coming to Cornwall every summer, Her Majesty was in the news, and Liz the barmaid was being particularly imperious. One of the regulars teased that she was as bossy as the Queen, and from then on Queenie she was. She pretended to be annoyed about her new nickname, but secretly she loved it. It made her feel special.

She came back with drinks, and settled herself down next to me on the window seat. 'But, Queenie, haven't you got to work?' I asked her.

'No, I'm on a break. Bill will hold the fort for a bit. I want to talk to you.'

I looked down and took a sip of my drink.

'Molly. I don't want to intrude, or make you feel bad. But you haven't been back here for ages. And because of what happened to Joey, we thought we'd never see you again.'

I wondered if I wanted even to talk to her, to get into this. But Queenie was so full of warmth; everything about her exuded goodness and welcome. And I'd had enough. I'd tried so hard to keep my sadness inside the family. I'd been so private; my grief about Joey had been mine alone, shared with Adam and Danny, but no one else.

And now here was Queenie. She was just an old friend, more of an acquaintance really. But I felt so burdened, so desperate to shed some of my load. And she was there, in Polperro. She had witnessed my meltdown after Joey was lost.

My throat was dry. I felt sick with the mess in my mind. Queenie sat there before me, her face genuinely concerned; I felt she really wanted to know how I was feeling. And, God knows, I wanted to tell someone.

But there was little time to confide anything. We didn't have long before I was due to meet Ben. I told her he was coming to the pub to talk about the day Joey disappeared. She frowned. 'Ben, Molly? Are you sure you want to talk to him?'

'Well, of course. He was the last person to see Joe alive; who else can tell me what happened?'

Queenie was quiet for a while. Eventually she let out a breath and said, 'I do understand that, but I'm not sure Ben is the right person for you at the moment. I mean, given your state of mind.'

'What do you mean? You don't even know my state of mind.'

'Molly, love, it's obvious. You looked so sad when you came in. And utterly lost.'

Was I really that transparent? I stared at her. I realised she was echoing Adam's words, his warning that I was getting into deep waters.

'Look, Queenie, is there something about Ben I should know?'

'No,' she replied. 'Not really. He's a good lad now. But . . . ' She shrugged. 'It's just there are murky depths out there. And I don't think it will do you any good at the moment to start probing.'

Queenie looked up at the pub door behind me. Her face changed. She gave a small smile.

'Hello, Ben,' she said in a calm but distant voice.

'Hi, Queenie. Hello, Molly.'

Ben. He looked much the same as the sixteen-year old boy that Joey had asked us to take in, vulnerable but forceful all the same. This young man had a powerful presence, but he was obviously ill at ease. He looked at Queenie and me, and asked if he could get us both a drink. Queenie shook her head.

'I'll get back behind the bar now. Bill needs some help.'

He certainly did. He was inundated with tourists demanding drinks and food. Queenie joined him, and instantly the pub settled. Requests for crab sandwiches, ham and eggs and fish and chips were immediately noted and promised swiftly.

As Ben sat down beside me, Queenie looked over and locked eyes with me. 'I'll see you before you go, Molly. Don't leave without telling me,' she ordered.

Ben didn't notice. In fact he looked dazed, so pre-occupied I wasn't sure he knew exactly what was happening. He shook himself. 'Do you want something to eat, Molly?' he asked politely.

I shook my head. 'No thanks, Ben. Not hungry. But what about you?'

'No, I'll get something when I go home.'

Home. That was a strange thought. His home was here in Polperro. Where Joey vanished.

Chapter Sixteen

'Look,' said Ben after an awkward couple of minutes. 'Do you mind if we go for a walk? I can't really talk about Joey here. Too many memories.'

'OK. That's fine. Some air will do us good. I just had such a need to see you, and to ask you about Joey's last day.'

He looked evasive, I thought. But this couldn't be easy for him.

We left the Blue Peter, down the steep stone steps, and turned left away from the harbour. I asked Ben where he was living, and he said at one of the Crumplehorn cottages up at the top of the village.

We walked, slowly and awkwardly. To break the silence that had descended upon us, I asked my first question: 'Ben, why did Joey go out on his own that day? Why weren't you with him?'

He snuffled slightly. 'We weren't joined at the hip. We were both competent sailors in our own right.'

'I know. But still, it seems odd to me. Where did he tell you he was going?'

'I have no idea. He just said he wanted to take the boat out on his own.'

'Didn't you mind? Weren't you curious?'

Ben was ruffled. 'No. We weren't babies. We each had our own lives.'

'Was he meeting someone? Did he want to be alone for a reason?' I pressed on.

Ben looked truculent. 'How should I know? Look, Molly, Joey told me he wanted to take the boat out and he'd meet me at lunchtime in the Blue Peter. What was I supposed to do? Throw a tantrum?'

I looked at him. This was strange. Why was this young man so defensive? I tried to mollify him.

'It's OK, Ben. I'm not implying anything, of course not. It's just ... I desperately need to know what happened. And I know you cared for Joey. I thought maybe you could give me some insight into how he was feeling that morning.'

'Well I can't, Molly. I'm sorry. I know how much you must miss him, how much you've grieved. Me too. I don't think you understand how much.' Ben swallowed hard. 'He was my best friend. I knew him right from when we were little. Can't you understand how horrible it all was for me as well as you? I'm sorry for your loss,' and he said this almost formally, 'but it was my loss too. I want to forget about it. I have a life to lead.'

And he turned and walked quickly away from me. Up the hill, towards the Crumplehorn Inn, with a youthful litheness I could not hope to follow.

I stared after him, then trudged back up the hill to the car park. Back in the Volvo I sat quietly, trying to work out what my abortive mission to Polperro had actually achieved. Very little, obviously, but something was wrong. I felt tired. I was desperate to get back to normality, to Adam's comforting solidity, to Danny, Lola and above all little Edie. I needed to hold her in my arms, to feel her wriggle and chuckle, to experience her warm little life growing as intimations of death claimed my thoughts.

I drove back to Coombe. I'd had enough. Warmth and love was what I craved. Luckily my family was there to provide it.

Chapter Seventeen

When I got back Adam was still watching the cricket, but Danny, Lola and Edie were sitting in the garden. Edie was drinking milk, but her parents had opened a bottle of wine. Lola poured me a glass and looked at me closely.

'What's up, Molly? Is everything all right?'

'Oh yes, of course. I didn't go to Fowey though,' I stumbled, as I remembered I hadn't brought anything back for dinner. 'Just didn't feel like it, so sorry, I didn't get the lamb. I went for a long walk instead.'

'Don't worry, Mum. We won't starve,' said Danny

easily. 'There's spaghetti bolognaise in the fridge, and lasagne.'

'Right, of course.'

'Mum. Are you OK?'

'Yes, of course. A bit tired, I guess.'

Lola's lovely face softened. 'Yes, I can tell. This is hard for you, isn't it? Being back here?'

'No, no. It's lovely to be here in Cornwall, with you and Danny and Edie. A new start, just as Adam said it would be.'

Lola looked as if she didn't believe me. She turned to Danny and said in a low voice, 'I told you. I said it was too soon. I knew she'd be unhappy. We shouldn't have come.'

Danny looked uncomfortable. 'Lola, leave it, will you? Dad and I thought it was right, coming back here. And I still think—'

Lola interrupted. 'I think your mum needs a break. Molly, why don't you go upstairs for a nap? I'll sort out supper. You go and have a rest. I'll wake you up at dinner time.'

I felt hugely grateful to be given permission to disappear. To be off duty, allowed to be myself, and not pretend to be brave. I smiled at Lola. 'Thank you, love. I would like a rest.' Then I looked anxiously at Danny. 'I'm fine, Danny, really I am. Just not a spring chicken any more. We older ladies need our naps.'

'You're not old, Mum. You're only fifty. Far too young to be a glamorous granny, even. You're the youngest grandmother I know.'

'Yeah, well, I started young with you. Only twenty-two when you were born.' I smiled at him affectionately.

'Gosh. You really had Danny when you were only twenty-two?' asked Lola in surprise.

'Well, Adam and I met at university. It was love at first sight. We got married straight after graduation. It was a bit of a surprise when you came along so quickly, but we were delighted really.'

'And then Joey came, just three years later?'

'Yes.' I stopped. 'I'm going upstairs for a rest, pets. I'll see you later.'

But I didn't. I did go up to bed, took my clothes off and sank on to the comfortable mattress. I fell asleep immediately, but I didn't go down to supper. When Adam came up to wake me, I felt ill. I had a raging temperature. My head ached and I felt totally sick. Whatever virus little Evie had had, I'd obviously got it.

I moaned apologetically to Adam. I felt so bad, like all mothers do when they're not living up to their responsibilities. I was letting everyone down. I should be in the kitchen, helping to serve up, being the perfect grandmother.

But I couldn't do it. I needed to rest. And when Adam left me, I drifted immediately into a feverish sleep. I got up twice during the night to throw up, retching into the toilet. I was vaguely aware of Adam coming to bed, settling down next to me, finding his way around the darkened room with the light from his phone. I was boiling hot; and when I finally managed to let go, I entered a world no mother should ever have to breach.

The island. What was this island? I did not know, but in my fevered dream it consumed me. He was there, my Joey, I knew he was there. Only I could find him, but why? How? What was there to discover? I dreamed of caves, raging seas and, as my feverish mouth craved water, I dreamed of him, my son, desperate with thirst.

Oh, Joey. Where are you? Let me find you, my love, let me rescue you.

Chapter Eighteen

Next morning I still felt very ill. I barely woke up, registering dimly the movement downstairs which meant the family was awake. But I was confused, surfing restlessly through a consciousness that phased in and out, dipping through awareness, and then retreating into the delicious warmth of a fever-induced sleep.

At some point mid-morning, Adam stuck his head round the door, a broad smile on his lips.

'Molly, are you OK?'

No, I thought. *I'm not OK.* I groaned, to show him I was awake but wanted to be left alone.

It didn't work. He was thrilled with himself, I could tell.

'Molly, guess who's here? It's amazing, you'll be so happy to see her.'

No, no, no, no, no, I thought. *I'm not happy to see anyone. I don't care who it is, I don't care if it's the Queen. I'm ill. I couldn't give a stuff who wants to see me, all I want is to sleep.*

'Go away, Adam. Please go away.'

'No, seriously, Moll, I know you'll want to see Queenie.'

Queenie? Dear God, no. Had she told Adam I'd met her and Ben at the Blue Peter yesterday? I prayed not.

'Adam,' I croaked. 'Really, I feel crap. I don't want to see anyone today. *Anyone.*'

Too late. Queenie had already stuck her head through the door.

'Hello, gorgeous. I heard through the grapevine that you were all back here at Coombe, and I couldn't wait to see you again.'

I closed my eyes. 'Sorry, Queenie, I'm not well.'

'I know, darling. I've asked Lola to bring you up some honey and hot lemon. What a sweetheart she is, by the way. Imagine little Danny being married! And as for Edie, she's gorgeous. You are so lucky, Molly, having a granddaughter. I still don't have any grand-kids, even though I'm older than you. My lot are so feckless and irresponsible, I doubt they'll ever get round to it.'

Lucky? Queenie actually thought I was lucky? I held my tongue, but inwardly I was seething.

'Anyway,' she continued, 'I thought perhaps we could have a little chat.'

I looked at her balefully. Adam disappeared down-stairs.

'What are you doing here, Queenie?' I hissed. 'I don't want Adam to know I saw you in the Blue Peter yes-terday.'

'That's all right, honey, I know. He thinks Linda and Bevis told me you were all at Treworgey again.'

Linda and Bevis Wright were the owners of this little holiday hamlet. They were discreet, lovely and totally trustworthy. But it didn't alter the fact that I was ill, and the last person I wanted to see at my bedside was Queenie. Queenie was magnificent and larger than life, but gossip was her currency and her joy.

Lola brought up the lemon and honey drink, and with a worried look at Queenie went back downstairs.

I struggled up. 'Look, it was really nice to see you again yesterday, but what do you want? I'm really not well.'

'I know, I'm sorry. But the thing is, there's someone who wants to talk to you.'

I sighed. 'Well, to be honest, I don't want to talk to anyone. Can't you see I'm not up to it?'

'Yes. Obviously you can't talk at the moment. But in a couple of days, when you're feeling better, you will really want to meet Len.'

'Len? Who is Len?'

'He's a Charmer, Molly.'

'A charmer? But who is he?' Visions of George Clooney and Brad Pitt swam into my head.

'You must have heard of Cornish Charmers, Molly. They're white witches. They've been healing people and casting charms for centuries down here, especially on Bodmin Moor.'

I sighed. 'Oh, Queenie, don't go all mystic on me. Please, just go and let me sleep.'

And then, flooding into my mind, scaring me rigid

again, came the terrifying image of the evil-eyed scare-crow at Jamaica Inn. *Queenie* had gone 'all mystic' on *me*? Who was I kidding? The idea of a white witch seemed quite tame, compared to the fiend I'd seen at the Inn; yes, on Bodmin, where Queenie claimed these so-called Charmers congregated. But I had no intention of cutting her any slack. *I'm not prepared to make myself vulnerable to the village gossip, barmaid,* I thought snob-bishly, then flushed with shame as I considered how genuinely kind Queenie was. She didn't notice my face had gone red, but she was insistent I listened to her.

'I'm serious, Molly. It's OK. I know you're poorly. But you should talk to Len. He's waiting for you. He's got things he needs to tell you. About Joey.'

I stiffened. 'What do you mean?'

'I'm not going to talk any more. You obviously need to rest. When you feel up to it, call me. I'll leave my home number with Adam.' She leaned down towards me. 'Molly, I'm not being frivolous here. Len can help you, he really can. I totally believe in him, and what he can see.'

I turned over. Although I felt something, some faint echo of intuition fastening onto her words, I couldn't take it in at the moment. I felt ill, nauseous. The room was swirling around my head; I had vertigo. I was desperate to sleep. Above all else, oblivion was what I craved. I felt, rather than heard, Queenie leaving. There were murmured voices on the landing. And then, mercifully, I was left alone. No one else disturbed my solitude. I was allowed to sink again into dreams, into the borne of peace I longed for above all else.

Later, much later, Adam crept into the room. 'How are you, love?' he murmured. 'I think you should have something to eat. You must be starving.'

'No, not now, Adam. I feel sick. I need to sleep.'

'But you've been sleeping all day. Should I get a doctor?'

'No. I'm just exhausted. I'll be better tomorrow, I'm sure.'

He sat down on the edge of the bed. 'Look, Molly. I know why you feel so bad, and it's my fault for bringing you down here to Cornwall. I should have realised how much it would affect you. We'll go back to Manchester, tomorrow if you like. Danny and Lola can stay on here. They'll still have a good holiday.'

I closed my eyes. Should I take Adam at his word? I

was tempted. Our house in Manchester felt like a beacon to me now, a haven of security and warmth. There, I was used to coping without Joey. I could resume my life. Here, I was beset at every turn with images of horror. Each time I looked at the sea I thought about Joey's boat as I'd seen it when we hurtled down here in such a panic more than five years ago.

The little fishing vessel was a wreck, completely smashed up against the rocks. It spoke of violence, abandonment and death. There was nothing of my son still on board, not so much as a drink carton or a sandwich wrapper. The deck boards were splintered bones, the hull a gaping hole.

How could I possibly spend any more time here, pretending that I was on holiday, that I was somehow enjoying this time spent with my older son, my daughter-in-law and my granddaughter, when every glimpse of the ocean made me nauseous?

My eyes were still squeezed shut. Adam stroked my forehead. 'It's all right, Moll. This is all my fault. We'll go back home. You'll wake up in bed there and think this was all just a terrible dream. I'm sorry, love. I really meant it for the best, thought you could cope, but I got it horribly wrong. We'll leave tomorrow, after breakfast. I'll go downstairs and tell Danny.'

He kissed my cheek and left the room, shutting the door behind him with a gentle click.

I lay there for a long time. Tomorrow I could escape. And I would never come back. A chance to leave this sadness, this emptiness, behind me for ever.

I drifted off to sleep. Dreamed that we were packing the car, waving goodbye to Danny, Lola and Edie. The Volvo was out of the lane, heading back to Looe, to Plymouth and the Tamar Bridge. We crossed the estuary, the sun glinting on the water, the boats bobbing bright and sprightly on the tide, and suddenly we were out of Cornwall. We had crossed over into Devon. I would never have to enter the hell where my son had been lost ever again.

And in my dream, just as I smiled with pleasure and relief that I was on my way home, the skies darkened. There was an enormous, terrifying thunderclap, and behind us the River Tamar frothed and rolled. Forked lightning crackled down on our car, the heavens opened and beyond the tumultuous noise I heard an unmistakable voice: *Mother. No. Don't leave. Find me.*

I woke in panic, convinced that I was on the road leading back to the north. Leaving my boy here behind me in Cornwall, unfound and unburied. And then the familiar room, the four-poster, the drapes, the chintzy armchairs showed me I was still here, still in Coombe, still only a couple of miles from the place where my son had been claimed by the sea.

And I realised I had a job to do.

Maybe I could only regain my peace of mind by being on my own, free of family obligations. Maybe I just needed to concentrate on me, and on Joey. Because it seemed to me that, after these five horrible years, I was the only one still suffering. Everyone else wanted to move on. I was the one stuck, still reliving that apocalyptic Easter when I was told my son had drowned.

Feverishly, I considered my options. I could move out, rent a holiday cottage in Polperro on my own. This was the way I would find peace; I knew it. Yes, that's what I would do. Tomorrow. I would tell Adam in the morning.

And then I slept; peacefully and dreamlessly, at last.

Chapter Nineteen

I woke up the next morning feeling much better, my high temperature gone. Adam's side of the bed was empty. I looked at my watch and saw it was nearly ten o'clock. I'd slept through until the fever broke, leaving my head blessedly cool and lucid.

I remembered what I had decided last night. I was going to find a holiday rental in Polperro, and move there on my own. Adam, Danny, Lola and the baby would stay here. I would ask them to leave me alone while I got on with the business of finding out what happened the day Joey disappeared, to finding peace from this torment at last. I would feel much better without the family pressure on me to be happy. I wasn't, and I was tired of pretending.

Adam pushed open the door with his backside. He was carrying a breakfast tray. I could smell toast, and realised I was ravenously hungry. He smiled at me and put the tray on the bed: tea, orange juice, a boiled egg, toast and marmalade. I fell on it as if I were starving – which of course I was.

Adam beamed as I wolfed it all down. He was so thoughtful I couldn't help but smile at the sight of him. 'Good girl!' he said approvingly, as if I was about ten. 'Now, if you'll just get ready and pack your things, we can get away right now. With any luck we'll be in Manchester by suppertime.'

He saw my face fall. 'Hey, don't worry, love. I've talked to Danny. He and Lola quite understand why we're going home. Danny said he feels guilty that he so wanted you to come down here. He said he was being selfish. He was so desperate to get back down now he has a proper family and he genuinely thought enough time had passed for you to be happy again.' Adam paused, and walked over to the window. Quietly, he continued. 'He's young, you see, Molly; full of hopes and dreams for the future. Too young to spend the rest of his life mourning for a brother lost so many years ago. Don't blame him.'

Adam turned to face me. 'Blame me, love. I'm not young and I should have known better than to put you through this.' He coughed and turned back to the window. 'Lola was quite firm with him. Told him to let you go with good grace. He's got a good one there, Molly. She's clever and kind. When she said that, she looked quite fierce. I think Danny even quailed a bit.' He chuckled, then turned to me. 'So Danny asked me to tell you that you should go home with no worries. He, Lola and Edie will stay on here and they promise you they'll have a lovely holiday. So, it's all fixed.'

I stared down the bed, looking at my feet where they had slipped out of the rucked-up quilt I'd disturbed in my feverish sleep.

'Actually, Adam,' I said tentatively, 'I'm not going. I changed my mind.'

He looked confused and worried. 'But I thought it was all settled. You've been in a terrible state. Are you sure you're not still ill?'

'No, Adam. I'm sorry to be so inconsistent, and cause you all such worry. But I'm definitely not going back to Manchester. Not yet.'

Adam whistled softly. He sucked in his breath, and gave a weak smile. 'OK then, that's great. That's marvellous. We'll all stay here and have a good, sunny holiday. Danny will be so happy.'

Now it was my turn to take a deep breath. 'The thing is, I'm not staying here.'

Adam looked confused. 'You mean you want us to move somewhere else? Why? It's perfect here. I thought you loved it.'

'I do. But I want to rent a place in Polperro.'

He looked thunderstruck. 'Polperro? For God's sake, Molly, that's where—'

I raised my voice. 'Do you think I don't know that? That's why I need to be there. I need to reach him. That's where he'll be.'

He was quiet for a moment. 'But, if you've been so unhappy here, away from the sea, how on earth will you feel in Polperro? Every time you look out the window you'll see the harbour, the place where Joey took his last breaths.'

I tried hard to sound calm, but it was difficult. 'I KNOW that. That's the whole POINT.'

There was a long silence. I lifted my head and tried to see Adam's face. Then I saw comprehension dawn. I watched his expression change, and a small smile creep across his poor, puzzled features.

'I see. I see, Molly. You want, finally, to come to terms with what's happened. You feel strong enough to face up to Joey's death. You've realised, at last, that to do that you have to be brave, to confront it. That's fantastic, love. I've been praying for this. We'll go down to Polperro this morning and find a cottage that's big enough for all of us. Actually, I walked down to the village the other day and there are still quite a few empty holiday lets. One of them is really pretty, slightly up on the cliff, directly overlooking the harbour. It's big, too. I'll call the letting agent right away and ask him—'

I could bear it no longer. 'No,' I said, trying to keep my voice firm but reasonable. 'No, no, no. You don't understand. I don't want somewhere that's big enough for all of us. I need to be on my own. Look, Adam, I can't do this any more, playing happy families, little games on the beach with Edie, buying ice creams and pizzas, pretending everything's all right. This is not a holiday, Adam. For me it's purgatory. It's best if I stay in Polperro, concentrate on finding out what happened to Joey without any distractions, without feeling I've got to be a perfect wife, a perfect mother, a perfect grand-mother. Because I'm not, Adam. I'm a wreck. I'm bleeding, I'm torn to shreds; sometimes I feel I'm dying with grief.' I paused, my throat aching. 'I should never have come here, Adam. You made me feel I had to do it, for Danny. But I can't cope with all the memories. My only hope is that I can find out where he is. Please understand. I need to be alone with Joey.'

I was sobbing by now. Adam looked hurt, upset. 'Molly – I think you're wrong. I think what you want to do, going off on your own, leaving us all behind, will hurt Danny very much. It's selfish of you.' He paused. 'You're not the only one who's lost a son. And your other son has lost his only brother. I can only think you're having some kind of breakdown. This is all just nonsense.'

He left the room, closing the door firmly behind him. I thought he was right. I was having some kind of breakdown. It had been a long time coming. I had tried so hard not to collapse after Joey's accident. Five years of half-living. Five years of pretending I could cope, carry on. What was that old wartime adage? Keep calm and carry on? And that is what I'd done. I'd gone back to work the following Autumn term, presenting a tranquil face to the world. I had prepared my girls for A-level, achieving the usual excellent results and a record number of places at Oxbridge. There was praise from Ofsted for the sixth form's achievements, flattering articles in the more serious newspapers.

To my colleagues I appeared stable and steady. In fact it was surprising how few people remembered what had happened at all. It quickly faded from the minds of even my fellow teachers, no doubt partly because I never alluded to it myself. I kept myself apart, and I acted a part; that of the noble professional who would not allow her most private emotions to intrude upon her work.

And all the time I acted as if I were a whole, unwounded woman, I was crying inside. The magnitude of Joey's loss was insufferable to me. One day, I half knew, it would tear me inside out. And here in Cornwall, that day had come.

Chapter Twenty

I stayed in my bed at Coombe, allowing myself to cry properly now Adam had gone. Was I mad? Had my sanity, stretched to breaking point, finally snapped? Was that why I had 'heard' my missing son call out to me in a moonlit Cornish garden; why I had thought I would find him at Jamaica Inn, and instead found a bewitched malevolent scarecrow crouched against a broken old fence, which stared at me with evil glittering eyes and began to move. Madness seemed the only logical explanation.

And yes, I found myself blaming Adam and Danny

for bringing me back to a place where no woman who had been through what I had should ever have returned. Asking me to come here, selfishly, so they could have a seaside holiday, 'just like it used to be.' And blackmailing me emotionally, making me feel I would hurt Danny and Edie if I refused to come.

And look where it had got them. Look what they had to deal with now. A broken wife and mother, a woman driven half out of her mind because of their unforgiveable lack of sensitivity.

My sobs were interrupted by a rap on the bedroom door. It opened slightly and through the crack came a cultured, confident voice. 'Are you decent, Molly?'

I recognised that assured tone immediately. Dr Torrance, the local GP who had treated me in Polperro five years ago. Despite the horror I associated with that time, Jamie Torrance stirred a small patch of warmth in my wasted heart. He'd been marvellous. An oasis of comfort in a desert of grief, talking to him made me feel a bit better, the only person who could, back then.

I scrubbed my eyes dry with the edge of the sheet. A hopeless task. I knew I looked pathetic, my face blotched and swollen with tears.

'Yes, I'm decent,' I croaked. 'Come in, Jamie.'

And in he walked, tall, broad, and handsome as ever. Even in my vulnerable state, I felt embarrassed by the way I knew I must look. Jamie Torrance was a ridiculously good-looking man, possibly the best-looking doctor in Cornwall. His dirty-blond hair, bleached into streaks of dark gold by the Cornish sun, his eyes as bright and blue as the sea in which he spent all his spare time, and the mahogany tan acquired during the endless hours he spent surfing on his days off, all enveloped him in a kind of shimmering glamour. His surgery was in Looe, and rumour had it that there was always a long queue of eager ladies in his waiting room, excitedly anticipating the ways in which he would make them feel better, although those fantasies, no doubt to their disappointment, remained only in their heads. I bet he was aware of them, though. Back in the days when Adam would stand on the harbour wall skimming stones with Joey and Danny, Queenie and I would watch them from the Blue Peter, giggling about all the women who had a crush on him.

Jamie sat on my bed, and reached for my hand.

'Hello, Molly. Adam says you're in a bad way. He called me. I hope you don't mind.'

Oddly, I didn't. I'd been cross when Queenie poked her nose around my door, but Jamie was different. I had spent hours with him years ago, talking and crying. He was a good listener, not like most GPs who wanted to fob me off with Valium and Temazepam. He did give me sleeping pills, but he was there for me whenever I needed him. He visited me every day, listened and comforted when my grief was at its most raw, when I talked to him about suicide. It can't have been easy, comforting an irrational woman sucked into a vortex of shock and horror, but somehow he did it. When he left me every day, I always felt a little calmer; I felt more practical, more able to discuss the necessary next step with Adam. Adam was convinced Joey had drowned, even then. His certainty made me angry. We had to *look* for him, I told him.

'Where, for God's sake?' he'd say in despair. 'At the bottom of the ocean? They've had professional divers down there for days. They haven't found a thing.'

But by looking for Joey I didn't mean searching the seabed. He wasn't there, I knew it. He was somewhere else. I was certain of it. And I knew where, I did; it's just that I couldn't remember.

Jamie Torrance had witnessed all this back then. His patience was inexhaustible; his gentle warmth soothed us both. So now, in my bedroom at Coombe, my poor tortured brain relaxed a little, reflexively reacting to his presence with memories of the comfort he had brought me when I was most in need.

I poured out my heart. I told him how coming back to Cornwall had precipitated a spiral of hysteria that I couldn't control. I told him about hearing Joey's voice begging me to find him, about my visit to Jamaica Inn and the evil vision that had sprung upon me in the neglected little field.

'Adam says he wanted to take you home to Manchester because he could see how upset being here was making you. But he told me you don't want to go. You want to rent a holiday let in Polperro by yourself?' Jamie's voice was gentle, but questioning. 'Why, Molly?'

'I just need to. I don't know why, but something is telling me to do that. Or someone. I think it's Joey.' I looked at him desperately, aware how loopy I must sound.

'And what if you do stay all on your own in the place where such a terrible thing happened to your family?'

he asked gently. 'Don't you think that being alone with your thoughts and sadness, without the others to talk to about ordinary things, and without that gorgeous baby to cuddle, you will feel pretty bleak? I think I know you enough to feel you need at least some warmth and normality in your life.'

Like a red rag to a bull, I thought. All my warm feelings towards him disappeared in an instant.

'You don't know me at all, Jamie. You treated me briefly for – what? A few weeks until the inquest was over? Weeks when I was going through the worst time of my life? You only ever saw me as a bereaved mother, and that's how you see me to this day. You don't know the real me at all; you only see the broken husk that Joey left behind. I've coped for five years, you know. I will certainly cope in Polperro. It's what I want.'

Jamie looked unconvinced. 'Molly, I know I've asked you this before, and I well remember what you said, but I really do think you need to see someone—'

I interrupted rudely. 'A psychiatrist, you mean? No, actually, I suppose you're thinking of a "counsellor" or a "grief therapist" who's probably twenty years younger than me and doesn't know his arse from his elbow. I told you then and I'm telling you now, I don't need that kind of help. I don't need anything except to find Joey.'

I stopped for a moment, desperate to straighten my head, to try to tell Jamie about the deep conviction I felt about Polperro. I had to unlock some secrets there – I didn't know what. But they were there, and those secrets were hiding Joey, shrouding him, keeping him away from me. Ben could help, I knew, but it would be hard to get him to talk to me. In Polperro, on the spot, living so close to him, I had a greater chance to wear him down.

Secrets, conspiracies even. They were teeming in that magical little village, clustering invisibly around the self-consciously come-hither shops selling twee little good-luck charms. Plots and sinister plans, breathing thick as cigarette smoke from the wonky old walls of local alehouses: boiling, as busy as the teeming narrow rivers rushing beneath ancient pubs perched picturesquely on stilts, their wooden doors adorned with fantastical pictures of pirates and wizards. Secrets swirling round the chocolate-box white cottages, eddying in a vortex above Merlin's Land of Legend, and clinging like golden dust to the children who swarmed the summer lanes, heading down to the rocky harbour beach, uplifted by the enchantment which held its guests in thrall each year; thrilled by romantic stories of bloodthirsty pirates and desperate smugglers, their lanterns highlighting ashen faces, men who daily risked their lives for lucre.

Children, I thought. *Yes, there is something about children connected to Joey.* All this I knew absolutely, and with a shiver I locked it tight inside my heart. There was no point in trying to explain to Jamie. This was a vision for me alone; a vision not for sharing, lest it evaporate on the sea breeze.

I looked up and shook myself, aware that I'd been in a daze. Jamie was staring at me speculatively.

'Molly,' he said briskly, 'I'm sorry, but you do need help. The therapist I had in mind is actually a very nice woman, a little older than you, professionally trained of course but with a lot of life experience. As a matter of fact she lost a child herself, to illness. That's why she took up counselling. I think you'd like her a lot.' He smiled and looked at me encouragingly.

I shook my head. 'No, Jamie. I know what I need to do.' I hesitated; then, trying to placate him, said, 'Listen.

I'm sorry I was so rude about shrinks. I promise that if I do strike a blank in Polperro I'll see your lady. Just give me some time first.'

But I won't strike a blank, I thought, hugging my secrets to my chest. I was suddenly excited. I had a plan.

'How long?' Jamie asked.

'How long what?' I asked, knowing perfectly well what he meant.

'How much time do you want before you'll see Thelma?'

'I have no idea. A couple of weeks, maybe. That's how long I'll rent the cottage for.'

He sighed. 'OK. Well, at least that's something. Do you mind if I tell Adam?'

'No, that's fine.' *In fact, it's perfect*, I thought. Thinking Jamie has persuaded me to see a therapist would be music to Adam's ears. It should get him off my back.

'All right, Molly. I'll go now. Will you let me know when you've found a holiday let? I'd like to come and visit you, if I may?'

'For professional reasons, or just to be sociable?' I asked, almost flirtatiously, so light was my heart now after my sudden Polperro epiphany.

He laughed. 'A bit of both, I hope,' he said. 'I do need to keep an eye on you though,' he added, more seriously. 'Give me a call when you know your new address.' He smiled, and left the room.

I could hear low voices as he talked to Adam downstairs. I felt relieved and glad Jamie had come. He would convince Adam that my plan to move to Polperro would work out OK, that he would visit and watch out for me. I'd stopped crying now. I felt fired with excitement and enthusiasm. I was on my way to find my son.

Chapter Twenty-One

I slept like the dead for twelve hours, then rang the local letting agent first thing and told him what I wanted; he said he had a couple of places he thought might suit, and I agreed to meet him outside the Crumplehorn Inn.

Adam had told Danny and Lola about my plan. It was clear that Adam was deeply hurt, and Danny was upset and confused. Nevertheless my son announced he would drive me to the Crumplehorn to meet the letting agent. I was at once glad and dismayed. Of course I wouldn't have a car in Polperro, not that I expected I'd need one. The village is tiny, and I didn't have any intention of leaving it. I had been going to ask Adam if I could take the Volvo to meet the agent, but he, distant but courteous, had said at breakfast that he was going to play golf with one of the men he used to hang out with here when the children were small, one of the holiday friends we met up with every year. He and his wife had lived in Hertfordshire, but now, retired, they'd moved down to Cornwall permanently, living in a beautiful house in Fowey. Perhaps, I thought, if the boat had never been wrecked, Adam and I might have one day retired to Fowey. Danny and Joey would visit us, and hordes of grandchildren would romp through our sunny garden every summer, running down the steep lanes to paddle on Readymoney Beach.

With an effort, I shifted my attention to Danny. It was nice of him to give me a lift, but I knew there was an ulterior motive. He wanted to talk to me. Although he knew I was looking for a place in Polperro, I hadn't told him why I needed to be alone, and when Lola declined to come with us, saying she and Edie would stay behind at Coombe to watch CBeebies, with the feeble excuse that Edie was tired, even though she was currently rampaging round the house in her usual Formula One crawl, it was obvious Danny's gesture was an ambush, although with the kindest and gentlest of motives. I can't say I looked forward to it, but I owed him this conversation, and was at least grateful I didn't have to have it in Adam's presence.

We got into the car, Danny driving. Edie's car seat looked oddly forlorn in the back seat. We turned out of the pretty little courtyard and headed towards the coast. The May bluebells and cow parsley were long gone, along with the cool colours of spring. Wisteria, lilac and pale clematis had given way to the vivid blooms of summer. Red-hot pokers soared like flaming torches in the hedgerows, purple foxgloves and hollyhocks nodded knowingly in the breeze, and luscious fairy bells of fuchsia, pink, red and deep mauve glowed like tiny gems beside our path. They were beautiful, these cultivated plants, which had somehow escaped their orderly well-tended gardens, flown over the hedges and come to rest magically beside us like gifts to brighten our journey. I sighed with pleasure, handing my brittle sadness briefly over to some other universe, overwhelmed with the sheer glory all around me, unable to fight a delighted response to nature's gorgeous flowering. I let the beauty enter me. Fragrant tendrils delicately massaged my neck. All the aromas of this small piece of paradise filled me, and brought me peace.

I opened my eyes when Danny spoke to me. He was smiling. 'Gorgeous, isn't it, Mum?' I could sense the relief in his voice. 'It's so good to see you relax.'

'Oh, Danny,' I said. 'It breaks my heart to think of you worrying so much about me.'

He was serious now. 'I have been worried about you, Mum. More worried than I was five years ago when Joey's accident had just happened.'

'You think I'm worse than I was when I first found out?' I was astonished. How could my admittedly odd behaviour this summer possibly have upset Danny more than the overwhelming grief of that horrendous Easter?

'It's not really that, Mum. It's just that the way you were back then, when it first happened, well, that was natural. But now, the way you've been acting, it seems so strange. It's come out of the blue.'

Out of the blue? What could he possibly mean? Surely he knew, they all knew, how deeply my grief was buried? Surely they hadn't thought that I'd all but recovered, barely five years after I'd lost my child, the most eviscerating event that could ever happen to a woman?

And then I remembered my determination to 'keep calm and carry on'. My achievements at work, my solid reputation as an inspirational teacher, my kitchen suppers, my steady demeanour. I knew that Danny felt he couldn't talk to his father and me about Joey, but suppose he didn't want to? Suppose he found our lack of drama, our sheer normality, comforting? And he had Lola to share his deepest emotions with. He was twenty-three when Joey disappeared, not a child, not a small boy to be cuddled and comforted. I suddenly realised that he couldn't really express his grief, except to his girlfriend. There was only one time he totally broke down with me, and that was the night Edie was born, when he had told me how desperately he wanted his little brother to see his firstborn, how guilty he felt for being so happy to have a brand-new family when Joey was dead, and would never share this joy. Joey would never have his own family, his own baby; how could he, Danny, exult in his good fortune when his brother lay lifeless at the bottom of the sea?

And I'd embraced him, told him not to feel guilty. I told Danny I believed Joey knew about Edie. I wasn't just trying to comfort my eldest son; at that moment I truly felt my youngest was aware of the baby's birth. I had a strong intuition that Joey, in whatever form he had now taken, felt his brother's joy. In that moment I began to see Edie as a kind of bridge that would take me to Joey, and that feeling had persisted ever since.

Danny soon forgot his small meltdown, lost in the happiness of new fatherhood. He and Lola revelled in their 'babymoon' and he never again mentioned his feelings of guilt.

So, Danny's life found its balance once more. He was happy. He thought I was too, my aura of calm deceiving him that I'd 'got over' Joey. Adam, of course, played along with this. It suited his undemonstrative nature. If he worried about the fact that we never made love any more, he didn't show it.

What could I do to reassure Danny that I needed to do this to find peace? I would have to come up with an explanation about moving to Polperro that didn't worry or bewilder him too much.

'Danny, love,' I began, carefully, 'the thing is, and now

you have Edie you'll understand, that as a parent ...' I
paused, swallowed hard, started again. 'As a parent,
losing a child is the worst possible thing that can happen
to you. It drives you a bit mad. At least, it drove me
mad. All that time, back home in Manchester, when you
thought I was OK, well, I wasn't really. Oh, I was carrying on, teaching, living; functioning as best I could.
But I had no choice. I could have gone to pieces, had a
breakdown. In some ways that would've been easier than
waking up each morning, feeling normal for a couple of
seconds and then, wham, it would hit me. Joey was
dead – that was my first thought every day. And then I
began to refuse to think that. No, he wasn't dead. Where
was the proof, where was his body? And I convinced
myself he was still alive, waiting for me to rescue him. It
was the only way I could keep going. The thought that
I would find him, or he would find me, became central
to my survival.' I paused. 'I hate to tell you this, Danny,
but without that conviction, or delusion as your father
calls it, I'm not sure I could have carried on.'

Danny looked shocked. 'But what about me? What
about Dad? What about Edie, for God's sake? Don't any
of us matter to you too?'

'I told you, Danny, losing a child drives you mad. It wasn't that Joey was any more special than you, of course he wasn't. I'm just telling you what I went through. The thing is, I started to think I was getting better, slowly. I hadn't forgotten Joey, how could I? But I was beginning to think about the future more positively.' I paused. 'After Edie was born I felt much brighter, thought I saw a new purpose in life.'

Danny listened closely as I continued. 'Everything was sort of going along okay – well, you know, I felt I was pretty stable. Until we came here, to Cornwall. And, I guess, with all the memories, I kind of imploded. Everything came back to me and I couldn't face it; I need to do this. Sorry, Danny.'

Danny drove quietly. We were nearly there, the houses on the outskirts of Polperro staring down at us from the hill over the valley. Any minute now, we'd pull into that vast car park at the head of the village, and this conversation would be at an end.

'I can understand all that, Mum. I'm sorry you felt so alone grieving for Joey. I don't want you to think I wasn't grieving too.'

'Of course I knew you were grieving, Danny. The

thing is, this grieving business is something you have to do alone. It's really hard work, and you just have to get through it.'

'Is that why you want to stay in Polperro by yourself? To grieve for Joey even more?'

I heard the slightly impatient note in his voice. He obviously thought I'd done more than enough mourning to appease the gods of grief, who knelt keening in the skies with their requiems, black robes and crucifixes.

'It's hard to explain. I need to be in Polperro alone with Joey's ... spirit. I'm hoping if I stay here for a while, where it all happened, I'll get some kind of ... closure.'

Oh horrible, horrible word, implying that grief and death come in a neat parcel, to be wrapped and sellotaped, and, who knows, even tied with a bow and a consoling little label advising you your 'closure' has arrived at last. Enjoy!

But right now I had to comfort Danny, had to tell him what he wanted to hear. And he had to accept it.

Chapter Twenty-Two

We left the Peugeot in the car park and walked the short distance to the Crumplehorn Inn, the big ancient pub with an old watermill in the front courtyard which marked the top end of Polperro before the lane slopes languorously down to the harbour. The Inn is just across the road from the attractive row of little houses, roses wreathed round every door, known as the Crumplehorn cottages – where Ben now lived. I felt nervous. Ben was the last person I wanted to see at the moment. Later, yes, but right now, with Danny at my side knowing nothing of my previous meeting with him, I hoped the fact that it was only ten-thirty in the morning meant he wouldn't be in the pub.

We could tell immediately that our appointed guest had arrived; he was sitting by himself in the Inn's front courtyard drinking coffee. We'd never met him before, but Eric Mayhew Esq. couldn't possibly have presented a more flamboyant picture of a seaside estate agent, specialising in properties in quirky historic villages such as this one. He wore a crumpled beige linen summer suit, a paisley cravat and a battered Panama hat. He would have managed to look slightly louche and arty, were it not for the mousey little moustache on his upper lip, which he fussily kept dabbing with an ornate art nouveau handkerchief. He sprang to his feet as soon as he saw us.

'You must be Mrs Gabriel,' he drawled in an unconvincing upper-middle-class accent. I acknowledged that I was, and introduced Danny.

'Aha! The protective son, come to keep an eye on Mummy. That's the ticket,' he said offensively. I watched him sourly, said our time was short, and could he show us what he'd got.

'But of course, of course, although I had hoped to

buy you a coffee first and tell you all about this wonderful, unique village of ours.'

I told him I was very familiar with Polperro, had been coming here for years with my family, and so I didn't need an introduction. He looked disappointed, then arch. He wagged his finger at me like Leslie Phillips in an old black and white movie. I half expected him to wink and say 'Ding, *dong*!'

'Don't you even want to know about our pride and joy – the Miniature Village and Merlin's Land of Legend?' he twinkled.

I smiled thinly. 'Mr Mayhew, I think Danny here could tell you more about the Land of Legend than you could bear to hear. Added to which, we're hardly the target audience, knocking on a bit as we undoubtedly are.'

'Ah yes, Mrs Gabriel. But a lady of your age is bound to be expecting grandchildren soon, don't you think?' And he actually winked at Danny. 'I'm sure this fine young man has a twinkle or two in his eye, don't you, lad?' And he actually nudged Danny with his elbow.

Danny, more patient than I, was trying hard not to laugh. I, on the other hand, had had enough. I drew myself up to my unimpressive full height of five foot five, and said in my most school-marmish voice, 'I'd like to see these properties now, if you don't mind, Mr Mayhew. We don't have much time. I believe you said there were two I might like?'

All the time Mayhew was wittering on, I'd been in an agony of suspense about Ben. I didn't know which of the cottages he lived in, and I half expected him to materialise beside us any moment. And then – oh God – he would see Danny and I would have to explain to my son that Ben lived here now. Everything would get hideously complicated and Danny would think my decision to stay in Polperro was even stranger than he'd imagined. Surely he would find my prior knowledge of Ben's presence in the village inexplicable, even sinister. And he would feel he had to tell Adam, which didn't bear thinking about. My husband would sweep down here in a fury, accusing me of going behind his back. Which I had done, but I wouldn't have had to if he'd only agreed to meet Ben in the first place.

We left the Crumplehorn at a cracking pace, set by me. Danny and Mr Mayhew scurried to keep up. Of course, staying here in the village I knew I could bump into Ben at any time. Everyone here lived in each other's pockets, used the same post office, the same newsagent's, the same baker's. But if I were on my own it wouldn't matter so much. In fact it was an important part of my plan to make friends with Ben, to slowly gain his confidence so he would gradually reveal more details of Joey's last day. If Adam was right and Ben was keeping something back. I was determined to discover what it was.

We walked swiftly down the main street, past the bed and breakfasts with their gaily painted front doors and the tiny ornamental bridges which led to each house, allowing B&B holiday guests to arrive with their feet dry as they picked their way gingerly across the little brook which ran through the whole village. After a few yards, Danny laughingly begged me to slow down, because he wanted to reminisce about our family walks along this small but tumbling stream when he and Joey were very small. They found it endlessly fascinating, and after we explained about the constant tiny waterfalls that interrupted the burbling water's fast and furious flow, they would run ahead and stop at each one, shouting, 'Is that a little weir?' And, 'Is that a little weir?' And, 'Is that a little weir as well?' It drove us bonkers then, in an amused and indulgent kind of way, but looking back, what lovely times; how perfect and wonderful they were, those short and vivid parts of our lives. Unremarkable and trivial as they happen, we don't yet understand that we should hold onto them, grab and engrave them on our hearts; because they are precious beyond rubies, and we shall remember and mourn them for the rest of our lives.

When we reached the post office we ignored the lane branching off to the right that led to the harbour and the Blue Peter. I marched swiftly straight ahead, glad not to have to see either of those haunted sites again, and soon after we'd passed the newsagent's, we reached our destination. It was the Warren, a narrow lane of tiny cottages, some ornately decorated with seashells. I trembled slightly. Joey and Ben's final ill fated holiday-let had been close to the Warren. My mind had blanked out the exact location, but I really didn't want to stay anywhere so near.

A few doors on, Mr Mayhew stopped in front of a little whitewashed dwelling that looked charming and cosy, but some deep primitive instinct made me loathe it on sight. Eric Mayhew turned the key in the lock, opened the door and in we went, the agent cheerful and enthusiastic, me hesitant and reluctant.

'Here we are, Mrs Gabriel. I'm sure you'll agree that this little place is deeply romantic and very picturesque.'

I tuned him out, looking round with a dismay that was quite unreasonable. The cottage was pretty enough, with attractive interior stone walls painted white, what looked like amateur but jolly little pictures of fishing boats on the walls, and simple rustic furniture. There was a tiny but functional kitchen, and the whole place was immaculate and obviously freshly decorated. Mayhew informed us that there were two bedrooms and a small bathroom upstairs, if I'd like to take a look. But somehow, I didn't like. For no real reason, I couldn't imagine living here, even for two weeks. And it was so dark. Of course, most of the old cottages in this particular row were dark because there were so few windows. These seamen's houses had been built for shelter against winter gales and storms, not sunny summer holidays. The only view was of another cottage opposite, now empty, and encased in scaffolding. Shabby, with peeling paintwork and neglected damp grey walls, it was obviously undergoing extensive renovation. I imagined workmen on the scaffolding all day, looking into my little sitting room. I tried to see myself living here, listening to constant noise, clatter and shouts from the small building site just yards across the narrow path, and I shuddered.

When I looked at Danny he was frowning, and shook his head. He'd picked up on my mood. He didn't like it either. I squared up to Mr Mayhew. 'Sorry, but I don't think this one is right for me.'

He looked put out. 'Oh, but you haven't seen the upstairs yet, which is so pretty. I know it's small, but you have to admit it's quaint, and so atmospheric.'

'No, my mind's made up. You did say you had another place to show me?'

Nettled, the agent pushed open the door, let us out and locked up noisily behind him, with a bad-tempered twist of the wrist. He then led the way, pushing on through the Warren, while my heart sank. For the first time I began to see how ill-considered my impulsive decision had been. In my state of mind, there was every reason to expect the next property would be equally as depressing. If so, I would have to go back to Coombe and Adam with my tail between my legs, my dream of finding Joey in tatters, and my failure to jump the first hurdle of finding somewhere to live in Polperro proof of Adam's conviction that I was the victim of a stubborn and impossible delusion.

After a few steps, Mayhew seemed to reconsider his petulance. He turned round and beamed at me. 'Well, well, I'm sorry that cottage wasn't to your liking, Mrs Gabriel. I can quite understand it, of course. Although many of my clients love it, finding it quite charming and picturesque, it *is* a little on the small side, and rather dark if you are hoping for a sunny sea view.' He smiled to himself. 'And I think, I do think, that I have the perfect place for you, my dear. I think you'll love it.'

Danny and I glanced at each other, rolling our eyes. I was glad he was here. I'm not sure I could have coped with smarmy Mayhew on my own. By now, I may well have run back to the car park and called the whole thing off.

We walked briskly on down the path, past Sunny Corner, a cottage that vividly caught the sun. *I wish I could rent that one*, I thought wistfully, but alas Sunny Corner was spoken for. After a few more minutes, the view opened up and to our right the sea appeared, stunningly blue and silver. I stopped for a moment, my spirits suddenly soaring. Ahead of me, Mr Mayhew was talking again.

'So, up there on the cliff are some of the most beautiful houses on this part of the coast,' he said. I caught up with him, interested now. He pointed up to the left. 'That's The Watchers, and next to it is Seaways. Did you know that when they built it, they had to use donkeys to pull the stone up the cliff?'

Seaways, a giddily steep rocky climb up from here, looked breathtakingly lovely. I imagined, and envied, the astonishing view of the ocean the house must command.

A few yards further on, Mayhew abruptly stopped. 'And this, my dear, is Hope. I think it's just what you're looking for. It's not usually rented out, but there are ... unusual circumstances.'

And there, a dozen steps up from the coastal path, set back in a lovely garden bursting with summer flowers and shrubs and enclosed by a white picket fence, was a little yellow wooden house. Pale sunshine yellow, built of clapboard, like the oceanside homes in Martha's

Vineyard and Cape Cod; like a doll's house, or a child's painting: the perfect seaside cottage, its door and window frames painted in a soft but jaunty shade of blue-grey, mirroring the clouds and water it so gloriously faced.

My heart stopped. *Oh, yes*, I thought. *Oh yes*.

Chapter Twenty-Three

When I arrived back at Coombe, having told the agent I'd take possession of 'Hope', as he'd called it, on Saturday, two days from now, the atmosphere in the old farmhouse was very tense. Adam was barely speaking to me. I realised he'd hoped my property search in Polperro would turn out to be a wild goose chase, that I wouldn't find anywhere I wanted to rent. He must have told himself it was so late in the season that the probability of discovering an attractive empty cottage was remote. All that would remain, he thought, would be what was left on the scrapheap, too unappealing for me even to consider.

So when Danny and I arrived home soon after midday, my face wreathed in smiles, Adam was seriously put out. Coward that I was, I let Danny tell him we'd found a smashing little place, and I was moving in the day after tomorrow. Adam looked from his wife to his son in disbelief. It was obvious he thought we'd formed a conspiracy to betray him. As Lola, rocking Edie on her hip, looked on anxiously, Adam turned on his heel and walked out of the house.

After his father left, Danny looked upset, and I felt dreadful. Faced with the blank reality of my family's hurt feelings, my resolution to leave Coombe started to falter. I was aware of how selfish I was being; the euphoria I'd felt when I first saw the little yellow house with its glorious view had been written all over my face when I walked into the kitchen. I realised I was acting like a tremulous newlywed, enchanted at finding my dream home. Something about this cottage called Hope had aroused in me an almost romantic vision of my quest to find Joey.

Analysing my emotions, I knew how easy it would be to call me deluded. And surely heroic flights of fancy had no place in the grim business of rescuing

Joey from whatever frightful place he was stuck. Yes, that was it. He was stuck, unable to leave, unable to get back to me.

Lola interrupted my thoughts to say she and Danny were taking Edie out for a late lunch, and did I want to come? I longed to put Edie on my knee and make silly faces at her, listening to her croon and chortle while she grabbed at my nose and earrings. But I knew Danny and Lola would want to talk about me, what I'd told my son on the way to Polperro, so I declined and said I had a longing to go back to Talland Bay, and would they mind dropping me off? I thought I could walk on the beach and visit the old church up the lane. Perhaps that would centre me, and I'd be able to find some peace.

The kids dropped me off at the beach car park, but I decided to walk up to St Tallanus straight away. The eleventh-century church had always held a powerful attraction for me, partly because of its extraordinary location, perched on the cliff top. The sleepers resting in its ancient graveyard were truly blessed to lie amidst such beauty, the sky and the sea sweeping vast and eternal before them.

I didn't go inside the church today. Instead, I felt pulled to walk among the weathered, lichen-stained gravestones staring out to sea. From here, the rocks on the shore looked a deep, glowing purple. The whole vista was a glorious palette of yellow, blue, green and vivid indigo. I looked down at the graves beneath my feet. Most of them were very old, bearing witness to mothers and babies who had died in childbirth; and to children who'd been snatched from their keening parents at a blisteringly tender age, the inscriptions on their headstones betraying the heartbreak left behind. And yet these simple engraved verses also breathed something else, something more strengthening: a sense of resignation to the inevitable, of serenity and conviction; the devout belief that their little ones were safe in God's arms; that their early departure from this earth had spared them much hardship, and that, after all, they were better off with the angels.

That serenity was what I'd wanted for Joey. However terrible his fate, however shattered my heart, if I could only have visited his grave in this beautiful place, brought flowers, talked to him, I would have felt soothed, comforted. The knowledge of his presence, resting beneath my feet, might have been almost enough; a sad but peaceful resolution to a beloved life.

I'd never been a regular churchgoer, but I'd had a quiet faith until Joey disappeared, a typical educated middle-class belief in goodness, kindness, benevolence. A muddled sense that if you did your best, behaved well, and genuinely tried not to hurt anyone, then you were on the right side. Do as you would be done by, and all would be well.

Afterwards, shouting at God in bitter anguish, I asked Him how He could expect me to believe in a deity who inflicted such barbarous cruelty on children and parents throughout the world, in war or through simple tragedy? In other words, I reacted like every other victim of a terrible disaster. 'Why me? Why my child?' And I wouldn't listen to those who tried to counsel me by asking 'Why not?'

And yet, as I stood in the graveyard at Talland church, my weeping eyes raised to the soaring sky, something began to happen to my body. It stilled. My heart, initially beating fast and furious with anguish, slowed down. Without any conscious effort, I was filled with a deep sense of peace. And I became conscious of light stealing into my body, and a strong awareness of grace granted from – somewhere, some place way beyond me. I was calm, suddenly and completely. Here, in this holy place where so many souls lay at rest, I was receiving a message. And although I heard no words, no heavenly visitations, no glorious visions and neither sight nor sound of Joey, I knew I'd been heard, that my instincts were sure. I knew I was absolutely right to be searching for my son.

Filled with a calm certainty, I left St Tallanus and walked down the steep lane to the beach, listening to the tiny stream of water that dribbled down the hill to my left, running constantly past wall and hedgerow. All Celtic churches were built near running water, the staff of life; also the weapon of death. However you looked at it, water was key here – the most important single element in Cornwall's past, present and future.

Down on Talland beach, sitting at a wooden table in front of the little café, watching the children shrieking with their happy parents as they paddled in the wavelets of that oh-so-deceptively calm and pretty sea – the same sea that could rise like an ogre if it wished and swallow those little mites whole, leaving their parents bewildered and bereaved – I shook myself into practicality. I ordered tea and a sandwich from the boy helping out the owners, kept my eyes on the car park and waited for Danny.

Chapter Twenty-Four

Late that evening, as the roses in Coombe's small court-yard smelled their sweetest and lengthening shadows crept towards the front gate, I stood in the porch and worried about Adam. He was still out, and hadn't called all day. I could tell Danny was bothered at not being able to reach him on his mobile, but Lola was reassuring about the lousy signal down here and said Adam just had a lot to think about, and would be back soon. Lola had a wonderful knack of normalising things. It was impossible to panic when she looked you in the eye and spoke in her low, soft voice. Danny smiled and kissed her. They went upstairs to bathe Edie and put her to bed, and I felt so grateful to have such a strong, sweet daughter-in-law. She was a loving presence in the house, constantly helping us all to keep calm and positive, even though the stress levels in our holiday home were palpable.

Later, as I stood at the door, she came down again and said she and Danny were going to have an early night. Would I be all right waiting for Adam on my own? I said I'd be fine. Then she kissed me and said if I felt at all lonely, I must knock on their door and she'd come down and join me for a drink. There was no false pity in her voice, no obvious anxiety about my state of mind, just warm kindness. When I thought about the derogatory way in which some of my female colleagues talked about their daughters-in-law, the bitchy claims that their sons could have done so much better, I knew the Gabriel family had scooped the jackpot. Kind, wise and beautiful; that was Danny's Lola.

I closed the front door and went into the kitchen. I stood by the table and stared through the window into the back garden; another soft warm night. This long stretch of golden weather had gone on for a couple of weeks now. Even in Cornwall's sunny microclimate, where palm trees grew in every garden, this was unprecedented. It would surely break soon and we'd have a tremendous storm. I shivered. I'd be in my little yellow house the day after tomorrow. Would the weather turn while I was there? How would it feel to be alone in an unfamiliar place, the sea heaving and thrashing outside my window, the skies cracking and splitting above my head?

I made myself a gin and tonic and stepped through the kitchen door into the garden. At once I remembered the night, such a short time ago, when I had done just this, and heard Joey calling to me. That, I said to myself, had been the start of the journey I needed to take. That night in this silvery garden was why I took off for Jamaica Inn the next day, some strange impulse driving me there to gain knowledge of my son's fate. Instead what I found waiting for me was half an hour of theatrical horror in a misty, muddy garden, pursued by an animated scarecrow. I wanted to laugh now, but I couldn't. The sheer evil of that hallucination was with me still.

Tonight, I thought, would be different. I wouldn't

panic, I would try hard to relax and breathe deeply. The feeling of peace and lightness, of stillness, which had crept into me that afternoon in the graveyard at Talland church, was still with me. I sat on the stone bench and sipped my drink. Night-scented stocks filled the air with heady, insistent perfume. Silvery shadows stretched in the moonlight beneath the trees. I felt dreamy, tranquil; on the edge of a great adventure, calm and hopeful. Drowsily, I gave thanks to the sleepers resting quietly in their graves at the church for letting me share their peace that day. I stood up from the little bench and sat on the warm grass. Hugging my knees, I looked up at the black sky, pregnant with millions of tiny shining stars. *Soon*, I thought, sleepily. *Soon. Very soon.*

The hillside was suffused with a pale golden light. From the gravestones all around me streamed bright ribbons of starlight, twinkling and pulsing, as if all these loving monuments had become sentient beings. And in among the stones darted soft white drifts of air, barely visible until they moved, always swiftly, up and down, swirling round trees and bushes, sometimes getting snared as they caught on the branches. There was a feeling of gaiety in the air, a sense of celebration; of welcome.

A tall priest I'd never seen before walked silently towards me. He stopped just a few steps away, bowed his head. And then I saw what he saw. A void, a dark deep hole in the grass. It was a freshly dug grave, and the priest was here to conduct a burial. Behind him walked a small procession. Leading it was a polished wooden coffin, its lid crowned with a mass of white roses. Like the ones climbing round the door at Coombe, I thought drowsily. Carrying the coffin were four pallbearers, tall men in dark suits and black ties. Without surprise, I realised that the two men bearing the front end of the casket were Adam and Danny. Behind the coffin was a small cortege of mourners. I recognised Lola, holding Edie close on her hip. Next to her, to my astonishment, walked Ben. Behind him were a man and woman I didn't know, holding the hands of a young woman between them. She had red hair, and the lights kissed her face with kindness. She laughed at the darting flickering flames, which danced like the guttering gleams of a Christmas candle, joyful and gay; she let them tease and tickle her eyes and mouth. Then came Queenie in a smart black hat with a feather, next to an elderly man who shuffled sorrowfully along. He didn't look well; his face was white and gaunt. The playful white lights in the graveyard darted quickly round him, as if they were trying to comfort him. No, that wasn't quite right. They weren't trying to comfort the old man, they were trying to cheer him up. They brushed like will-o'-the-wisps around his head, touching his face with mirthful jollity.

Jamie Torrance walked behind Queenie, handsome, tall and erect. And behind him, quiet and sad, were streams of people, young men and women. I knew them all. They were friends of Joey and Danny from school and university. Until I saw them, I'd thought the procession was short, but now the boys' friends filled the churchyard, fanning out among the headstones. It seemed there were hundreds of them, and the sight filled me with joy.

At the very back, a small young woman not much more than a girl walked holding the hand of a little boy. She looked sad; the boy, like all the children gathered here in this mystical dreamland graveyard, skipped by her side, his face wreathed in smiles, unaffected by the solemnity of the woman by his side.

And then I too was among the mourners, and the darting white gusts of air joined me, lifting up my hair, caressing my cheek. They made me smile; they dried my tears. They made me happy. The coffin by now had been lowered into the grave and Adam and Danny stood beside me, holding my hands. And one by one, all these wonderful hushed people — not a sound had disturbed the silent hillside since I first opened my eyes — came to the graveside, smiled and gently dropped a white rose on top of the casket. Adam, Danny and I went last, and as we stood over the grave, my husband and my son stepped back, leaving me alone on the edge, but not before Adam handed me a bouquet of red roses. I kneeled down, and it seemed I could easily touch the coffin lid. I placed the roses carefully on top, and suddenly there was something else in my hands; also red. It was Joey's favourite winter scarf. I turned the soft wool round and round, twisting it, knowing I had done this before, but unable to remember when. I kissed it, and laid it gently on the roses. I whispered goodbye, and looked up; the golden glow grew warmer, and the swift whispering ribbons of starlight darted into the grave, and wrapped around the two of us; to me they offered peace; to Joey, they promised eternal rest.

Chapter Twenty-Five

Someone was shaking me. I groaned, reluctant to leave the churchyard where I felt so tranquil. I didn't want to wake up somewhere else, somewhere dark. I wanted to stay in the warm golden glow that filled me with love and peace. I struggled to stay on the hillside among the welcoming gravestones and my children's friends, but the pale beckoning light was fading, and I opened my eyes. I was lying on the grass in Coombe's back garden; the night was black and I was cold. Adam was kneeling next to me, grasping my shoulders and calling my name, his voice anxious.

I shivered. 'Oh God, what happened?' I moaned. 'I'm freezing.'

Adam sighed with relief and pulled me roughly to my feet. 'Let's get you inside. You feel cold as death.' He pushed me towards the kitchen door, his words puzzling me: cold as death? But death was warm, comforting. He propelled me through the kitchen and into the sitting room. A log fire blazed brightly in the grate. Surely I hadn't lit it? It was a warm night.

I said so, and asked, 'Who lit the fire?'

'I did, before I realised you weren't in bed,' Adam said gruffly. 'It may have been warm earlier, but it's gone midnight, for Christ's sake. What on earth were you doing out there? I was worried sick when I went upstairs and saw you weren't in our room. I woke up Dan and Lola and they said you were here when they went upstairs to bed. And then of course the baby woke up and started screaming. Jesus, Molly, I nearly called the police. Then Lola looked out of their bedroom window and saw you lying in the garden. I thought you'd had a heart attack or something. God almighty, Molly, you don't half put us all through it.' He subsided, gave an exaggerated sigh, and disappeared into the kitchen.

I sat shivering in an armchair, seeing the fire but not feeling it yet. Lola came into the room wearing her dressing gown and carrying mine. She draped it round my shoulders, and then handed me a soft woollen throw from the sofa.

'Oh, Lola, I'm so sorry I woke Edie up when you were going to have an early night,' I said, my teeth chattering from the cold. She put her fingers to her lips and kissed me on the cheek. 'It's no big deal, Molly, honestly. Everything's fine; stop worrying. Get yourself warm and go to bed. You just need a good night's sleep.' She sounded in charge, like a nurse, but I was grateful for a bit of well-meant bossiness. Adam came back with a bottle of brandy and two glasses. He raised the bottle questioningly towards Lola when he saw her, but she shook her head. We heard her weary footsteps climbing the stairs.

Adam poured us both a brandy and sat down in the armchair on the other side of the fireplace.

'We need to talk,' he said.

'You keep disappearing,' I replied ungraciously.

'*I* keep disappearing? What about you? And now you're going to disappear into a strange house in

Polperro for God knows how long. Jesus, Molly, the last time we talked, you were screaming at me, telling me all your bloody strange behaviour since we got to Cornwall was MY fault. I mean, you go charging off to Jamaica Inn and come back with stories about being haunted by an evil scarecrow, and you blame ME? I've told you before, Molly, you need to see someone. I hoped Jamie Torrance would make you see sense, even if I can't. But no, he said he couldn't budge you. You're determined to have your own way. Well, fine. On your own head be it. Just don't say I didn't warn you.' He took a large gulp of brandy and angrily poured himself another glass.

I realised I didn't want this. Anger would destroy everything good that had come to me in the graveyard. I took a sip of brandy, then leaned back into the chair and closed my eyes. I concentrated on the vision of peace and comfort I'd just had. I wanted to hang onto it. The fire and the throw had warmed me through, the brandy had made me calm. I held my glass out for a refill. Adam's hands were shaking slightly as he poured it.

'Adam,' I began. 'First of all, this – this – rift between

us is my fault. You're right, I did go a bit mad at Jamaica Inn. I had some kind of hallucination, a terrifying one, brought on by all the stress caused by the memories of this place. When we first got here, I thought I could handle all that. I even enjoyed myself at first, playing with Edie and feeling happy for Danny. But the feelings in my head started to build. The longer I was here, the more I felt – possessed by Joey. I know that sounds ridiculous, and it's certainly irrational, but that's the way it felt. And I got angry with you because I felt you didn't understand how unhappy I was, and that trapped me into a cycle of "good" behaviour because I felt I had to pretend to everyone that I was having a good time. So that's why I blew up at you the other day.' I paused. 'This sounds inadequate, but I'm sorry, Adam. I'm not myself.'

He huffed. 'Well, that's all too obvious,' he muttered. He stood up and walked around the room, saying nothing for a while. He pulled the curtains apart at the front window. The courtyard was gently lit by carriage lamps mounted both on the house and on the old grey-stone wall separating the farmhouse from the lane. From where I sat, I could see the white climbing roses wreathing the window, and I thought of the flowers dropped gently onto Joey's coffin by his multitude of friends. Was that part of a vision? Or was it all a dream?

Adam spoke with his back to me, still watching the front yard. His voice was gruff. I knew what he was about to say was difficult for him. 'Does this mean that you won't be moving out to that place in Polperro?' he asked, then swiftly downed another swallow of brandy.

I hesitated. I thought of the feeling I'd had that afternoon in Talland church's graveyard. Not the strange enveloping comfort of the – dream? – I'd just had, but the way I'd felt in broad daylight before I left the church. I'd felt I'd been sent a message that my instinct to find out what had happened to Joey was right. I'd also left with the absolute conviction that I was on the right track. And what track was I on? What had I done this morning? I'd rented a cottage by the sea in Polperro. And I'd been told, by some mystic messenger, that it was the right thing to do. I knew what Adam wanted me to say, but I couldn't do it. I took a deep breath.

'I'm sorry, Adam,' I said for the second time. 'I'm afraid I have to go through with it. I can't explain. I only know I must. Please believe me. This is because of Joey, because I think if I concentrate on him, speak to Ben, find out exactly what happened that day, I might be able to find him.'

Adam had stiffened. 'Speak to Ben? So that's what you're up to. I thought I'd forbidden you to talk to him again.'

'*Forbidden* me? Do you really think you have the right to do that?'

I looked at him, then got up and walked to the coffee table before the fire. I picked up the bottle of brandy and poured a generous amount into my glass. I paused, and sloshed in another hefty slug for good measure. 'Adam,' I said, 'this is impossible. I would have liked you to humour me by letting me go, knowing as you do how close to a breakdown I've been for so long. It'll only be for a couple of weeks. I've already promised Jamie Torrance I'll see a therapist after that, if . . . if I don't feel better. I want your support with this. I'm going to bed.'

I left him in the sitting room, and went upstairs. I pulled the curtains, undressed and brushed my teeth in the en suite bathroom. Wearing a scruffy old T-shirt, I got into bed, listening tensely, waiting for Adam to come up. At last his footsteps sounded on the landing; I stiffened, dreading another confrontation, and then I heard him open and close the spare-room door. With a sigh of relief, I glugged down the enormous brandy I'd brought up with me, and almost instantly fell asleep.

Chapter Twenty-Six

I felt terrible the next morning. I never drank brandy, except at Christmas lunch when I poured it onto the pudding so I could light it and triumphantly bear it, flaming festively, into the darkened dining room. Edie, at six months, had been too little to pay attention last Christmas, but I knew how excited she'd be this year as a real little toddler, utterly enchanted by fairy lights, glittering Christmas trees and gaudily wrapped gifts. But here I was, midsummer, no festive excuses, floored by a hangover of mega-dimensions, crippled by the worst headache I could remember. I dragged myself out of bed and into the bathroom, wondering if I was going to be sick. I turned on the shower and stepped into it, swiftly switching the tap onto cold. I stood under the icy flow, gasping at first but then grateful for the power of the freezing needles sluicing down my back. I could feel my head, then my neck, relaxing as my nerves responded to the arctic onslaught.

Numb with cold, I staggered out of the shower, wrapped myself in towels, and brushed my teeth. In five minutes I was heading downstairs, toasty again in my dressing gown, headache much better but definitely in need of food.

In the kitchen, I realised the house was empty. On the table was a note from Danny.

Hi, Mum. Popped my head in to see you and realised you were dead to the world, so didn't want to wake you. We've gone to St Michael's Mount; Lola's always wanted to see it. It's a bit of a way, so I guess we won't be back 'til late afternoon. Dad wanted to come with us. He's

left the Volvo in case you need to
shop or anything.
    See you later, love Danny.

His note was an unpleasant surprise. I tried to tell myself it wasn't abrupt, just practical, but it hurt that they'd gone to St Michael's Mount without me; to the spectacular, awe-inspiring place where our two boys had spent so much time exploring the castle and steep hill-sides. Where they'd been scared by the enormous silver spoon that was said to belong to the evil giant who lived there and terrorised the local people, until Jack the Giant-Killer climbed up the castle walls and managed to trick the fiend into throwing himself out of the window. Many hundreds of feet below, a huge grassy mound supposedly marked the spot where the giant had fallen to his death, slain by the doughty Jack. Danny and Joey had loved the legend. I would have given a lot to revisit the Mount with my son and his family, showing Edie the super-sized silver spoon that had so intrigued her daddy and uncle.

Still, they were gone and I couldn't have it both ways. I was the one who'd opted out of this family holiday, the one who'd hurt them by deliberately setting myself apart. I couldn't complain like a cross child when I missed a special treat. My festering head throbbed and thumped. There was nothing to be done except try to cure it with a large fry-up.

Ten minutes later I was sitting down to scrambled eggs, bacon, a pile of toast and a big pot of tea. I looked at my watch. It was nearly midday. That would teach me to neck large brandies gone midnight; now I faced a wasted morning. I swallowed two panadol with my third mug of tea, took my plates to the sink and washed up.

Still wearing my dressing gown, I carried my tea out to the front porch and sat on the wooden bench beside the door. The white roses cascaded down the soft grey wall, their smell delicate and nostalgic. All those years visiting Coombe with the boys, and always that sweet scent welcoming us back home from the beach.

What should I do? I asked myself. I couldn't sit there all day, waiting for Adam to get back, waiting to have another row. I leaned back against the wall; yet again it was sunny, the sky blue, and the call of the coast irresistible. On impulse, I decided to go and have a look at my little yellow cottage in Polperro. I was moving in tomorrow – I didn't have the keys yet, but maybe a cleaner or odd-job man was around preparing for my arrival. Perhaps I could persuade them to let me have another quick look round. My impression of the interior of Hope Cottage had been delightful, but vague. I was so bowled over by its prettiness that I hadn't retained much detail. For example, would I need to bring towels, sheets? I didn't think so, but I needed to know before I arrived, carless, the next day. Taxis would have to do me while I was there.

I felt excited at the thought of a sneak preview of my new home, and rushed upstairs to get dressed. Soon I was in the Volvo, and twenty minutes later I was driving into Polperro car park. I wound my way down the main street, following the rushing stream as it tumbled down the hill. Before long I was in the Warren, walking past the quaint old cottages. I paused outside the little whitewashed dwelling I'd seen just yesterday with the letting agent, which I'd found so dark and hostile. Today, my earlier reaction seemed inexplicable. The small house looked charmingly warm and welcoming. I peered through the window and saw the sun slanting across the wooden floor, brightening the interior and illuminating the attractive cream-upholstered furniture and the pretty seaside paintings on the walls. I couldn't imagine why I'd found the place so alarming. Even the scaffolding-clad cottage across the way looked in better condition than I'd previously thought, with bright new tiles now laid across the roof, and a gleaming coat of sky-blue paint on the walls, contrasting with the white trim of the door and windows.

I shook my head and walked on. The mind plays strange tricks; for some reason I was not meant to live in that very sweet-looking house. For some reason I'd been prevented from seeing it in its true, non-threatening colours. How would I feel when I saw my yellow cottage again? Disappointed? Unable to fathom why only yesterday I had found it so enchanting? My stomach, still queasy from the midnight brandy, heaved a little. *Please*, I prayed, *let it still be perfect. Let it be the place I've been guided to.*

And then I was on the coastal path. The sea swung out to my right, huge and breathtakingly blue. And suddenly, there was Hope Cottage. And the front door was open. I felt ridiculously excited.

A woman came out of the house, carrying a large basket of cleaning materials. When she saw me at the gate, she put the basket down on the porch and gave me a brilliant smile. 'Mrs Gabriel?' she asked.

I nodded. 'But please call me Molly.'

'Molly. Yes, I thought it was you when the letting agent phoned. You used to come here every year with your family, didn't you? I was working as a chef at the hotel next to the Land of Legend, and I remember you were always there with your two gorgeous little boys. They must be enormous now!'

I gulped. She obviously didn't know about Joey, and I didn't feel like explaining. I returned her smile in what I hoped was a winning way. 'I thought you looked familiar. Yes, that's right, my boys are huge,' I said lamely.

'I'm Josie Sutherland. I own this cottage— oops!' she laughed. 'Hope would kill me if she heard me say that. Have you come to check inside? Don't worry, you won't need to bring anything like bedding or towels, it's fully equipped. I'm so glad you're renting it; it's always nice to have someone you know – not that I really know you, of course, but at least I remember you and that makes me feel happy for the house. Sorry, I'm babbling. Always did talk too much. Anyway, come on up. I've just washed the floor inside and it's wet through but let's sit down here on the porch and have a chat. Which reminds me.' She paused and walked over to a wicker picnic basket sitting on a bright green wooden table at one side of the porch, fumbled inside and triumphantly produced two scalloped wine glasses and a bottle of Pinot Grigio. She winked at me. 'Can't get through a day's dreary cleaning without a drop of this. It's still nice and cold.' And she unscrewed the lid, and began pouring. I somehow felt it would be rude to make an excuse and leave, despite my unwillingness to talk about my sons. After all, I was renting her cottage; I would have to be courteous. I took a breath, and decided to wing it.

The porch was another reason I'd loved this little gem of a house as soon as I saw it. It was wide and stretched the width of the front, bordered with a low wooden fence. Like the clapboard outside walls, the porch reminded me of Cape Cod or the Hamptons; a pocket American Dream, obviously carefully and lovingly designed by someone who knew exactly what she wanted. She? Oh, yes, I was sure it was a she. Only a woman could create such a perfect childhood fantasy, straight out of a fairytale.

I sat down on one of the comfortable cushioned porch-chairs: four classic American Adirondack rockers painted blue, yellow, deep pink and green. Josie settled next to me and handed me a brimming glass that miraculously felt almost icy to the touch. I hesitated before I drank, the memory of last night's slide into the brandy bottle making me wonder if drinking again this lunchtime was a good idea. *Oh well, hair of the dog*, I thought, *and I did have a huge breakfast.* I sipped the wine cautiously; it was absolutely delicious. 'Are you a witch?' I asked my hostess. She looked at me quizzically. 'It's so lovely and cold,' I explained, 'and it's a hot day.'

She laughed. 'Oh, I've got a plethora of miracle cool boxes. We run a B&B, you see, and the guests love nothing better than a gourmet picnic lunch with lots and lots of properly chilled bubbly.'

I raised my eyebrows. 'Gourmet picnic lunches with champagne? It must be a very upmarket B&B, then?'

Josie looked embarrassed. 'Well,' she said, 'Tony – my husband – and I thought there was a gap in the market here in Polperro. Cheap and cheerful's all very well, and in fact very popular, of course, but we wanted to try something different. We opened it four years ago, and it's going better than we could ever have hoped. Word of mouth, and we're in some posh guide. For discerning people, you know.' And she burst into peals of laughter. I decided I liked Josie. 'We've only got eight rooms to let,' she said, 'but that's good because we can give it all our attention without being dead on our feet. And amazingly they're all full, not just in the summer but autumn and spring too. Older people like it here when the holiday families have gone. Of course, 'cause it's a farm and we've got animals – lambs, goats, chickens, pigs, horses – kids love it. But when the babes are back at school, couples enjoy being here, all quiet and sophisticated. Not only the oldies either; we get a lot of dirty weekenders.' Her eyes gleamed with naughty enjoyment. 'And we try to make it special. You should see us at Christmas – I don't think the Ritz could look more festive.'

She was laughing, mocking herself for her grandiose claims. She looked at me, slightly apologetic. 'The thing is, I know it's all a bit pretentious, this luxury B&B stuff, but it works. People really want to feel special, part of a privileged club. And I can cook and do all of that stuff really well, so why not, if we can make a profit? And we're not really just a B&B. We do evening meals too – in fact we've started opening the restaurant to the public; we're in yet another foodie guide for that. I like to cook good, honest food with fresh local ingredients. Anyway, that's what everyone who comes here seems to want, so we're quids in – so far,' she finished, holding her hands up and crossing her fingers.

I smiled. 'And do you?' I asked. 'Make a profit, I mean?'

'Yes, we do, astonishingly,' she said quietly. 'It's amazing. The old farmhouse has belonged to Tony's family for ever; a couple of hundred years. And he's always wanted to live here; he would never leave Cornwall. At first we lived in a cottage near the harbour, but after his mum and dad died we took the farm on and tried to make ourselves self-sufficient. You know, a smallholding, goats, hens, pigs. And there I was, me, believing I was Mrs Beeton manqué, wringing chicken's necks for the pot and growing all our own veg. But it didn't work. Tony had to drive a taxi to make ends meet. So then I had this idea to run the farm as a B&B. I love cooking and all that stuff. Looking after people. Making them love the place, want to come back the next year. And it was hard work, but we did it. Had to take out a bank loan to convert the old place into eight en suites, but we're paying it back, and still making money.' Josie stopped. She looked down, and smiled at me. 'God, I'm going on. I'm sure you don't want to hear all this good-life stuff. I don't normally talk to new guests like this. I guess you've got a really sympathetic face.'

I smiled back. 'So what about this cottage, then? You rent that out, as well as taking B&B guests?'

'Well, actually no, not usually. I mean, the cottage is Hope's, and she doesn't like strangers staying in it when she's not here.'

I left the question hanging in the air. Josie went on sturdily. 'She's in hospital. Derriford, actually. She does have to spend quite a lot of time in there.'

'I'm sorry,' I said quietly. 'I hope it's nothing too serious.'

'Oh, no,' said Josie heartily. 'It's just routine; part of her condition. She'll be back in a couple of days.'

I took a sip of wine. I wanted to ask the obvious

question: who's Hope, and what's wrong with her? But I sensed the moment wasn't right. I'm good at reading between the lines; very good at knowing when someone, however verbose, is using words as a smokescreen. God knows I've done it often enough myself.

Josie went very quiet then, as if she'd read my mind.

'I mean it's no secret, Hope going in and out of Derriford. Everyone knows what's up with her. It's just I tend not to talk about it much when she's away – I get anxious, and I don't want to let on. What I really want is everyone to think I'm fine. You know, good old Josie, always so on top of things, nothing fazes her. When in fact sometimes my knees are knocking with fear. God, I've never told anyone that before, except Tony.' She looked up at me, slightly defensive, and gave a small laugh. 'I said you'd got a sympathetic face; I don't know why I'm burdening you with all this when I hardly know you.'

'Perhaps because you recognise a fellow traveller on the road of parental fear?' I asked, keeping my voice light.

'What do you mean?' Josie's voice was guarded, but I sensed she hadn't completely shut me out.

'Is Hope your daughter?' I asked. Her head shot up, taken by surprise.

'Hope? My God, yes of course she is. I thought I'd told you.' I shook my head. 'Stupid me,' she sighed. 'Somehow I thought you knew. I forgot I've only just met you.' She tried to blink away the tears in her eyes. 'It's only ... in my everyday life here in Polperro, with a business to run, I can't afford to let anyone feel sorry for me. So when I'm worried, I mostly talk to the nurses and the other mums at the hospital – and I've got a lot of people I can talk to online, you know, when things get bad. I'm lucky really ...' Her voice trailed off.

I leaned over my chair, brushed her hand. 'Josie, what's wrong with Hope?' I heard Josie draw breath, saw her straighten up.

'She has Down's Syndrome. I mean, it's not too bad, not really. I see plenty of other kids at the hospital far worse.' Obviously trying to change the subject, she stood up briskly, turned away and walked over to the picnic basket. She reached inside and brought out a Tupperware box. 'Are you hungry?' Her voice was thick. 'Smoked salmon sandwiches OK?' she offered.

Here was the other Josie climbing back into the saddle, asserting control, trying to keep calm and carry on. How well I knew about all that, and I admired her; deep inside I congratulated her. *Well done, Josie,* I thought silently. *Ten out of ten for effort.* For now, I thought, I'd play along, let her feel she was back on top, that she was manipulating the conversation.

'Yes, please. I'm starving,' I said. We paused for a minute as she found napkins and charming little china plates painted with tiny blue and yellow dolphins that matched the cottage. Another totally unexpected lunchtime treat. I ate, glad of the nourishment – breakfast felt far, far away, and the Pinot Grigio was making my head swim. As I swallowed, my stomach settled and I thought about what to say next. The moment was delicate: two mothers standing on either side of a whirlpool black with sad emotions. Could there be a bridge across? Josie wanted to talk about Hope, and yet she felt she shouldn't, in case she lost her strength and became just another wounded mother, the world on her shoulders. And I, on the opposite side of that frail bridge, didn't want to talk about Joey; didn't want to share the grief I'd felt for so long. But I did feel a need, strong enough almost to be irresistible, to confide in this pretty woman, with her long dark curls and fierce green eyes.

I started first. 'Josie, when you said you remembered me with my two small boys on holiday here years ago, where did you see us? Did you meet us, talk to the boys?' Now it sounded as if I was trying to change the subject too, and I saw disappointment in her face. Then, with a brief shake of the head, she rallied.

'No,' she said briskly, immediately donning once more her preferred disguise: the jolly, capable mistress of a highly regarded luxury B&B. 'No, I just saw you on the beach a few times, and at the old Land of Legend place. Your kids were so enthusiastic about that daft little attraction, so full of energy.' Josie's voice changed. She sounded slightly tremulous. 'And you and your husband looked so happy and proud of them. I remember because it was such a terrible time for me. I was traumatised by Hope's birth. And to me you looked like the perfect family. I remember thinking that you were the perfect family. I envied you so much,' she said wistfully.

'How old was Hope then?' I knew I sounded abrupt, and Josie looked startled. 'Oh, she was tiny; only three or four weeks old. Funnily enough, I remember the day because it was the first time she wore an incredibly expensive little pink dress my mother bought at Harrods. It was French, a baby designer number and it cost a fortune. It was gorgeous, but I thought it was a complete waste of money. Well, I was depressed, so I couldn't find pleasure in anything. Mum had come down to stay, and so she insisted Hope wore it.' She stopped.

I chivvied her. 'How do you remember so well, Josie? And where were we when you saw us?'

'I told you, Mum made a fuss about the dress, cross that I obviously wasn't appreciative enough. So I put Hope in it, and then Mum wanted to take her to the Land of Legend – Merlin's so-called Magic Kingdom,' she scoffed. 'I mean, really. I didn't want to go, but Mum insisted. Said Hope would love it.'

I smiled at her. 'Bit small for witches and cauldrons, wasn't she?'

Josie didn't smile back. 'I didn't ... well, it was my mother really; her first grandchild and all that. But when we got there, I found I did want to go in, not to see all the little tableaux or anything. I was pretending, you see. I was trying to imagine how it must feel to be a normal mum, with a normal child: one that would grow up loving silly kid's stuff like Merlin and witches. That's why, when I saw you and your family, I remembered you so strongly. Your boys were so fascinated: laughing one minute, jumping out of their skins the next. That's what I wanted, for Hope to be like them. And I suppose then I was looking for a miracle. I used to take her to the Holy Wells; there are so many of them in Cornwall. I used to try and baptise her in them, dipping my fingers in the water and tracing a cross on her little head, hoping somehow I could change her. Poor Hope. She screamed her head off when I nearly dropped her in the well at St Keynes. I think I was a little bit mad then. Tony never wanted her to be any different than she was – is. He fell in love with her right from the start, as soon as she was born. I thought at first he hadn't realised, hadn't seen her face. I did, straightaway. Her little face. I thought the bottom had dropped out of my world.'

'You didn't know, then? You hadn't been tested?'

She shook her head. 'No, no antenatal tests. We didn't think I needed them, not for Down's. I was only thirty. Besides, I couldn't bear to think anything would go wrong when I was pregnant with Hope. My last baby had been stillborn. And I'd had two miscarriages before that, and two more by the time I finally got lucky with Hope. I lost two of them when I was quite far gone; and then there was little Rosie, who was full-term but never breathed. It was beyond traumatic, I was beside myself with grief. So I suppose I blinded myself to the idea that anything could go wrong this time. That's why I called her Hope, even when she was still in the womb. Hostage to fortune, I suppose, but I thought I'd had my run of bad luck. I thought God couldn't possibly punish me again.'

She stopped, shifted in her chair, and drank some more wine. 'You must think I'm a terrible mother, talking like this,' she said, very quietly. 'The thing is, after she was born, the madness didn't last. After a few weeks I somehow stopped panicking. I began to look at her lovely little face and see what Tony had seen from the start. I saw how beautiful she was, and I saw how much she loved me. And it melted my heart. Up until then, all I'd seen was her neediness. And of course she was needy, totally dependent on me for her life. But what I suddenly realised was that every baby is just as helpless as Hope. It didn't matter if they would grow up with an IQ big enough to join Mensa. Right at that moment, and for a very long time to come, my daughter would require no more of me than the cleverest baby in the world. All she needed was my love; and suddenly I had buckets of it. Since then, I've never felt cheated, never doubted my ability to cope. I'd move mountains for Hope. I love her more than I've ever loved anything.' Josie sighed. 'But I still do panic now she's older. It's her heart; like a lot of Down's kids she has serious cardiac problems. She's got a hole in the septum – that's a wall in the heart. It's not going to get better at her age; she's twenty-two now, and she's had so many operations, poor girl. She gets a lot of chest infections as well, which put a terrible strain on her whole vascular system. That's why she has to keep going into hospital, so they can stabilise her and keep an eye on her breathing. She has to be ventilated quite a lot; masks, oxygen tanks and all that. It's happened dozens of times, but I feel sick with anxiety every time she's in there. I'm always terrified she won't come out.'

I patted her hand. She looked at me with something

like astonishment. 'I don't know what it is about you, Molly. I never talk about all this, except to Tony. There's something about you; it's not just that you're a good listener. I feel as if you know me inside out.'

'Ah,' I said. 'I think I do, Josie. It's to do with motherhood: love, panic and grief.'

She rocked in her chair, swaying gently on Hope's little American porch. She closed her eyes for a minute, then she abruptly stopped rocking and stared at me. Her eyes were sharp and focused, as clear and green as the sea.

'What do you mean, Molly? Tell me. It's your turn.'

And I did. I told her everything.

Chapter Twenty-Seven

It was two days later, and I was finally installed in Hope's cottage. Predictably enough, the glorious weather had come to an end the previous night with a storm of gigantic proportions. The lightning was not just forked but horizontal, viciously cracking open the sky, its flickering glare separating the black, still heavens from the foaming sea beneath. The noise grew terrifyingly loud as the furious waves began to roar in protest, clamouring to rejoin the calm skies above. I shivered in my new bed. My picturesque little house, Hope's miniature version of her idealised view of America's apple pie culture, seemed pitifully small to stand against the wild Cornish elements. I worried that the roof might crack along with the sky. Then I remembered that she'd modelled her cottage to recreate the sturdy coastal houses of Cape Cod, which had stood for centuries unvanquished by gale or blizzard. Which was comforting until I thought that robust New England seaboard dwellings did not look as if they were auditioning for *Toy Story*.

I managed to sleep in the end, but when I woke up on my first morning in Polperro, the prospect before me was utterly dismal. The rain thrashed down, and my plans to eat breakfast on the porch were aborted. Instead I hunched over the kitchen table and pecked at a slice of toast.

By late afternoon, I was a mess. I lay sobbing on the sofa, totally consumed by my folly and hopelessness. The deluge continued, the coastal path outside my front door surged with a torrent of angry water. I had no car, nowhere to go, nothing to do. I had no idea where to begin with my enquiries about Joey. I'd tried to call Ben three times, but he wasn't picking up. I could have left a message, but somehow I couldn't find the words. I felt he wouldn't respond to yet another request to meet and talk. He'd made it pretty clear he wasn't interested. Somehow I would have to force a meeting, but how? I realised I'd got no further with my grand plan than moving to Polperro, and now I was here, the cloudburst outside beginning to resemble a Biblical flood, I was absolutely clueless. And pathetic; I hadn't even brought any wellington boots, let alone a raincoat or umbrella, so snugly had I been wrapped inside my sunny seaside bubble. Well, now I saw the reality of what I was trying to do. I envisioned Joey as wet as I was dry, drenched, bravely trying to control his storm-tossed boat, terrified at the fate that was about to befall him. That was his truth; mine was less heroic, huddled up inside a duvet, crying my eyes out on my holiday home sofa. And I was lonely. I longed to be back at Coombe, where they would have lit a fire. I imagined my family playing with Edie on the hearthrug, the rich smell of a casserole in the oven. I was feeling horribly sorry for myself.

The doorbell rang; naturally Hope had chosen the American national anthem, and the cottage filled with the bit that went *Oh, say can you see/By the dawn's early light?* I reluctantly shrugged off the duvet, wiped my face with a shredded tissue, and opened the door. In the porch stood not President Obama but a dripping and grumpy Queenie from the Blue Peter.

'Don't just stand there, let me in. Can't you see I'm soaked?' She tut-tutted as she entered, battling to let down her dribbling umbrella, which left a dank puddle of water on the hardwood floor.

'What do you want?' I asked rather ungraciously, returning proprietorially to my sofa and wrapping the quilt around my shoulders.

'What do I want?' said Queenie, and she was obviously in a mood. 'I want to know why you are being such a bloody fool, leaving your poor family back at Coombe while you go off on some wild goose chase and hole yourself up here?'

'How did you know I'd left them?' I asked moodily.

'I went round there, of course. I didn't know you'd packed up and gone. Danny gave me your address, poor love. They all seem a bit shell-shocked.'

I dug deeper into the duvet, as sulky as a two-year-old. Queenie stared at me, then said, 'Have you had anything to eat today?'

'A slice of toast,' I muttered.

'Oh, right. That's sensible at nearly six o'clock in the

evening. And you look freezing. Why isn't the heating on?'

'Search me. Could it possibly be because it's supposed to be summer?'

'Don't get smart with me, young lady,' said Queenie unbelievably. I stared at her, my lower lip jutting in a petulant pout. She stared back, and then we both burst out laughing.

'"Good God, will you look at us?"' spluttered Queenie in an Irish accent. 'That's what old Paddy down at the Blue Peter says every time he has a stupid row with someone. Now then, Molly, you look a bit peaky. I'll light a fire and put something in the oven. I got some nice lamb chops from the butchers, fresh peas and Jersey Royals.' She busied herself with kindling and logs.

'No, Queenie, don't be silly. You don't have to do that. I can look after myself.'

My friend – and yes, in my gratitude to her for caring about me, I realised that she was indeed a friend – gave me what my mother would have called an old-fashioned look, full of affectionate scepticism, as she started to lay the fire. 'It doesn't look like that to me, love. Besides, I've invited someone to dinner.'

'For God's sake, Queenie. Who?'

'Len, the Charmer I told you about. He wants to meet you.'

I was put out. 'You really shouldn't spring this on me, Queenie. I can invite my own dinner guests.'

'Come on, Molly. You'll like him. He's a real sweetie, a gentleman. It'll do you good to talk to him.'

She got up off her knees; the fire was already spitting happily, and the smell of wood smoke filled the room. The warm golden glow transformed the cottage, obliterating the driving rain that was darkening the windows.

'The woodcutter's cottage. Hansel and Gretel,' I murmured sleepily, spinning my own fairytale around the flames.

'Yes, well, if you don't cheer up I'm going to turn into the wicked witch and cook you for dinner instead of the chops. Here,' Queenie said, handing me a glass of red wine. 'Drink this. It'll put you in a nicer mood.'

'Thanks, Queenie. This is so good of you. I'm sorry I was such a grump.'

Queenie called from the kitchen, clattering pans. 'It's

OK. Sometimes you just need someone to give you a kick up the backside.'

'With a lamb chop?' I asked.

Queenie chuckled. 'Needs must. Close the curtains and shut out that horrible weather. Len should be here in no time.'

Half an hour later the cottage looked snug, as welcoming as a young girl's idea of an old-fashioned American doll's house could possibly be. The fire leapt and danced in the grate, throwing shadows on the pretty gold and emerald rug that covered most of the sitting-room floor. The blue and yellow curtains, woven in a soft pattern of sand and sea, were closed; soft creamy wall lights shimmered low, the dimmer switch turned well down; and scented candles glimmered on every surface. The sitting room smelled of Jo Malone roses, the kitchen of home-made chicken soup.

I raised my eyebrows at Queenie. 'I thought we were having lamb chops?'

'We are, but it's an awful night, and you can't go wrong with chicken soup when it's nasty outside. I make it myself in batches, and put it in the freezer. It's really good, though I say it myself.' Queenie smiled proudly, and, pleased with herself, poured two more glasses of red wine.

Oh, say can you see/By the dawn's early light? the door-bell chimed patriotically.

The Charmer had arrived.

Chapter Twenty-Eight

We had dinner at the small kitchen table. Len was indeed a true gentleman, as Queenie had promised. He was an impressive sight. When he came through the front door, drenched and covered in fisherman's oil-skins, I was struck by his height. Six foot three at least, I thought. And he was shrunken now by age, so he must have been at least a couple of inches taller in his prime. But he walked slowly, shuffling out of the night into our warm, golden room. He was old; a man of great age; possibly in his nineties? I wondered how far he'd walked in this transport-less village to get to my house. I knew he lived locally, but it was a bad night, and Polperro was hilly and long.

Len told us tales about previous Cornish storms: families trapped in caves on the beach, foolish tourists out fishing in rock pools who ignorantly failed to monitor the tide and the relentless lowering of the sky. They survived, though, these naive out-of-towners; rescued by local expertise and diligent lifeboat volunteers. He talked about floods, and seaside houses destroyed by water. I suppose you could say his stories were a bit gloomy, especially as the rain was still crashing on the roof with no immediate promise of respite.

And yet, his voice was so gentle and rumbling soft, his manner so humorous and warm, that he transformed these perilous adventures into arcane fairytales, always with a happy ending. I liked Len a lot. Queenie was right. He was a sweetie.

After dinner we went back to the sitting room. I offered Len some wine. He shook his head, saying that like all true Cornishmen he drank only whisky and beer. I had neither, but he said not to worry, and produced a hipflask from his pocket. 'Never leave home without it,' he twinkled, 'unless I'm going to the Blue Peter.'

'Well, you've certainly drunk us dry there before, Len,' said Queenie in a hearty voice, and I could tell she was egging him on, encouraging him to unleash his old Cornish 'charms', or 'spells', whatever you wanted to call them.

I fetched a glass and a jug of cold water from the kitchen. He accepted the first, but declined the water. 'You only want to drink a good malt straight, my dear,' he said, and poured the Scotch into the heavy glass. He patted his pocket again, brought out a pipe and asked if I'd mind if he smoked. I felt totally nonplussed. I couldn't let him light up inside; this was not my house, and a notice by the door stated unequivocally that guests were requested not to smoke. I stumbled apologetically that smoking was not allowed in here, but he gracefully gestured towards the porch. 'Oh, don't be silly, Len,' said Queenie disapprovingly. 'It's pouring down. You'll catch your death.'

Len smiled, cocked his head, and raised his fingers to his lips in a shushing motion. We listened obediently. The spew of pelting rain seemed to pause, take a breath. The heavy splashing drops receded, like the fading soundtrack at the end of a movie. A minute later, there was absolute silence. The rain had gone. Len opened the front door to a moonlit night. The clouds had disappeared. The stars crowded round the moon like a milky shawl, pulsing tentatively, trying to magnify their brightness, infants in cross competition to impress their silvery mother. The wind had dropped. The night was warm. Cornwall had imperiously changed its mind. Summer was back.

Queenie looked at me significantly. She whispered, 'See, Molly. That's what Charmers do. They can control the weather.'

'Pity he didn't do it earlier,' I replied cynically. 'He could have saved us a hell of a day.' Queenie actually stuck her tongue out at me. We were regressing into childhood by the hour.

We walked out onto the porch, Queenie bringing tea towels to dry off the chairs. I brought out the cushions I'd hastily removed the previous evening when the storm began to crackle in the distance. Len sat down with his Scotch and lit his pipe. Queenie and I poured more wine, and settled on the porch with sighs of contentment.

'Cornwall is so amazing,' I sighed. 'Just when you least expect it, everything is perfect again.'

Len turned to look at me, and leaned deeper into his chair. I'd left the front door open, and the soft candlelight and fierce blaze of the fire looked safe and welcoming behind me.

Lulled by the moonlight and the wine, I snuggled back into my cushions and asked, with the faintest hint of insolence, 'So. What's a Charmer, Len? Are you a sort of magician, or a white witch?' I smiled.

Len puffed on his pipe, silent and perfectly at ease. He raised his eyebrows at me and I immediately felt a fool.

I finished my attempt at conversation; Len sipped his whisky, and Queenie began a sort of formal, self-conscious introduction. This seemed ridiculous, since we'd all just shared supper, but I soon realised it was necessary for both of them. Queenie was cross with me for being sceptical and needed to bolster her friend's credentials. And Len? Well, Len just needed to drift for a moment, zone out; as I watched him smoke, his eyes contentedly closed, I tried not to think about school kids, students, Ben and my boys, puffing on spliffs, turning on and tuning out. But Len needed no illegal substance, just his tobacco and Scotch. He sat on the porch, wheezing slightly, smiling gently, rocking back and forth on his chair.

Queenie said, apologetically but also full of self-importance, that she'd told Len about Joey and his accident – also that his body had never been found.

She'd told him about me too, my anguish; my conviction that my son wasn't dead, and my belief that he was begging me to find him; that Joey was not at the bottom of the sea, but trapped in a place from which he was desperate to escape.

I felt a bit upset. Joey's accident and my grief were hardly news, and yet I felt the story was mine to tell, not Queenie's.

From Len there was more silence, more rocking and supping. I wondered if he was getting drunk. I looked at Queenie, raising my eyebrows and signalling that I was not enjoying this. She shook her head, raised her fingers to her lips and mimed *Shh!*

'Look, Queenie,' I said quietly but truculently, 'all I want to know is what exactly is a Charmer? You're the one who keeps telling me about them, and to be honest I'm still none the wiser.'

'Molly,' said Queenie, trying to sound lofty but

starting to get annoyed, 'You've been coming down to Cornwall for years. Surely you know what Charmers do?'

'Actually, no, I don't. I'm sorry, Len. I don't want to be rude, and it's lovely to meet you. But to be honest, this is all getting a bit much. Queenie's right about one thing; I'm desperately unhappy about my son Joey. I've never been back to Cornwall since he disappeared, but my family persuaded me to come here this summer. It was meant to be a healing process, but for me it's turned into a nightmare. Since I came here, he's come back to me – he needs me; I have to find him, and if I don't, well, I think I shall probably lose my mind.'

Queenie opened her mouth again, but Len stopped her speaking with a peremptory gesture.

'Molly,' he said, and his voice was gentle. 'You say your family meant this stay to be a healing process. Well, they call the likes of me "Charmers", and that's what we do. We cure. We have a gift, God-given, not magic or witchcraft but holy, which tells us what to do to stop people hurting. Not just people, mind you; animals too. There are those who say we cast spells, or charms, to end suffering or bad luck. And yes, I suppose it's all a little medieval; we use stones, bits of material, people's hair, whatever, to help the spell along. We write down incantations too; the power of language to soothe suffering humans has always been very strong. But to be honest, although I'll do all of that to make people feel better, I know that some of us, just a few, are rooted not only in nature, but in something else, something just as profound, every bit as fundamental, and yet more difficult to understand. The supernatural, we'd call it. And I don't mean witchcraft, although the old belief in Wicca, using nature's own magic to help prevent misfortune, is at the root of what we do.

'The point is, Molly, that we try to help. And I'd like to help you.' Len paused and poured himself more whisky from his hipflask.

'Of course,' he continued, 'I remember what happened when your son's boat was found wrecked near Looe. Everyone was talking about you, how you were staying in your boy's cottage in Polperro and used to walk the coastal path every day, down past Talland beach, and on over the path to Looe. Do you remember that?'

'Not really,' I replied. 'That time is just a blur to me.

I do vaguely remember walking every day, as if I was possessed, but not where I was going to, or why.'

'Do you remember the place you always used to stop?'

I shrugged. 'No. Well, I suppose Looe, to get a cab back to Polperro? It's a long walk there and back.'

'Yes, it is. But no, you never even went into Looe, and you always turned straight round after you'd finished looking at ... the place you sought, and walked back to Polperro. The whole trip took you at least a couple of hours, depending on how long you stopped.'

'Stopped where?' I asked sharply. I knew this was important.

'You stopped at a place on the footpath where you could get a good view of the island. Looe Island, just a couple of miles offshore from the mainland. You really don't remember?'

'No. I've never heard of it.'

Queenie leaned forward. 'Oh, Molly, you must know Looe Island. You can't miss it.'

My heart began to thump. I tried very hard to remember an island near Looe. For the life of me I could not.

'What's it like?' I asked.

'It's small,' Len said, 'only about a mile in circumference, twenty-two and a half acres in all. It's very ancient;
geologically the rocks in the area were laid down some
three hundred and fifty million years ago. It has a very
interesting history.' Len paused. 'It's also known as St
George's Island. But its original name, back in the earl-
iest times, barely remembered now even among folk
who've lived here for generations but fortunately passed
down in ancient scripts, is the Island of St Michael of
Lammana. That dates back to the thirteenth century.'

Lammana. The name wound its way through my
head. I felt absolutely rigid with terror. My head ached,
my stomach filled with sourness. I wanted to vomit.
And then there was clarity; and I found I knew.

St Michael of Lammana was the place I dreamed
about, the place from which Joey's desperate voice
called. *Mother. Mother. Find me. Find me.*

I asked Len to excuse me. I needed to go to bed. Would
he mind leaving? He said he needed to show me the
island; it was the right thing to do, he told me, the only
way forward. To persuade him to go, I agreed he should

meet me here at the cottage tomorrow morning after breakfast. I watched him leave. When he got to the bottom of the steps he turned, saying goodbye with a slight wave. The porch light caught his face, and in that moment I knew I'd seen him before. His eyes, his mouth, his shuffling walk, were infinitely familiar to me. And yet I was sure I'd never met him, or laid eyes on him before this night.

I found myself shivering as I watched him walk away down the path. I closed the front door. Queenie was still there, pouring more wine, in the sitting room. She gestured that I should sit by the fire, and reluctantly I obeyed. I was glad she was there; I was spooked, and her presence was a comfort.

The old grandfather clock, sturdy and strong, struck the hour with its mellow chime. Eleven o'clock. I couldn't believe we had been talking for four hours. The whole evening seemed like a dream; I couldn't remember what I'd said, or what Len had tried to tell me. My head was as muddy and confused as it had been in my haunted sleep at Coombe.

Queenie told me gently that I needed to go to bed. I was all too willing, and yet I wanted her to leave first.

It was clear from the way she was fussing around me that she intended to stay. There was a comfortable spare bedroom, and I could tell all too easily she had her eye on it. I felt a bit weak, but determined she should leave me alone. I didn't need a nanny on this strangely eventful night. I needed to be in a quiet, solitary bower, all humans banished. All I wanted was to wrap myself in a dream and see Joey.

Eventually, Queenie got the hint and prepared to go home to her cosy house next to the Blue Peter, telling me she would be back with Len in the morning. She closed the front door. I heard her footsteps leaving the porch, and twitched the front curtain. I watched her turn right and walk sturdily towards the village. I felt both sorry and relieved to see her go.

I went up to bed and fell instantly asleep. All I dreamed of was last night's storm. It crashed around the house, and in my sleep I watched through the bedroom window. The sea was black and grey, the lightning crackled and shot out bolts of broken silver. The waves were terrifying, high as mountains. And bobbing around on the tumultuous ocean were dozens of boats, small, fragile, completely unequal to this massive

Atlantic tsunami. One by one, the boats disappeared; they broke up, shattered like matchstick toys as the waves devoured them, and I saw them sink down to some dreadful fate, to be swallowed up for ever by this inexorable and merciless emperor of death.

And then there was just one left, one small child's boat; just a tub really, with a jaunty red flag tied to its mast. This one looked like it might make it, so determined was it as it sailed over the towering seas. The little ship had an air of dogged confidence, as if it could conquer all, as if it would climb up the massive foamy crests as easily as Jack scaled the beanstalk. And as I looked, I cheered that tiny boat as it fought bravely against the massive odds around it: the furious ocean with its insatiable jaws; the monster that would always win, would always triumph over a small vessel and a small human life. And I watched as that little boat broke, snapped, smashed; and I watched as the small figure sailing it fell into the waves, and drowned.

Chapter Twenty-Nine

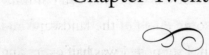

When I woke it was daylight and I was safely tucked up in bed at Hope Cottage. Outside there was no storm, no tumult. All was quiet. I walked to the bedroom window and pulled back the curtains. Cornwall had vanished. All that was left was a dead grey mist. A fret had followed the storm. Beyond the cottage, beyond the ghostly picket fence cowering against the invisible sky, was a swirl of nothingness. No footpath, no white rocks or stones bordering the lane down to Talland beach, the trusted markers warning walkers away from the treacherous edge. No ocean, no swelling god of the deep surging up to claim his earthly kingdom.

There was nothing; nothing at all. Just silence, and a world without point – a world in which I felt completely lost.

My mobile rang. The signal worked in Polperro; it was only in Talland and at Coombe that cell communication was useless, some quirk of the landscape and topography. It was Len. I suppose I was half expecting his call. After all, in this weather our hike over to Looe wouldn't be any fun. Surely he was ringing to cancel?

Len spoke gruffly. 'Molly? There's no point going out to the island today. You won't see a thing from the path, not with this sea mist. And none of the fishermen will take us over there in this weather. Landing is quite tricky at the best of times. In conditions like this, it's just too risky.'

My heart thudded. Landing? Len hadn't mentioned actually visiting the island last night. I couldn't cope with that; everything was going too fast. 'Right, Len,' I said sturdily. 'Another time, eh?'

There was a pause. 'Look, Molly – let's not play silly

buggers. This is important. Believe me, you need to get to the island as soon as possible.'

'Yes, I know, I'm sure,' I replied almost merrily. I was so relieved not to have to visit the bloody place today that I wanted to cheer. 'I really appreciate all your help.'

Another pause. Then Len actually growled at me. 'Molly. I'm not messing about here, girl. I tried to be gentle last night but to be frank, I don't have that much time left. I have to take you to Lammana and tell you about Joey very soon.'

I stiffened. I assumed Len was telling me he was not in good health. Did he mean he was dying?

'Are you ill. Len?' I asked. 'Look, if you're not well I don't want to be any trouble. Forget about me. Just say what I can do to help.'

Len sighed. 'Molly, dear, you don't understand. I'm not ill, but I am very old. The lights are dimming. I know I'm fading; I won't last that much longer. I have one task left, and I can't rest till it's done. It's you, Molly: you and Joey. I've known I had to do this for a long while. I was just waiting for you to ask, because we can't do anything without permission.'

'We'? Was he talking about Charmers? If they were

white witches, as Queenie had said, I supposed they had to get consent before they cast their spells. After all, white witches were benevolent and ... What rubbish was coursing through my head now, I thought crossly. I seemed to be always ready to swallow everything and anything: that stupid scarecrow at Jamaica Inn. I'd believed in that, hadn't I? Next I'd be thinking that ...

Len was talking again.

'We'll sort it out, my dear, for good or bad. I'll call you tomorrow. Please prepare yourself. This can't wait long.'

And he rang off.

I stood looking out of the window at the leaden world outside. What should I do? This business about the island; it was what I'd wanted, wasn't it? This was the first step in the quest on which I'd embarked. Len sounded certain that I must go to Lammana, but I was terrified. A voice in my head screamed at me to leave the place alone. I was sure that what awaited me there was nothing but sorrow.

Wait, I told myself, *wait*. The instinct that had led me to look for Joey, my certainty that I should move to Polperro and wait for guidance, was surely paying off. Len had offered to show me the way forward, and his was the only suggestion since my son had disappeared which pointed confidently in a positive direction. I realised that if I funked it, if I cowered here in my pretty seaside cottage and refused to risk the short journey to this mysterious island, then I might as well have stayed in Manchester. And although I wished I had, although I'd cursed Adam for bringing me back to Cornwall, now that I was here I was committed to following a plan. If I didn't see it through, I would be denying Joey's call for help. I would be forsaking him, and I would blame myself for that until I died.

Queenie called. She had spoken to Len and agreed that the weather was too bad to walk down the cliff path to Looe. She suggested that instead I should join her at the Blue Peter for lunch. Although I knew she meant well, trying to offer me company and comfort, I refused. She had a good heart, but she was a bossy woman, and the more I saw of her the more I felt she would try to influence me, tell me forcefully what she thought I should do. I could do without that at the moment. Self-preservation and dislike of being pressured while I was so stressed made me put her off. She sounded disappointed, but said a graceful goodbye.

I was hungry. I put the kettle on and made breakfast; tea, toast and a boiled egg. I missed the newspapers. No home delivery in Cornwall; at Coombe, Adam or Danny had driven into the nearby village of Duloe every morning to fetch them before breakfast. I'd have to go to the newsagent's, and I realised I needed to buy food as well. I'd meant to shop yesterday, but the storm had reduced me to childish tears and impotence. I hadn't left the house since I moved in, and this morning the cupboard looked very bare.

I looked out of the window again. The sea mist was still intimidatingly thick. *Mist, my arse*, I thought crossly. It looked more like an old-fashioned pea souper to me. Or rather a white-onion souper. At any rate, it was very damp out there, and I remembered again I hadn't brought a mac or wellies with me. Belatedly summoning my initiative, I began to delve in cupboards and wardrobes, and of course practical Josie had provided plenty of wet-weather gear. I tried on a vivid red PVC poncho with a matching hood and wellies. I looked at myself in the mirror, smiling at my reflection. *Little Red*

Riding Hood, I thought. *Hope I don't meet a wolf before I get to the baker's*. I opened the door and walked down the steps to the path.

The silence was eerie. The mist felt tangible, as present and unnerving as a spectral companion. I couldn't see the sea, and the cliff side on my right loomed above me, shrouded as a sepulchre. I passed the iron gates leading to the steps that climbed upwards through the gardens of Seaways and The Watchers. The big, beautiful houses on the cliff top were invisible. Not so much as a matchstick glow announced their presence. Walking through the Warren, nobody was about, although now I was on the same level as the cottages, I could see lamps glimmering dully through windows. I caught the occasional glimpse of a television, as comforting to me as it must have been to the stranded holidaymakers inside, drinking tea and watching *This Morning* instead of showing their children how to go crabbing with special lines dangled down from the harbour wall.

At the village shops, normal life resumed. Local residents went about their business, unfazed by the mist that deadened their footsteps and wrapped itself around the street like curtains billowing across a stage. Each glowing shop seemed to frame a rural Cornish scene, the dramatic action taking place upstage at the cash till and serving counter. Customers busily bought meat, eggs, fish and vegetables. Bread and newspapers rapidly changed hands; and before long I'd left the stage and was back on the street with a full shopping bag, on my way back to my little cottage, Hope. My hooded head was down, and I was feeling dreamy; I felt as if I were an extra in a Charles Dickens story, perhaps a version of *A Christmas Carol*, set not in the London snows of December but the rolling, sinister mists of summer on the Cornish coast. And as I passed, another scene caught my eye, framed by a wide bow window, paned and mullioned like a Victorian toyshop. The shop's interior was artfully lit with golden lamps and electric candles, which contrived to flicker like the real thing. The window was full of magical junk; brass piskies, swords with the legend EXCALIBUR emblazoned on the shafts, while a helpful sign above pointed out that these were 'replicas' of King Arthur's enchanted weapon. There were plastic dragons that promised to breathe smoke; knight's helmets and plastic cloaks; tiny ornamental wishing wells, and, next to them, just a few books. It was these that arrested my gaze. They weren't what I'd call proper books; no novels, except for a rack of paperback Daphne du Mauriers, the only writer summer visitors associate with Cornwall. But next to these was a shelf of local tourist guide books; there were flimsy offerings about Cornish ghosts and legends, spells and wizards, and one small booklet which stood out so vividly it was as if it reached forward, tapped on the glass and beckoned me in. This was *The Looe Island Story*, written by someone called Mike Dunn. On the cover was an aerial shot of a small, green, scrubby chunk of land, surrounded by a grey, baleful-looking sea. I didn't recognise it at all. In fact, I was sure I'd never seen it in my life. This cheered me up a bit. So this was a photograph of Looe Island, previously known as St George's, and before that, way, way back, as the Island of St Michael of Lammana. It meant absolutely nothing to me, any of it, and emboldened by ignorance I marched into the shop and bought it. The girl behind the counter slipped it into a paper bag, but as soon as I got outside I took it out, leaning against the window as I flipped through the pages.

'Molly! How great to bump into you, even on such

a lousy day.' It was Josie, muffled up in a poncho identical to mine, except hers was bright green, matching her eyes.

'God, can you believe this weather? Now, what have you got there?' she asked with a grin, snatching the little book out of my hand. 'Cornish fairy tales, ghoulies and ghosties from the local tourist trap?' She peered at the title. 'Oh no. This one's quite respectable. Are you interested in Looe Island?'

Before I had a chance to think what to say, she waved the book around, and said, 'If you are, you must meet my husband, Tony. He knows everything there is to know about St George's Island. That's what everyone used to call it.'

'And before that,' I asked faintly, 'St Michael of Lammana?'

'That's right. Such a fascinating place, steeped in legend – holy as well. Jesus is supposed to have visited Lammana with his uncle, Joseph of Arimathea, trading spices for tin. Joseph was a merchant seaman, and the legend goes that when Jesus was just a boy, he came along as his uncle's ship's carpenter. That's why the island has always been so special to religious orders. The monks attached to the monastery at Glastonbury kept a mission there for centuries, right from the early Middle Ages. It's a mystery what actually happened on Lammana, but there are all sorts of stories about ghosts, smugglers and wreckers – and worse.' Josie winked and gave a dramatic fake shiver, an enormous grin on her face. 'Anyway, let's not stand here getting wet through in this nasty old fret. Come back with me: Tony's home, and Hope. You can meet them both over a coffee, and let Tony bore the pants off you with his terrible tales of the monks of Lammana.'

I wasn't sure if Tony's tales would help, but Josie was so full of fun and laughter that the idea of coffee with her and her family was very tempting. And I'd get to meet Hope; I was dying to hear why she had designed her cottage like a tiny Disney Ride. I suddenly felt quite sociable; a couple of hours with Josie seemed infinitely preferable than sitting alone in my little holiday home, sheltering from the sea mist and watching daytime TV.

So the two of us walked off, looking like overgrown elves in our brightly coloured ponchos with matching pointy hoods and wellies; one of us poppy red, the other emerald green. And that was appropriate actually, because as we cut through the dead grey shroud of mist, our rain gear glowing as if we were a pair of neon plastic toys, Josie told me the name of her home, the upmarket gourmet B&B: Emerald Point. I thought it was a beautiful name, but didn't sound like an old farm. Josie chuckled. 'Oh that's because Tony's great, great, great something-or-other grandmother, Bridget she was called, had delusions of grandeur when they first built the farm in the early nineteenth century. She wanted a gentlewoman's house with a fancy name, not a common old farmhouse. So Emerald Point it was. Actually it works well, because from the house the sea looks a really vivid green. It only happens at that vantage point, something to do with the ocean currents, but just at that particular spot the colour's really intense, varying from emerald through to deep sage. It's gorgeous; and the guests love it. They think the name's dead romantic.'

And, chattering on in a way that soothed my soul, Josie led me home to Emerald Point, just a short walk from Hope Cottage, but higher up the cliff. When we got to the front door, I looked back to see if from here the sea really was a deep green, but in the mist I could see nothing but a vast grey wipe-out of the horizon. But all the lamps were on, and when we closed the door behind us the big house was golden, warm and filled with lazy chatter; children shrieked as they played board games, grown-ups talked and laughed good-humouredly, and the delicious smell of coffee wafting through the house made my mouth water. This was clearly a happy place.

Josie took me into the kitchen, whispering that because of the weather most of their guests had stayed put that day, although a couple of adventurous souls had retrieved their vehicles from the big car park at the top of the village and set off away from the coast in search of blue sky and sunshine. 'They'll probably find it too,' said Josie. 'We've got a real microclimate here. If they drive a few miles inland they should get better weather.' I immediately felt homesick for Coombe. My family was probably in the garden playing with Edie.

Josie's kitchen was huge, and as befitted a room where she churned out gourmet meals, it boasted every modern professional appliance. But it didn't look off-puttingly sophisticated; there was more warm wood than stainless steel and chrome, and one end of the kitchen was furnished as a cosy family sitting room, with a comfortable sofa and armchairs, a big flat-screen TV and an old-fashioned farmhouse range in which glowed a polished wood-burning stove. It was lit, and I sank down gratefully into a big old leather easy chair while Josie hung our dripping ponchos up to dry.

I was suddenly aware of a small movement on my left, and when I glanced round I saw a flash of bright red hair, a pair of eyes as green as her mother's, and a wide grin. 'Hello,' said Hope. 'Are you the lady who's in my house? And why were you wearing my red poncho?'

Chapter Thirty

The colour of Hope's hair was explained as soon as her father walked in. Tony was tall and rangy, his strongly muscled arms revealed in a white T-shirt emblazoned in green with the legend EMERALD POINT. His eyes were a bright pale blue, and his hair was almost as red as the poncho I'd been wearing, but darker and richer.

'Tony, this is Molly, who's renting Hope's cottage,' said Josie as she brought a tray of coffee and homemade biscuits from the kitchen, and settled down next to Hope on the sofa. Tony shook my hand and sat in the opposite armchair. 'Ah yes, Josie told me about you.'

Not too much, I hoped. But he didn't look pitying, just cheerful and friendly.

'And how do you like our Hope's little place?' he asked, his voice a soft Cornish burr.

'I love it. Thank you so much, Hope, for letting me stay in it,' I said.

Hope looked proud. 'You're welcome,' she said politely. 'I don't normally let anyone stay there, but Mummy told me you were really nice, so I said it was OK. And I can't stay there at the moment because I've been in hospital.'

'Yes,' I replied. 'Your mum told me. Are you all better now?'

'Oh, yes. I won't have to go back for a while, will I, Mummy?' she said, turning to Josie.

'That's right, sweetie. The doctor said you're doing very well.'

'So will you go back to your house soon?' I asked. I saw Josie shake her head briefly. Tony watched her and said cheerfully, 'Well, we'll give it a couple of weeks, shall we, Hope?'

Hope nodded gravely. 'Yes. I have to wait 'til my cough's gone first, though it nearly has.'

Josie added, 'Yes, it has. But we have to wait until Mummy or Daddy can get a weekend away from Emerald Point as well. You know we're very busy at the moment, honey.'

'All full up,' nodded Hope. 'Because they all love it here. And I love playing with the children,' she beamed.

'Yes, you're such a big help with the little ones, Hopie. I don't know what their mummies would do without you,' smiled Josie.

'I want to be a mummy, too. Can I, Daddy?'

'I don't see why not, but not for a long time yet, eh? We can't lose you here to go off and look after a baby, Hopie. There's too much work for us to do here, and we need you.'

'I won't go off, Daddy. I'll stay here with the baby,' Hope beamed.

Tony turned to me. 'Hope can't stay in the cottage on her own, you see. So she goes there when one of us or the staff here can be spared to stay with her.'

'Well,' I said to Hope, 'if you want to come and see me while I'm staying there, just ask your mum to give me a ring to make sure I'm in and then you can tell me all about your house and why you chose everything in it.'

'Yes,' she said, pleased. 'I will come and show you round my house.'

Josie smiled at me, and then turned as a little girl in shorts and sweatshirt coughed apologetically from behind the sofa. 'Please can Hope come and play with me and show me the animals?' she said shyly. Josie looked doubtful. 'I'm not sure that's a good idea, Victoria. It's so misty out there I don't think you'll be able to find your way.'

But Tony had stood up and crossed to the window. 'No, I think it'll be OK, Josie. It's clearing up. Look.'

And it was true. The fret was lifting. I could see their garden now, and a hazy blue patch had appeared in the sky. Hope jumped up from the sofa and grabbed the little girl's hand. 'Come on, Victoria. I'll show you the piglets.' And giggling, they both rushed off.

'She's gorgeous,' I said. 'She looks like a little doll.'

'Yes,' smiled Tony. 'We keep saying we should make her a pair of wings and put her at the top of the Christmas tree.'

'How did the cottage come about?' I asked.

'It was while we were taking this place apart, converting it into a guest house. Hope got it into her head that she wanted a house too,' said Tony.

'And Tony's really good at doing places up,' continued Josie, 'so he and his mate Alan, who's a terrific carpenter, built the little house themselves.'

'Yeah. Alan did the walls, I did the plumbing and the electrics, and we did the roof together.'

'And I did the painting and decorating, and made all the curtains,' finished Josie.

'Wow,' I said, impressed. 'It's beautiful. Congratulations.'

Tony shrugged. 'It's really just a big Wendy House. But it makes her happy.'

'What about the Cape Cod design, with the porch and everything?' I asked.

'Oh, Hope just loves America. We took her to Disney World in Florida, and then the next year we went to New York and spent a week in the Hamptons,' said Josie. 'She went on and on about the houses there, so when we asked her what sort of cottage she'd like, she looked at some travel brochures and drew the ones she loved. We just copied the one that looked least complicated.'

Josie took a breath. She poured more coffee into all our cups. There was something deliberate and slow about her. She obviously wanted to change the subject.

'Anyway, Molly,' she said in a controlled voice. She didn't want to talk about Hope any more. I wondered why. 'Let's have some more coffee and Tony can tell you about Looe Island. I told her you were an expert, love.'

'I don't know about that, but I've done quite a lot of research on it.' Tony sounded serious but humble. I wasn't deceived. I could tell this man was quite confident that he knew what he was talking about.

'The island's history has fascinated me since I was a boy,' he continued. 'What do you want to know?'

Two hours later I was back at Hope's little house. I had left Josie and Tony beginning to serve up an emergency lunch for their weather-bound guests. 'Homemade soup, pâté and cold meats, cheese and fruit,' hissed Josie as I left. 'Not very gourmet, but all I can rustle up at such short notice. And we're open for dinner tonight. I haven't even started prepping.'

I suppose I did at least have a sort of lunch to hand; instant chicken noodle soup from a packet, cheese and salad, and a glass of red wine. I sat on my sofa, holding the booklet I'd bought about the island. After what Tony had told me, I was steeped in the mystery and other-worldliness of the place, but none the wiser as to how all the legends and scary ancient rumours could help Joey or me. The island was clearly a place of deep significance to mystics and believers; it had represented a sort of holy shrine to them since the thirteenth century. But I couldn't see where my dreams fitted in. I believed Len when he told me I used to walk the path to stare at that little rocky shore every day right after Joey disappeared. Why did I become so obsessed with the place? I didn't remember. At least, I thought, if I knew enough about its history I would be a match for Len. I was sure knowledge was important; I couldn't just believe everything I was told. My own insight would be crucial; of that I was certain.

I settled down, wrapped myself up in a warm blue and yellow checked throw, and began to read the story of St Michael of Lammana.

Chapter Thirty-One

Ben

Ben lit a cigarette, sat down on the steps at the foot of the War Memorial on the cliff path above Talland Bay, and stared out to sea. Yesterday's mist had completely cleared; the waves played gently, liltingly soft, and small fishing boats were plying their trade again, bobbing cheerfully on the silvery surface. He tried to make himself think of nothing, as the book he'd borrowed from the mobile library had advised. It was about 'mindfulness', the current craze in psychiatric circles, and the subject of a recent avalanche of self-help books. The idea was not to think but simply sense being in the present, to be aware of one's breathing, one's surroundings. By concentrating on his physical sensations alone (the stir of the breeze in his hair, the warmth of the sun on his skin, the movement of his diaphragm as the air was sucked into his lungs, then slowly expelled) the thoughts poisoning his mind would somehow melt away. After twenty minutes or so of Buddha-like meditation, he would be revived and reborn into a state of calm relaxation. All the horror, the sense of guilt that churned so endlessly in his head, would have been banished by breathing.

If only it were that easy. Every night he woke in the early hours drenched with sweat, trying to swat away the dreams that tortured him and filled his mind with a fear so deep that he could find no rest. Desperate to escape his memories, he would stumble into the kitchen, make tea, gulp it down fast, pull on his trainers and run away from the house, still wearing the sweat suit he'd slept in. He would jog down the main street, carefully avoiding the harbour and the Blue Peter, past the village shops still wrapped, these short summer nights, in the stillness of dawn, then through the Warren, where already there were signs of wakefulness. As the sky began to lighten, doors opened; gnarled old fishermen stood on their front steps smoking, passing the time of day with other early risers; eager DIY types emerged to take advantage of the fine weather, getting an early start to their day's work, brandishing ladders and paint pots; white-haired women of unfathomable age let their cats in or out; and the dog-walkers, brisk, tanned and fit, began their twice-daily walk along the cliff path down to Talland Bay and back.

Talland was also Ben's destination. The old men dragging on their cigarettes would call out to greet him. 'Early start again, Ben? Youngster like you needs your sleep.'

'Training for the London Marathon, are you? Don't overdo it now. Pint at the Blue Peter later?'

Ben would nod and smile but never break his stride, and after he'd passed, the old women would look meaningfully at each other and shake their heads. 'Not seen him restless as this for a couple of years now.'

'No, poor lad. Something must have rattled him – brought back bad memories. Did you hear . . . ?'

And they would go into a huddle, watching Ben's retreating back with a mixture of pity and speculation.

Sometimes Ben would make it down the path as far as Talland; sometimes he would carry on, skirting the Bay and jogging along the flatter path to Looe. But when he went that far, he never stopped to look at the island. He pelted past it like *an agitated pony in blinkers. This run was supposed to calm him down; allowing himself even to look at the quiet, brooding presence a couple of miles offshore would destroy any peace of mind he'd gained. Exercise, said the self-help books, that's the key. That's what you did to lift your mood when your mind was troubled. Running created endorphins, the body's natural high. What with his mindfulness breathing techniques and the exercise-induced serotonin flooding his brain with happy, optimistic feelings, he should have been feeling on top of the world by the time he got back to his little house at the top end of Polperro.*

Except he never was. Oh, the run did calm him down a bit. He felt exhausted when he got home, too shattered to think. But then he would collapse onto his bed, and even before he stepped into the shower, the endorphin high was beginning to wear off. The temporary euphoria was quickly deserting him, as if pleasant emotions knew they didn't belong in his mind and were slinking away, ashamed of the brief, jolly party they'd just started to throw in his head. The memory of those few days in April 2009, the horror, grief and self-hatred he'd lived with ever since, would never leave him. He could try to live the quietest, most serene life possible in this little Cornish village, he could try his damnedest, every day, to make amends for what he had done, for his part in that terrible tragedy. But it was no use. Who was he kidding? Certainly not himself.

Now he finished his cigarette at the War Memorial and stood up. He wasn't in the mood for meditation this morning; had been unable to find the energy to do anything but jog since he'd spoken to Molly at the Blue Peter. It had been an enormous shock, hearing from her out of the blue like that. And he'd behaved like a total prat, striding away from her in the street like a guilty child.

He would have to face Molly eventually, he knew. He would walk, not jog, back to Polperro, shower and escape to have breakfast at the Crumplehorn. He couldn't face the others at home, not yet.

Chapter Thirty-Two

Molly

I spent the morning in a total flap. Len had telephoned, suggesting that we should head over to the island now the weather was calm and sunny once more. I found my throat close up with tension as soon as he began to speak. My stomach churning, I told Len I wasn't feeling well. I'd been sick, I lied, and was going back to bed. Maybe we could do it tomorrow? It was obvious he didn't believe me. His voice was gruff with disapproval as he confirmed he'd call me later, once again adding that time was running out.

When I put the phone down, I rushed to the bathroom. Although I'd felt fine before Len's call, speaking to him had indeed made me ill. So much for lying, I thought grimly. It served me right that I was now throwing up, my nerves were so jangled. I brushed my teeth, then lay down on the bed and tried to sort out my muddled thoughts.

Why was I so reluctant to let Len take me to the island? I knew all about the place now, both from Tony and the book I'd read the previous day. Although it had a spooky past, full of stories about smuggling, dark hauntings and foul play, its history was really only as colourful as the legends attributed to Jamaica Inn. The aspect of Lammana that most intrigued me was its religious significance, the holy awe with which it had been regarded by monks for centuries; so important to them that after the original site of worship on the island had to be abandoned – the unforgiving elements imposing a harshly cruel environment that made it impossible to carry on living there – the Cistercians built another monastery on the mainland, keeping the island firmly and perpetually in view. It seemed that the holy friars felt they had to keep watch over Lammana, almost as if they were expecting something astonishing and momentous to happen there.

Although this mystical distant history somehow resonated with my own dreams about Joey, especially the vision I'd had of the mysterious ceremony in the graveyard at Talland church, and the sense of peace and deliverance it had brought me, I still couldn't make out why Len was so determined to get me there. It was as if he knew something, but what could he possibly know? If it were something about Joey, surely he would have told the authorities, the police, the harbourmaster, long ago?

But then, I had walked to stare at the island myself, apparently, back in 2009. Len had told me that practically everyone in the village saw me make that journey on foot compulsively every day of my stay. If that was true, why had nobody questioned me about it, including Adam? Were they all too embarrassed to tell me they thought I was losing my mind? Were they just being polite? Were they keeping a secret? Restlessly I got up and went into the kitchen to put the kettle on. Taking my tea into the sitting room, I jumped as the phone rang again.

It was Adam. I sat down with a bump when I heard his voice. He sounded strained, but I could tell he was trying to be kind.

'Molly, we need to talk. Could we meet for lunch? I can pick you up from the car park and we'll go somewhere quiet. We could eat outside at the Talland Hotel; in the garden we can talk privately.'

'I don't know, Adam. Every time we talk we have a row that ends in stalemate. I'm not prepared to leave Polperro yet, if that's what you want.'

'No, I accept that. But I haven't seen you for three days.' There was a pause. 'I miss you, Molly,' he said quietly.

That shook me a bit, his tenderness. I stammered something about missing him too. I wasn't remotely sure of this. In fact, I knew Adam had barely crossed my mind since I moved into Hope Cottage. Embarrassed and a little ashamed, I said I'd really like to see him and agreed to meet him at the car park at half past twelve.

After I put the phone down, I stood for a long time looking out of the window. I watched the sea, now as calm and translucent as a village pond. Mindlessly I marvelled at its beauty, letting my thoughts wander, making shapes out of white woolly clouds, wondering idly about the small sailing boats I could see in the distance and the kind of families that were on board, enjoying the sun and the salt-tinged breeze; simply having a wonderful time together at leisure in a beautiful place.

I thought of my own reduced family: Danny, Lola and Edie, and felt a violent and distressing pang of longing to hold my granddaughter in my arms. It was Edie I missed. I hadn't really missed Adam at all.

Chapter Thirty-Three

Adam and I sat together at a table in the hotel garden. We'd deliberately chosen a spot as far from other diners as possible, right at the front of the large paved patio. The hotel was behind us; before us, a wide sweep of lawn, curving down to a superb view of Talland Bay. After a young waiter had taken our order, we sat in a silence born not of awkwardness but rapt delight. On a summer's day like this, not even a famous celebrity-packed five-star restaurant in the south of France could provide a more perfect vista.

An attractive, smiley girl brought out a jug of Pimm's.

Adam had insisted on ordering it, although I thought it was a strangely frivolous drink in the circumstances; oddly celebratory for a lunch during which some difficult things were bound to be said. Adam poured us each a glass, and smiled. 'A lot better for us to be sitting here on a beautiful day drinking Pimm's than shouting at each other in the middle of the night necking a bottle of brandy,' he said, raising his glass to mine. I had to agree, though I still felt uncomfortable. This man sitting opposite me was my husband, and yet I felt as distant from him as I would a stranger.

Adam leaned into me. 'What's your cottage in Polperro like?' he asked pleasantly.

I just about forced myself not to shrug. 'Lovely. Very picturesque.' He looked at me expectantly. I realised he was expecting an invitation. I couldn't give it. As it dawned on him that I wasn't going to ask him round, his smile began to fade.

I looked steadfastly at the pretty fairy dell that Vanessa, the hotel owner, had created for children in a little copse to the left of our table. There was a life-size fairy queen, delicate and shimmering silver, waving her wand out to sea as if it were her dominium and she was summoning mermaids to join her from the waves. Elves danced around her, and a giant Alice in Wonderland mushroom stood guard. Closer to the edge of the enchanted glade were a white horse sprouting silver wings, and a gigantic bronze snail. Somewhere further along the winding path stood a grinning pink pig, and dotted about suspended from trees were tiny flower fairies and dragonflies made from glittering wire, shining like silver bells as they hovered in the sunlight. Set against the glorious background of sweeping green lawns, deep blue sky and cobalt sea, the effect was enchanting. More Cornish magic, this time restrained, delicate and full of childlike wonder.

Dreamily, I found myself thinking about Edie. We'd brought her here, of course, but she was far too little yet to appreciate the fairy dell. Forgetting the awkwardness between Adam and me, I said, 'Won't it be lovely to bring Edie here in a year or two, when she's old enough to enjoy all this?'

I shouldn't have been surprised at his ill-tempered reply. 'What do you mean, bring her here when she's old enough? You've told me in no uncertain terms you don't ever want to come back here again. Have you suddenly changed your mind now you've found your *picturesque* Polperro cottage? Will you be staying there again next year? Alone? Oh, I'm sorry, I forgot. With Edie, of course. And I suppose Danny and Lola. Just not with me. I'm not allowed, because everything's my fault. It's my fault Joey died, isn't it?'

I started to protest but he silenced me with a furious gesture. 'Oh, please don't tell me it's nothing to do with me that you've moved out of Coombe, that you're grieving. That's bollocks. I've been thinking about this, you know, on and off for years, but especially now. What do you think it's like for a man to go without sex for five years? For a husband to be rejected by his wife time and time again, when he's lost his son, when he desperately needs comfort? Because he knows his wife is punishing him for something he didn't do? Don't pretend, Molly. You know that's why we haven't had sex since that bloody Easter. You know it's because you blame me, you can't forgive me for his death. Admit it, for Christ's sake. Just admit you hate me, you've hated me for five long years, and then let's talk straight and get a divorce.' His face red with fury, Adam got up from the table and stalked off along the path towards the lawns leading down to the sea.

I was dumbfounded. Sex? How had we got on to this? And what was Adam talking about? I didn't blame him for Joey's accident. And the reason we hadn't had sex for so long was because we were both grieving. The idea of making love was impossible. I remembered the night we came here for dinner, and went back to Coombe, both of us feeling tender towards each other and hoping we could be lovers again. But though we fell asleep in each other's arms, sex eluded us; Joey's spirit loomed outside the bedroom. It was impossible to ignore.

And yet – had we both felt Joey's presence, or was it only me? Had we both felt it was wrong to make love, or only me?

Adam was nowhere to be seen. I dug a notebook and biro out of my bag, and scrawled him a note. I couldn't bear to sit here any longer. Other people on the terrace had seen Adam's anger, they must have done. I looked around, and sure enough several couples were looking at me, whispering to each other behind their hands. I wrote on the note that I had gone down to

Talland beach. I would either meet Adam there, or if he didn't want to see me again, I would wait half an hour and use the phone box on the lane to get a taxi. I left enough money on the table to cover our bill, walked quickly to the gate and turned left down the lane. My face was flaming and my eyes stung with embarrassed tears. I would never, ever be able to go back there again.

On the beach, I found a secluded rock and sat down, trying to make myself as unobtrusive as possible. I probably should have called a cab straightaway, but I needed some time to compose myself. Even a taxi driver would see I was upset. And I had to think. I had to think about what Adam had said. I looked down at the little rock pool at my feet. Tiny fish and minuscule crabs darted across the water, all busy, completely self-contained in their miniature world. I thought how secure and snug they looked. Around me children swarmed all over the rocks with their dads, their buckets and little fishing nets. Any minute my contented fishy companions could find their small haven in turmoil as the children's nets plunged into the pool, stirred the sandy water and scooped them all up. Then they would be dropped into plastic buckets and triumphantly carried back to Mum. A compassionate mother might encourage the kids to return their little captives to the water, and some might obey, but for most of those baby crabs and fishes, it would undoubtedly be curtains. And so the world turns. Snug environments become hostile in an instant. Everything changes and nothing, no one, is safe.

Had I really blamed Adam for Joey's accident?

When our safe environment imploded and I lost my son, had I somehow, illogically, thought it was my husband's fault? I didn't think so. I stood up restlessly and began to walk up and down the beach. I thought back to that hideous day at the start of the Easter holidays when I had screamed in our Manchester garden as Ben told me what had happened. I tried to remember what I did next, the sequence of events. But everything was scrambled, a chaotic mess. Adam must have come home, and he must have called Danny, but all I really remember of that night were flashes of the journey down to the West Country, blurs of blackness on the motorway when I dozed off (Adam had got our family GP to come round and give me sleeping pills and tranquillisers before we left). When we arrived at Joey's cottage, Ben was waiting for us. I remembered his white face, his trembling hands, but not what he said. Adam put me to bed, heavily dosed with pills. The next day, the next weeks, were hazy, without definition. I remembered vaguely talking to the police, the harbourmaster, and Ben. But I couldn't recall the conversations, just as I had no memory of my mysterious walks along the cliff path to the island every day. But Adam must have known, surely? Why didn't he stop me, or come with me? Why did he just let me wander round the coast on my own? What had we said to each other during those tortured days?

Adam failed to materialise on the beach, and eventually I got a taxi back to Polperro. I was miserable, and thought of calling Josie. Then I felt I couldn't talk to her about Adam. I didn't know her well enough. In fact there were no girlfriends I could discuss such an intimate problem with. My sanity for the past five years had depended on keeping my distance, on pretending everything was fine, including my marriage. If I told anyone we hadn't had sex for five years, what would they say? They would know our marriage was a charade; that it had broken down. They would have breached my defences.

I sat on the porch for most of the afternoon, trying to read one of the piles of novels I'd brought with me from Coombe, but I couldn't really concentrate. I drank tea at first, but soon succumbed to white wine; trying to numb myself, avoid the impact of Adam's devastating accusation. People wandered past the house, up and down, heading into the village or going the other way, towards Talland beach. They smiled and waved, their dogs barked happily and their children yelled and screeched with laughter. I dutifully waved back, trying to find pleasure in these charming little families enjoying their summer break, but I felt glum and distant.

Later, I watched television with complete lack of interest. Impulsively I decided to walk to the Blue Peter. I wouldn't know anyone there, except perhaps Queenie, and I wasn't in the mood for conversation about Charmers, Looe Island or Joey. But Queenie could be a very entertaining gossip and I could certainly do with a laugh. I needed company, noise and laughter, and all the Blue Peter regulars were friendly. I would repress my normal shyness and try to have a good time.

Daylight was fading as I walked past the harbour, the bright colours of the fishing boats darkening into a uniform grey. But their prow lights were on, joining the moonlight reflected in the pewter waves, creating nautical jolliness even in the gathering gloom.

I pushed the pub door open; the place was thronged with fishermen and, of course, summer visitors, thrilled to be included in a genuinely nautical crowd. They liked local colour, the holidaymakers – who could blame them? The Blue Peter and its regulars provided as attractive an atmosphere as Disney's Pirates of the Caribbean, while being totally, authentically, Cornish. Admittedly there were no animatronic sailors chasing local maidens and brandishing brimming jugs of ale while bellowing about the joys of a pirate's life. But the laughter was real and raucous, and I stepped inside with a lighter step.

I saw Queenie straightaway, talking nineteen to the dozen as she served drinks with astonishing speed. I waved and she saw me, beckoning me to the bar, which was heaving as always. By the time I'd pushed my way through, she'd already made me a gin and tonic and she pointed towards a tiny corner table. The chairs had been grabbed by a couple of flushed young men, but just behind the table was a narrow window seat. I squeezed myself into it, and, after I'd people-watched for a while, Queenie, with extreme difficulty, managed to squash her round body next to mine.

'I'm really glad you're here,' she said without preamble. 'I was going to call you as soon as I got a break. Len's in hospital.'

I stared at her. 'Why?' I asked with deep foreboding.

'Pneumonia,' said Queenie crisply. 'I knew he shouldn't have walked through that terrible storm to get to Hope's place.'

I gawped at her. 'What do you mean? You invited him.'

Queenie tried to shift her squashed body, and shook her head. 'Well, I didn't want to, not on a night like that. I knew he'd get drenched, and he's an old man, you know. But when he heard you were there, he insisted I should arrange something.'

'How ill is Len? And where is he?'

'He's in Derriford. They took him in an ambulance a couple of hours ago. He gave the ward sister my telephone number and she called me.' She looked shifty. 'He'd told her about being caught in the storm and she was very cross. Said I ought to know better than to let a man as old as Len get wet through. I told her, I said,

'"Don't you blame me, Sister. He was going to see a friend and he said it was urgent. I was merely acting as the go-between".'

Queenie took a sip of her wine. 'He's ninety-two,' she continued. 'Pneumonia's about the worst thing an old man like him can get. Sister said he's very weak right now, but not critical yet.'

I drained my gin and tonic and stood up. 'Right,' I said. 'I'll go and see him first thing tomorrow morning. Thanks for the drink, Queenie. I must get back.'

'I'll come with you in the morning, shall I?' she said eagerly. 'We can share a taxi.'

'I don't think so. Not tomorrow. He needs to talk to me. I should see him alone.'

And I left; Queenie looked crestfallen. When I reached the old blue door, I found my way blocked by a group of men in their forties, all pretty drunk. 'Hello, love,' slurred one beefy-looking bloke in a striped faux-matelot sweatshirt. 'Fancy a drink?'

'No thanks, I've just had one. I'm leaving,' I said, trying to push my way past him.

'Don't leave, love, a pretty lady like you, all on your own. I'm on my own too, bloody wife's left me.' As he said that, his mates drunkenly cheered. The matelot leered at me. 'Where's your hubby, darling? Has he left you all alone? Shame. Come and have a drink with me and let's talk about our shit spouses.'

The other drunks cheered again. I drew myself up, pushed through them and escaped down the steep stone steps. I walked quickly past the harbour, turning round to make sure I wasn't being followed. The sozzled group of beery fools stood on the rocky stairs, still cheering my departure, one of them starting to sing.

'When you walk, through the storm . . .'

They harmonised, heads close together, locked in devoted brotherly love.

At the end of the line came a befuddled crooning. Clearly the impromptu choir had forgotten the rest of the lyrics. They all had their arms around each other now, nodding their heads, triumphant when they finally got to the bit they all remembered, the bit everyone remembers. Suddenly, after a mish-mash of mumbling, they all looked up. Together, they raised their drooping heads, looked at the sky as if they were in church and roared with sentimental fervour:

'YOU'LL NE-VER WALK, AAH-AAHLONE.'

I walked home slowly, thinking about men, thinking about Adam. And about Danny and Joey. How much had I really understood my sons? What did I know about their private lives, their deepest worries? If I'd had daughters, perhaps I would have automatically shared their emotions, their anxieties. But my boys were not like women. I loved them both to distraction, but their DNA made them incomprehensible to me. And Adam? Oh, Adam.

The Blue Peter and its melancholy drunks faded away into the hushed harbour; the sounds of life ever more noiseless as I slipped along the quiet lanes to Hope. Once back at the cottage, I went straight to bed. I would visit Len tomorrow, and face whatever it was he had to tell me. It had been a difficult day. I hoped I could sleep.

I did, for a while.

And then I remembered why Adam thought I was punishing him. It came like a bolt of thunder. I was dreaming about Edie; I was showing her round the fairy dell at the Talland Hotel. She was in my arms, and we stood beneath a shiny silver dragonfly floating under a bush. She was chuckling. She was also talking. 'Nanamoll,' she said, and my heart quickened with pleasure. It was the first time she had called me any-thing. Nanamoll was just about perfect. 'Nanamoll, why is Poppa Adam so sad?' she asked me.

'I don't know, baby. Is he sad?'

'You know he is, Nanamoll. It's because he thinks you don't love him. You DO love him though, don't you?'

'Of course I do, sweetheart. Of course.'

'Then why do you blame him for when my Uncle Joey was dead in his boat?'

'Edie, I don't. I really don't.'

Edie looked at me gravely, and shook her head. 'Don't fib, Nanamoll. You do think Poppa made Joey deaded. You told me once, when I was a baby.'

And then, stuck in my dream, Edie twined around my neck, it all came back. I remembered everything. And I sat up in bed, reached for the bottle of water on my bedside table, took a long draught, closed my eyes and leaned my head back against the woven headboard, embroidered with sunny yellow boats sailing joyfully on an emerald green sea.

I remembered. And I thought, God forgive me.

*

We'd arrived in Polperro that terrible April evening and moved in to Ben and Joey's rented cottage. The first night I was catatonic, drugged up to my eyeballs with tranquillisers and sleeping pills. I had a vague impression that the next day, I was completely assaulted by other people's theories and explanations. I couldn't understand any of them; the only emotion I felt was a compulsion to walk. So I did, I went off, ignoring Adam's increasingly strident instructions to stay at the cottage. I wouldn't even talk to him, I remember that. I was completely out of it, refusing to engage in any kind of discussion. I just left him, distraught as he was, stranded on the doorstep as I moved purposefully away, completely estranged from whatever my husband needed from me; totally immersed in the son who was calling me.

I don't remember where I walked.

I do remember, shockingly, what happened later when I came back.

Somebody fed me, I don't know who or with what. Eventually, someone put me to bed; I insisted on sleeping in Joey's room, hugging his sweater and his scarf, wrapping my head in his pillow. Everything smelled of him; young, tough, athletic. His odour was full of life, packed with energy; my boy's future filled the room with his essence, full of promise and adventure. His soul was so strong; if he'd been a candle, I could have lit it and watched him materialise in the glow.

I woke, sobbing. Adam was lying next to me on the bed, kissing my hair, stroking my face. I twisted away from him. I was furious that he was there, disturbing my deep communion with Joey. I wanted him to go; and I said what I had blotted out ever since. I told him that Joey's accident was all his fault. I said that if only he hadn't encouraged the boys to love sailing so much, Joe would still be here now. I told him, and this was a lie, that I'd heard him talking to Joey before he and Ben left for Cornwall; that I'd heard my son confide his worries about sailing to his dad. He had a feeling, he said. He thought that something bad might happen to him and Ben. He was thinking of calling the holiday off, but he was worried that Ben would think he was an idiot.

I told Adam that I'd heard him laugh Joey's worries away, telling our son that he was being superstitious and silly. He and Ben were great sailors, really experienced. They would have a terrific holiday. These anxieties are normal, Adam said, but meaningless. The thing was to grasp the nettle, carpe diem, and get on with it.

The thing is, this wasn't true. Joey had never discussed his sailing holiday with his father. It was I in whom Joey had confided his insecurities about the Easter break with Ben. I now remembered the conversation in crystal-clear detail; the words I'd banished from my head for five years, unable to allow myself to acknowledge that I, Joey's mother, had dismissed his fears, and encouraged him to go on the holiday that took him away from me for ever. And until this night, I had erased it from my mind. Because if I remembered, I would have to accept that Joey's fate was my own fault. And to have believed that would have destroyed me.

Joey's worries were not just about sailing. Mumbling, reluctant, embarrassed, he told me that Ben was being 'strange'. He wasn't the same boy he used to be, said Joey. He was terribly moody; so ill-tempered at times that all Joe wanted was to get away from him. And he kept disappearing at night when a crowd of them, all university friends, were drinking together at the Red Lion in Withington. Ben was tense, restless and difficult.

Joey said he wondered if his friend was taking drugs again.

This should have raised huge alarm bells in my head, but it didn't. I'd worried about Ben for so long now; I'd been so relieved when Joey told me his friend was clean and sober; I couldn't bear to think this boy, whom I should have mothered, and whom I had failed to mother because Adam wouldn't let me, had screwed up his future because of a youthful experiment at university. I knew Joey wasn't taking drugs. I didn't feel that alarmed about Ben. So I told Joe to stop worrying. It was me, not Adam, who said laughingly that he should 'carpe diem'. Ben was his best friend, they both loved sailing, and would watch out for each other. I told Joey it did him credit to worry about his friend, but he shouldn't let these temporary glitches spoil their companionship. I stressed how wonderful Cornwall was, how important to keep our connection with it as a family and, so naively, I said that if Ben was in trouble, sailing in Polperro was the best place for him to heal.

I didn't manage to speak to Joey after that. He and Ben went off on their Easter break. I did have a postcard from him, sent three days after they arrived. *Thanks, Mum*, it read. *Cornwall is great, Polperro as much fun as ever. Having a fabulous time. You were right, as always. Ben sends love. Plus lots of love from me and see you soon, Joey.*

Nothing after that, until the day I took Ben's phone call.

I lied to Adam, that frightening night in our son's Cornish cottage after he had disappeared, that I had overheard his conversation with Joey; I told him I had heard him insisting that our son should go ahead with the sailing holiday, despite his misgivings about Ben. Not only had I told my husband a lie, I completely believed it. After Ben had called me in Manchester to tell me my son had disappeared, his broken boat found swept up on the rocks near Looe, my mind would not allow me to acknowledge that I bore any blame.

And so I remember, that same night, breaking down completely, telling Adam hysterically that I would never forgive him; that our life as husband and wife was over. He began to caress my shoulders, kissing me gently, telling me he understood why I was saying these things. I pushed him away and screamed.

'Listen to me, Adam. It's over. I will never forgive you – you pushed Joey to his death. I can no longer be your wife. How can I? You killed our son. This is it. If Joey is dead, then so is our marriage.'

And so it was. Our marriage had been over for a long, long time. It was my fault, and I'd never had the courage to face it. Life with me, having lost Joey, must have been unbelievably vile for Adam. What did he have to hope for? Why had he stayed with me for all those years? Was he hoping I'd change? Surely not. Not any more.

I thrashed around restlessly in bed, tangling the sheets into knots. When it was light I got up and made tea. I sat on the porch in the soft morning light and thought about what I must do. I should call Adam, I thought. I had much to apologise for. But first of all, I must see Len. That was urgent. He was ninety-two and in hospital with pneumonia. He might make a brief recovery, but he'd told me his time was running out; I knew if I didn't speak to him today I would never forgive myself.

Chapter Thirty-Four

An hour later, I arrived at Derriford Hospital in Plymouth. Within minutes I was shown into a small office adjacent to Intensive Care. A small woman with a fiercely competent manner bustled in after me.

'You're here to see Mr Tremethyk?' she asked abruptly, consulting a clipboard.

I blanched. 'Um, I've come to visit Len,' I said, cursing myself for not knowing his surname.

'Len Tremethyk, yes. I'll take you to him. He's not in a good way, but he should be able to talk to you. Are you a relative?'

'No, just a friend.'

The Sister pursed her lips and sighed. 'Well, God knows the poor devil needs someone to visit him,' she said. 'He told me he has no family living, and his old friends are either dead or far too old to make the journey to Plymouth to see him.'

'I've brought him some fruit and chocolates, if he can eat them.'

'Well, we'll see, although I don't see why not. I'm Sister Maynard, by the way. Come with me and I'll see if he's up to a chat.'

Len lay in his narrow hospital bed, bolstered by a bank of pillows behind his head. His eyes were closed, and he was very still. His face was white and gaunt. He looked more ill than I had ever seen anyone before. Sister Maynard bent over him and said in a gentle voice, 'Len? There's someone here to see you. Do you feel like talking?'

He opened his eyes, which were clear and full of intelligence. When he saw me he smiled. 'Molly. I'm glad you're here. Just in time, I think,' and his mouth twisted in amusement. 'I did tell you, my dear. I knew I didn't have long.'

I sat down in a chair beside the bed. Sister Maynard drifted quietly out of the room.

'I'm sorry, Len. I didn't want to believe that.' There was no point in trying to deny what he meant. He was dying. He knew it and I knew it. He started to speak, but coughed painfully instead. I looked wildly round for the Sister, but she'd gone. There was water in a jug by the bedside. I poured a glass and held it to Len's lips, but he waved it away. 'Wait,' he rasped, his voice barely audible.

After a couple of minutes he swallowed deeply, closed his eyes and gripped my hand.

'Molly, you must listen. When you went to Jamaica Inn, you had a bad fright, didn't you?'

I nodded, mute with surprise. I'd expected him to talk about the island, not the misty Inn on the Moor.

'How did you know I was at Jamaica Inn?' I asked him.

His voice was faint. 'You were seen. I was told by another like me.'

'Another Charmer, do you mean?'

He nodded. 'Another old man, yes. He lives on Bodmin, at Bolventor. He saw what happened to you.'

'What do you mean? What did he see?' Whoever saw

me must have witnessed my hysterical behaviour in the deserted field. He must have thought I was mad.

Len confirmed my doubts. 'He saw you running away; you kept stopping and staring back over your shoulder. You looked absolutely terrified.'

Sure I was, I thought. I shivered involuntarily. Death. It was here in the room, waiting for Len. I could feel it, and see a flash of movement, a brief impression on my retina. The grotesque figure of the rotting scarecrow stood leering behind Len's bed, its head bent down towards the old man, as if it were salivating at the prospect of bearing him away to its own stinking lair.

'Because he knows, a frightful fiend

Doth close behind him tread . . . '

Startled, I realised I'd said the words out loud.

'What was it, Molly? The fiend you saw? What shape did it take?'

'Your friend didn't see it?'

Len shook his head. 'He told me you were running away from something terrible, but it wasn't visible to him. Tell me, Molly. I think I can help if you tell me what it was.'

I swallowed, embarrassed, then remembered that the

old man on the bed believed in spells and charms, believed he could heal people and keep them from harm. His thoughts, his conviction were rooted in the supernatural. Besides, he was dying; and I knew that his compulsion to help me before he passed on meant everything to him.

'Are you afraid?' I asked him.

'Of dying?' he replied. I nodded. 'No. Why should I be?' Len smiled; then was overtaken by another coughing fit. This time he sipped the water I proffered.

'The process is difficult – harder, much harder than I thought it would be. Not a lot of dignity in bedpans at my age. And it's painful, though the morphine helps at night. But death is a physical event, it's not quick and it's not pleasant. No point in fighting it, though. It's easier if you open your arms and embrace it. As for afterwards, what's to be frightened of? Nothing, Molly, believe me.'

He looked hard at me; then closed his eyes again. It was a long speech for a man whose lungs were barely capable of allowing him to breathe. He drank more water, and seemed to doze for a minute. Then he was suddenly alert and focused. 'Molly, I won't get to see the island with you now. But you must go; you must face it. Not alone, though. Take your husband with you. You will need him.'

'But when I go, what will I find?'

'Nothing at first, perhaps. Not immediately. You won't understand straightaway. But seeing Lammana is the first step; the rest will follow. Your son's friend is important, I think. That should come next. Molly, I'm drifting off. I can't talk any more. You must go.'

I stood up obediently, but Len immediately became agitated.

'No, no. Not yet.' He muttered to himself, trying to lift his head up off the pillow. I put my hands gently on his shoulders and guided him back into a comfortable position. He coughed and spluttered, breathing as deeply as he could, a painful, shallow dry-throated rasp the only sound he could utter for a moment.

'You must tell me about the Inn. You have to say what you saw.' His voice was low and desperate. 'I need to dispel it, you see. I need to exorcise it. I can't go before I've done that. I can't leave it hanging over you; I must help. This is all I know.'

I felt his desperation, and was ashamed of my unwill-ingness to confess my weakness, my mental frailty.

'It was a scarecrow,' I blurted. 'It was evil, horrible, malicious. It stared at me, and then it . . . it moved, staggered; it pointed at me. I've never been so scared in my life.'

Len, his eyes closed now, sighed and nodded. 'It pointed? Had you ever seen it before?'

'No, never.' But even as I spoke, something shifted in my head. There was a change in my perception, a long-forgotten memory. Something danced before my eyes; a hazy, indistinct shape, surrounded by a blue-grey blur. That was the sea, I realised. And as soon as I half-glimpsed it, the apparition vanished. My skin crept with embarrassment. What imagined horror had I just glimpsed? A figment of fancy, surely, just the dim shadow of a lost childhood nightmare.

Len was staring at me. He closed his eyes once more. His lips moved in a rapid silent prayer. Was he praying because he was so close to death, I wondered? Should I go?

Then I knew the prayer was for me. It was an incantation. Len was casting a charm. He was asking the God he was so sure of to help me through him. He was a vessel, a channel, bringing me enlightenment and succour, as he had tried to bring others afflicted by illness or distress throughout his life.

The prayer, or spell, came to an end. Len lay silent, his breathing shallow, his eyes shut. Then he opened them and looked at me. It seemed as if he stared into my soul.

'Walk from Polperro along the coastal path to Talland. You will not need to go far. Look for a gate close to the beginning of the path. The ground is rough and stony beneath your feet. The gate is old, dark wood, to the right of the path. It is padlocked, but you will find it opens for you. Walk into the place the gate guards. The sea lies beyond. You will find what you are looking for.'

I stiffened with fright. My heart was thumping. Would I find Joey behind that gate? Is that what Len was trying to tell me? I leaned forward, urgently calling his name. But he was finished. He had nothing else to say.

There was a rustle behind me. Sister Maynard, ever vigilant, touched my elbow, signalling that I should go. I leaned over and kissed the old man's papery cheek. 'Goodbye, Len. Sleep tight. God bless.'

I walked to the door, paused and looked back at this gentle man, so full of wisdom and kindness. The morning sun caught his thin white hair. A darting silver beam of light played softly around his head, caressing and stroking his tired face. That darting gleam, that merry glow; I remembered a grave-strewn hillside, a soft darkness shot through with dancing rays of starlight. I remembered my vision of Joey's funeral, and I suddenly knew where I'd seen Len before he came to the cottage.

I never saw Len again. He died that night, peacefully, Sister Maynard told me. He lost consciousness as soon as I left; he didn't wake up after that. In the early hours, he breathed his last.

'But he was in no pain, dear,' the Sister said the next morning when I spoke to her on the telephone. 'He just went to sleep when you left him, and was perfectly calm right to the end. Before you came, he'd been a bit agitated from time to time. But after you'd gone, he slept like baby, bless him. It was as if he was waiting for you so he could make his peace. He was a good man, I think.'

'Yes – yes he was,' I said.

Chapter Thirty-Five

After Sister Maynard's phone call telling me Len had died, I went straight to the Blue Peter. Although it was only midmorning, the pub was open, Queenie at her usual station behind the bar. She was very upset about Len, and it took some time to calm her down. She asked if I'd seen Len before he went and I said I had, but I didn't tell her about Len's mysterious guidance, his information about my next steps. As I left the pub, preoccupied by Len's last instructions to me, I wondered what to do next. I should go to the island, but not alone. Who would come with me? Len had told me to take Adam, but I was still too raw. I had lied to Adam to salve my own conscience. The thought of facing him now, knowing what I'd done, was unbearable.

Not Queenie either; she was far too melodramatic. I thought about Josie, but at this time of day she'd be very busy organising lunch for her B&B guests. I shied away from asking her to come with me on what was probably a wild goose chase. I stopped, annoyed with myself. Did I really think that? Had I already dismissed Len's wisdom as the wanderings of an old man on his deathbed?

I knew I hadn't. I trusted Len, revered him in a way. I trusted his goodness, his transparent determination to help me. The only reason I was belittling his final directive was that I was frightened of what I might find.

I hurried through the Warren, well aware that the coastal path over to Talland began its rocky journey in just a few hundred yards. I had two discoveries to make, Len said: one, the island, which had haunted my dreams, locked in my subconscious for years. The other was new to me; a wooden gate, high and padlocked, which would open for me and lead me into the place it guarded, facing the sea; there I would make a discovery, find what I was looking for. When Len said this, I had immediately thought he meant I'd see Joey, but now I was calmer I realised that was ridiculous. Still, I was disturbed and shaken. I decided I wouldn't make either journey alone, and I realised that the only person I wanted beside me, the only person I trusted absolutely, was Adam, the husband I had spurned so mistakenly and cruelly. I had to talk to him.

I sat on a bench, facing the sea, and took out my phone. This was going to be a difficult conversation, but I would have to beg my husband's forgiveness. I would have to confess I'd been terribly wrong to blame him for Joey's accident. I would tell him that I now knew that it was I who had encouraged our son to go ahead with his Easter boating holiday, in spite of his anxiety about Ben. The responsibility for what had happened to Joey was entirely mine.

My stomach lurched at the thought of what Adam would say to me, but I had to bring him round; only he could help me now. I would ask him to come to Hope Cottage, and then I would ask him to accompany me, as Len said I must, on the next part of this frightening journey. And afterwards I would go with him back to

Coombe. I would move in again, be part of my family, build sandcastles with Edie, coo over her with Danny and Lola, wrap my arms around my husband, be his loving wife again.

Totally putting aside the nature of Len's last orders, the daunting implications of what he had asked me to do, the possibility of a dreadful and harrowing discovery, I began to focus instead on what I'd thrown away, the cosy normality of life at Coombe. Family dinners with Edie chuckling away in her high chair, watching her throwing breadcrumbs to the ducks in the farm pond, smothering her with kisses and tickles, making her laugh playing peek-a-boo. I had to get back there; I had to bring an end to this journey. I would do what Len had told me, and then, whatever happened, I would reclaim my family. I realised I couldn't wait.

In breathless anticipation I called the landline at Coombe. It rang for a while, and then Danny picked up. He was breathless, laughing, and I could hear the baby gurgling in the background.

'Hello?'

'Danny, it's me, Mum.'

'Mum! How great to hear from you. How are you doing in your cottage?'

'Fine, yes, the cottage is lovely. How are Edie and Lola?'

'Great. We've just been feeding the ducks with Edie. She can't stop saying quack-quack now.'

'Oh, that's lovely. I can't wait to see her again.'

'Do you want to come over after lunch? I'll come and get you.'

'I'd love that. But could I speak to Dad first?'

There was a pause.

'Oh. Didn't Dad tell you? I thought you knew.'

I felt sick. I sensed what was coming.

'Knew what? Isn't he there?'

Danny's voice became low and troubled.

'He went back to Manchester, Mum. Yesterday. He said he'd call you.'

I swallowed hard. My fault, all my fault. I should have realised Adam wouldn't stay in Cornwall after he stormed off during our lunch at the hotel. I should have called him before I went to see Len. I should have apologised. And now it was too late.

'He must have forgotten. Did he get back OK?'

'Yes, Mum, he's back home, safe and sound, don't worry.' Danny sounded upset.

'Did he ... well, did he tell you why he left?'

'Not really. I mean, I gathered you'd had a row, but he didn't want to talk about it.'

'No, right. Of course.'

'Mum, look, I'll come over and get you. Come back here and we can all have lunch, and talk.'

'No. No, that's all right, Danny. I want to see you all, of course I do. Maybe later, or ...' My voice trailed off. 'No, don't worry, darling. I'm just out for a walk at the moment. When I get back to the cottage I'll call Dad in Manchester. And then, well, I'll probably ring you back and tell you ... what I'm going to do.'

'Mum,' Dan's voice was worried. 'Come back here to Coombe, please. I know this is all about Joey, and you and Dad are so upset. It's my fault, I should never have got you to come back to Cornwall.'

'Danny,' I said forcefully. 'Nothing's your fault. And nothing's Dad's fault either. Please, love, just let me be for a while. I promise I'll call you later today.'

And I rang off. For a long time I stared at the sea, trying to make sense of the last couple of weeks. The ocean was empty, so was the path. There was not a breath of wind; I could see no waves on the still blue surface that stretched to the horizon before me. I felt cast away, thrown up and solitary in a bizarre, silent, Godforsaken world. I had lost my son and I had lost my husband. I had almost lost my mind. I wanted to go home, to Manchester, to my own house, my own garden, my own bed. I wanted Adam next to me. I wanted this nightmare to be over. If I couldn't go back to the way we were before Easter 2009, then I wanted to go forward. I was stuck here in a little hell of my own making. I couldn't stand it any more. I couldn't be alone any more. I wanted Adam. I had to talk to him.

Adam's mobile rang and rang, then went to voice-mail. I ended the call. I couldn't possibly leave a message. I imagined him angrily listening to my pathetic voice, begging him to forgive me. I thought he'd probably ignored the call, determined not to talk to me. Hadn't he said when I last saw him that he wanted a divorce? He might be meeting a solicitor right now.

I stood up unsteadily, grasping the bench for balance. I walked slowly back to the cottage. Not a soul crossed my path. It was lunchtime on a sunny August day; the village should have been thronged with families, children shrieking with excitement. But there was not even a dog in sight here in this dog-walker's paradise. Not even a cat. I was in a bubble, shut off from the world. Nobody wanted to come near me, and self-pity overwhelmed me.

But there was someone; a still silhouette, leaning against the porch at Hope's house. Josie? No, it looked like a man. Tony? I walked a little faster, mopping my tears with a tissue I found scrunched in my pocket.

It wasn't Tony. It was Jamie Torrance. The doctor had called.

Chapter Thirty-Six

He took one look at my face and said, 'Oh dear.' I opened the front door and walked ahead of him. I was, as always, embarrassed. He followed me in, closed the door behind him and stood looking at me, hands in pockets, shaking his head.

'I'm sorry to see you so upset, Molly. Is there anything I can do?'

'Sorry,' I muttered. 'I'll be all right in a minute. I'll go and freshen up. Please sit down.' And I rushed upstairs to the bathroom where I washed my face, repaired my make-up and brushed my hair. Last time

I saw Jamie I'd been in bed at Coombe, an emotional wreck. I couldn't let him see me like that again. I looked at myself in the mirror and breathed deeply, in and out.

When I felt more in control, I went downstairs. He was still standing, and when he saw me his face broke into a smile. 'Ah!' he said. 'You look much better. I hope you don't mind me dropping in but I was at Emerald Point, checking up on Hope. Josie told me Tony saw you at the Blue Peter, looking a bit miserable, with Queenie in tears. He saw you leave. Josie said she was thinking of coming to see you, but I said I'd pop in first. I've been meaning to see how you are.'

'Why were you checking on Hope? Is she OK?' I asked.

Jamie looked out to sea. 'She's not too well at the moment. There are one or two problems, I'm afraid.'

'Her lungs?' I asked. 'Has she got another infection?'

He shook his head. 'No. Her lungs are clear. It's not that. It's much worse, I'm afraid.' He heaved a deep sigh. 'I shouldn't really be telling you this, Molly. Patient confidentiality.'

'Yes, I understand. But . . . is there something I could help Josie with? Anything I can do to help?'

'I think Josie needs all the help she can get.'

'Is it her heart, Jamie? Josie did tell me she has serious cardiac problems.'

'Ah. She's told you about it, has she?'

I nodded. 'Yes. I know Hope was born with congenital heart disease.'

He grimaced. 'It's a known complication of Down's. She's had a lot of operations already. Now it looks as if she's going to need another.'

'Soon?'

'Yes. It would be dangerous to delay it much longer, although Josie and Tony are dreading her going back into hospital.'

'I know,' I said. 'Josie told me she's terrified every time Hope goes into Derriford. She always thinks her baby won't come out again.'

'Well. This time . . . ' He shook his head. 'I'm sorry, Molly. I'm being unduly pessimistic. Hope is amazing. She's defied every prognosis since she was born. She shouldn't have lived this long. But she has, and she's a joy. Not only to her parents, but to everyone around here who knows and loves her. But her latest tests aren't good; the full results are just back, and it's clear she needs more surgery. She'll be going in again tomorrow.'

'I'm very sorry. I'll go and see Josie later.'

'Yes, do. She's going to need a lot of support.'

'Would you like a cup of tea?' I asked.

'That would be great. And look, I grabbed some sandwiches from the baker's. I never get time for lunch when I'm on call. Would you like to share them?'

'Are you sure?' I asked. I was hungry but it seemed a bit cheeky.

He smiled his assent, and I went into the kitchen to put the kettle on. I'd left the front door open and the sea view was irresistible. When I got back with the tea, Jamie had settled himself in a chair on Hope's shady little porch. He opened his paper bag and produced a ham and cheese sandwich and a Cornish Pasty.

'Half each?'

We drank our tea and munched our scrappy lunch in contented silence for a while. After a while I noticed he was looking at me speculatively.

'How are you, Molly? How are you feeling? Any better now you've moved into Polperro?'

'Not really, to be honest. Things aren't working out the way I'd hoped.'

And, sustained by his sympathetic eyes, I found myself telling him everything. I told him how Adam had gone back home to Manchester, despairing of our marriage and threatening divorce. I told him about Len; about his insights into what had happened to Joey, and the connection he had sensed with the Island of Lammana. And I talked about my visit to Len in hospital yesterday, his last words to me; about his instruction that I should not visit the island alone, and what he said about something that awaited me on the cliff path behind a wooden gate; something that I urgently needed to find.

'Len said I should go there with Adam, but he's left. I'm on my own, and I don't know what to do. I suppose I could ask Danny, but it's a pretty grim kind of search. I'd rather not upset him.'

Jamie listened carefully, then said, 'Would you like me to come with you?'

I looked up, surprised. 'I . . . never thought of that. I

think it's a bit too much to ask you, Jamie. I'm sure you don't have the time to come with me on what ... well, it may just be a fool's errand.'

Jamie leaned forward. 'I'd like to help you, Molly. If you really want to do what Len said, I'm happy to be of service.'

I looked at him, and then at my feet, aware once again of how irrational I must sound. Islands, gates, instructions from a dying Charmer. What must this practical doctor think of me?

He intuited my feelings. 'Molly, in case you're feeling embarrassed about following Len's directions, don't be. I've known Len Tremethyk as long as I've been here. He was a Charmer, and if you've lived in Cornwall for a while you don't dismiss people like him. I'm a man of science, but I've seen Len and others like him heal people doctors could do nothing for. I can't explain his powers, but I certainly don't underestimate them.'

'Then you don't think I'm being naive and silly to trust him?'

Jamie stood up. 'Come on, Molly. If you don't do this you'll spend the rest of the day brooding about it.

Whatever happens, it will make you feel better to take some action.'

I smiled at him. He made me feel stronger and I was grateful.

We stepped down from the porch and walked through the little gate in the white picket fence, turning left when we reached the coastal path. We followed the stony, rutted footway which would take us first to Talland Bay, and then over the beach to Looe, and the island. I did not know what awaited me there, but for now the sun shone, the sky was sharp and radiant and the sea looked like blue ruffled silk. It was impossible to feel scared surrounded by such light and clarity. Nothing dark could exist here in this open breezy world smelling of salt and wild garlic. Seagulls swooped, butterflies fluttered in the hedgerow, the horizon lay bright and tantalising over the ocean. All was goodness and contentment. As I walked I felt clean, fresh and full of good health.

Suddenly to our right, a stout wooden gate materialised as if from nowhere. It was hidden from the path by a slight bend, and behind it lay a hazy vista of green trees and bushes, flitting butterflies and, just glimpsed between shady foliage and thickly leaved branches stooping gracefully to the ground, the sea, brilliant with silver-gold flashes as the sun sparkled flirtatiously, peeping down from its cloudless sky.

I stopped dead. There was a heavy-duty padlock on the gate. Just as Len had said there would be. This was the place.

'Here?' asked Jamie curiously. 'Is this the gate Len meant?' He gave an affectionate laugh. 'It's the allotments, Molly. Polperro's kitchen gardens, very popular and lovingly toiled in by the good folk of the parish to produce cabbages and courgettes.' His voice was suddenly serious; he bent down to me. 'Molly,' he said gravely, 'you must remember Len was dangerously ill when you saw him in hospital. He was confused, at death's door. I know you think he had certain powers, was a Charmer, and I agree with you. He was a lovely bloke and certainly very wise. Well, he was ninety-two; of course he was wise. But I don't want you to expect too much. Len meant well, but he was a very sick old man.'

I remembered Len's kind face, full of warmth and wisdom. Yes, he was dying, but he hadn't seemed confused to me. He had sounded absolutely confident, sure of his ground. He had wanted to help me. I believed in him.

'There's a padlock on the gate,' I said to Jamie.

'Yes, the allotments are always kept locked, to stop tourists getting in and pinching the veg. The folk who grow stuff here are very possessive.' He smiled. 'It's like a religion to them. They even have competitions to see who can grow the biggest marrow.'

'Len said there'd be a padlock,' I said, my voice slow, drowsy and insistent as I thought back to his last words to me as he lay on his deathbed.

The gate is old, dark wood, to the right of the path. It is padlocked, but you will find it opens for you. Walk into the place the gate guards. The sea lies beyond. You will find what you are looking for.

Jamie was looking at me carefully. 'You want to go in, don't you?' he asked.

'I must,' I replied, still in the slow voice that had appeared from nowhere but held my tongue firmly in its grasp. 'But it's locked.'

'That's not a problem. I'll just get the key from Annie Trelawney.' And he turned to his left and sprinted up a steep flight of steps leading to an imposing white house just opposite the sternly fastened barrier. I saw him ring the bell, and moments later a vigorous-looking elderly woman opened the door. She was delighted to see him, and I saw him kiss her cheek, and follow her inside the house. I stood still, staring at the gate and wondering what lay behind it. Then I turned back to the impressive dwelling into which Jamie had disappeared, and froze.

There was a sign attached to one of the two substantial pillars framing the long stone staircase that led up to the graceful, dignified old building. It was a large sign, bold white letters engraved on a slab of dark grey slate. It read JAMAICA HOUSE.

Jamie came running down the steps, a bunch of keys in his hand. He faltered when he reached me and saw how white I looked.

'Molly?' he said. 'What's the matter?'

'It's called Jamaica House,' I said wonderingly.

'Oh, Annie's lovely old place. Yes, it's belonged to the Trelawney family for generations. The Trelawneys were the major landowners in this part of Cornwall, very rich, very important. Two of them were successive governors of Jamaica, in the seventeenth century. That's how Jamaica Inn got its name.'

'I thought it was to do with smuggling rum,' I said in a daze, my preconceptions shattering.

Jamie laughed. 'That too, probably, but no, the Trelawney family's ancient association with Jamaica is the real reason. The family's not nearly as powerful now, but there are still quite a few of them about. Annie here is one of the last. She never married, had no kids, so she lives here in Jamaica House in solitary splendour. She's a lynchpin of the village, our local historian, chairman of the neighbourhood watch, of course, and she keeps the emergency keys to the allotments.'

'Emergency?' I stuttered. 'What sort of emergency?'

'Oh, you know, in case some drunken youths who think they're on holiday in Rock or Newquay instead of sleepy old Polperro decide to spend the night there with a few cans of strong lager. It happens sometimes. They climb over the gate, make a hell of a noise. And it could be dangerous – the allotments form part of a small headland; there's a sheer drop down to the sea. No one's actually fallen over it yet, but Annie always keeps a weather eye out in the summer for drunks. She may be old, but she's quite formidable. I've seen lads quail before her. She's got a shotgun too; don't think she's ever used it, but these daft young yobs don't know that, do they? Come on, I'll let you in. It's quite beautiful in here, in fact – they're probably the most romantic allotments in the country.'

Still chattering, he unlocked the gate.

Chapter Thirty-Seven

I followed Jamie, my mind locked onto what he'd called
Annie's emergency key. Could there have been an
emergency concerning Joey? Could something have
happened to him here, in these innocuous allotments?
No, of course not. If Annie had seen my son here she
would have talked to him, and if he'd subsequently disappeared surely she would have reported it to the
police? Everyone in Polperro knew about the boat
wreck, the missing boy. Annie's possession of the key
was for the simple purpose Jamie had outlined: so she
would have access to the gardens if some drunken kids

had climbed over the gate and needed a fearsome old lady to kick them out again. This pretty spot had nothing to do with Joey.

Except . . .

Jamie closed the gate behind us. I felt increasingly sleepy as I walked slowly ahead of him down a narrow paved path. On either side grew shady fruit trees, beginning to burgeon with growing apples, pears, walnuts and plums. Rose bushes perfumed the air; hydrangeas and fuchsia were lush with colour, and dotted among them were bird tables and nesting boxes. Wooden benches provided inviting places to rest, and, glimpsed through the trees, the sea sparkled like sapphires. Such a restful quiet place, full of peace like a graveless cemetery. I startled myself with the comparison, and yet the calm tranquillity of this gated garden did remind me of Talland churchyard; it had a hushed repose. As I walked, the drowsiness I felt became stronger. I could hear the birds, I could feel the sun warm on my face, I could see the winking turquoise ocean, yet I felt I was sleepwalking.

No, this charming spot could have nothing to do with Joey.

Except I knew I'd been here before.

I heard Jamie's voice, but distantly, muffled as if he spoke through cotton wool. He was telling me that we had almost reached the allotments. I saw a couple of potting sheds and a large greenhouse full of tomato plants and strawberry beds. I walked past these first signs of human industry, and the layout of the gardens immediately became less dreamy, more purposeful. I could see the individual plots were laid out in long strips, each of which were neatly tended and bursting with produce; carefully planted with all sorts of tender green shoots, budding kitchen delicacies, herbs, shallots, leeks, small marrows, runner beans. There were flowers, too: night-scented stocks, lavender and sweet peas climbing up canes and trellises; and amongst them idiosyncratic personal icons, small rural mementos placed affectionately on each patch: ceramic hens and cockerels, tiny pink piglets, ducks and geese and miniature baby lambs.

The whole place was enchanting – greens and reds, yellows and blues, and beyond this fecund little world the sharp intense cool blue of the sea framed a perfect picture.

Yes, I'd been here before. I wandered up and down the gravel tracks between each plot, and as I did my sense of ease and contentment began to falter. I grew cold under the hot sun. Something was wrong. Something was waiting for me, and suddenly I knew what it was. I didn't want to look but I had to. There was no escape.

Because he knows, a frightful fiend
Doth close behind him tread . . .

There was a rickety old fence running along the bottom of the allotments. I was surprised it looked so broken down; everything else in the kitchen gardens was sturdy and pristine. Beyond the fence shimmered the sea, and for a moment I saw that it had altered; it had become dull, dark and ominous. The rippling waves had disappeared. The surface was sluggish, moody, threatening. It surged towards me, urging me, telling me, forcing me to look. My eyes followed a breaking wave, topped not with crisp white surf but scummy grey dirt. The billowing ridge moved west, dragging its grimy muck with it, pulling my eyes towards where it finally disappeared under the headland. As it vanished, a spume of black sludge, thick with slime and mud, rose abruptly from the water. It hovered in the sky above the cliff like an exclamation mark, a sign. When it sank back down into the hellish depths from whence it came, it dragged my eyes down with it. I blinked. And there, right in front of me, leaning drunkenly against the sagging fence, was the scarecrow. My frightful fiend, dry, broken, and clad in black, come to haul me down below, come to take me to the monstrous lair in which it held my Joey, trapped and desperate in an infernal underworld.

I screamed. An inky jet of clammy mucous, stinking of rotting fish, blew in from the ocean, coating the scarecrow in a viscous jelly. It covered my face, my hair, leaving on me a foul stench of decay, a noisome stink forced from an abyss of pain.

I fainted.

When I came round, I was lying on the grass. Jamie bent over me, cushioning my head, feeling my pulse. I didn't remember where I was or what had happened, but it felt as if I'd been here for ever.

'Molly, Molly, you fainted. It's OK. You're all right now. But what happened? What did you see? What scared you?'

I remembered the slime, the vile jelly that had covered my face and hair, the awful stench. Surely Jamie could smell it too? And then I realised I could smell nothing but roses, stocks and lavender. I sat up abruptly, Jamie catching me as my head started to spin again. I put my hands up to my hair. It was clean, silky. There was no foul stuff clinging to my head or face.

I heard rapid footsteps coming down the path, and Annie Trelawney appeared, her face creased with concern.

'Goodness, Jamie, what on earth's happened?' she asked anxiously. 'I was watching you from an upstairs window, and I saw your friend collapse.'

'It's fine, Annie, don't worry. She just fainted; she's coming round now.'

The two of them hoisted me to my feet and guided me to a nearby bench. Annie handed me a bottle of water. 'I grabbed it from the fridge when I ran downstairs. Drink it. It will make you feel better.'

Gratefully I took the bottle and drained it. Jamie looked worried. 'You're shaking badly, Molly. What on earth happened?'

I shuddered. 'Didn't you see?' I appealed to him. 'You were right behind me, you must have seen it.'

'Seen what?' asked Jamie helplessly. He shook his head. 'Molly, I saw absolutely nothing; just the gardens and the sea beyond the headland.'

'No, no Jamie. The ... the thing I saw. The THING.' I was shouting, struggling to get to my feet. 'It's over there. Look!' Jamie grabbed me, but not before I'd managed to shakily turn round. I pointed a quivering finger at the fence, the rotting, dilapidated ...

The strong, neat and immaculately maintained fence preventing unwary visitors from straying too close to the cliff edge; the heavily padlocked gate bearing a stern notice: DANGER. DO NOT PROCEED BEYOND THIS POINT. THIS AREA IS NOT STABLE AND LIABLE TO SUBSIDENCE.

My shaking finger moved to the left, my body following my hand, until I saw ...

... a scarecrow. A scrappy old effigy clothed in tatty black rags; a perfectly ordinary, everyday scarecrow, with perhaps a slightly malevolent face, but really frightening enough to scare only birds.

I collapsed back onto the bench. I turned my head back to the frightful fiend of my imagination, now transformed into a pathetic figure even a child would laugh at. And I looked at the sea behind it, glittering and bright once again.

'What's the matter, dear?' This was Annie. 'Did the old Ancient Mariner give you a fright? Goodness, he's so decrepit now the birds even perch on his head. We only keep him out of sentiment, because he was the first scarecrow we put up when we dug the allotments. That's why we called him the Ancient Mariner, because we wanted him to be really scary, constantly telling the damned birds to clear off. We've got quite a few scary-men now, as the children call them, but he's the original.' She waved her arm around the gardens, and I saw she was right. There were half a dozen or more scarecrows spread out over the land, festooned with scarves and jumpers in bright colours. Only mine wore black.

Annie was looking thoughtful. She glanced up at Jamie. 'Do you think we could get her back to my house?' she asked. 'She needs some sweet tea and a rest.'

Hooking an arm under mine she pulled me up. Jamie did the same, and the three of us walked unsteadily back to Jamaica House.

Chapter Thirty-Eight

Annie's living room, or 'drawing room' as she called it, was delightful: big, with enormous bay windows looking out to the sea, and, at the back, to her beautiful garden. Light streamed in, illuminating the polished wood floor and shimmering on the huge cut-glass vases filled with flowers on every surface. The house smelled of roses and beeswax. She made me lie down on a red sofa. There was another, this time midnight blue, on the opposite side of the fireplace, and deep armchairs upholstered in white and pale grey scattered around in the window recesses. She plumped cushions behind my head, and covered me with a silver-grey fur throw. I protested, saying I was warm enough, but Jamie shook his head and said in fact I felt icy. It was the shock. It was the shock, too, which prompted Annie to make me drink a glass of brandy. *Brandy again*, I thought. I've never drunk so much of the stuff until I came to Cornwall. I'm always freezing or in shock here; I was tired of it. I wanted Adam. I wanted to go home.

Jamie pulled up a chair while Annie was out in the kitchen making tea. 'Molly,' he said quietly. 'The scarecrow you told me about, the one you thought you saw at Jamaica Inn. Did you see it again in the allotments? Is that what made you faint?'

I closed my eyes. Tears welled up. I felt foolish, drained. How could I possibly make sense of what had just happened? I had had another episode of madness. I had no idea where it came from. What was happening to me? I felt wrecked, out of control. Jamie was right. I should see someone, perhaps that therapist he'd mentioned before. But right now I couldn't bear to talk to him, or anyone. I'd had enough.

Annie came in with the tea. I sat up, and drank her very sweet hot brew. Together with the brandy, it worked. I stopped shivering, feeling warmth steal through my body. My heart stopped thumping. I almost fell asleep.

Annie's hesitant voice roused me. 'My dear, Molly – it's Mrs Gabriel, isn't it?' I opened my eyes. Annie was looking at me, gently and with profound sympathy. I saw Jamie's head jerk up and he stared at Annie.

'Yes, Molly Gabriel, that's right,' I said, wondering how she knew my full name. Perhaps Jamie had told her.

Annie continued, ignoring the doctor's intense gaze. 'I don't want to be intrusive, Molly, or upset you, but I remember you now. You used to walk past this house every day; it was a few years ago. I was usually sitting in the front garden reading, and I watched you go past. I would always say hello, but you never replied. You seemed in a world of your own.'

'Yes, I suppose I was. I'm sorry if I seemed rude but I don't think I was aware of anything or anyone back then. People have told me I used to walk every day, but I have absolutely no memory of it. I've blanked that whole period out. I don't remember you at all, I'm afraid.'

'But you remembered the allotments?'

'Not really.'

Annie looked puzzled. 'But you stopped today and asked Jamie to get the keys. Surely you must remember that you'd been inside the gardens before?'

'No – it's just that Len told me to look for the pad-locked gate. So when I saw it today I thought that must be what he meant.'

'Len? Do you mean Len Tremethyk?' she asked.

I nodded. 'Yes. I went to see him in hospital yester-day, hours before he died. He was very ill, but he told me I must find the gate, and that it would be padlocked but it would open for me. He said I would find what I needed inside the area it guarded. He'd asked me about the scarecrow, you see . . . ' Weary, I trailed off. I was too tired to explain about Jamaica Inn, and too horrified to link what I'd seen there with what had happened in the allotments. Jamie leaned forward.

'She's very tired,' he said to Annie. 'I think I should get her home.'

'No,' she said sharply. 'I knew Len very well, and I think I can help her. She needs to know what's going on.'

I burst into tears. 'Yes. Oh yes. Christ, I need to know what's going on, why I'm being driven mad with dreams and visions. It just happened again. I can't bear it any more.'

Jamie looked reproachfully at Annie as he handed me a wad of tissues, but she carried on.

'Len was a Charmer. Did you know that, and what it means?'

I nodded again. 'He told me about it.'

'How did you meet him?' Annie asked.

I explained about Queenie and how she invited him to dinner at Hope's cottage. Annie looked eager and interested to hear more, but my strength was exhausted. I looked pleadingly at Jamie.

'Will you tell her everything, Jamie? Everything I've told you?'

'Molly, I can't. You're my patient. It's confidential.'

'But I'm giving you permission. I want you to tell Annie everything. I think Len knew I'd meet her; that's what he meant when he said the gate would be unlocked for me. He knew Annie would be the one with the key. He knew she would be the next link.'

'Link to what?' asked Jamie, worriedly.

'I don't know; the next link in the chain. Please, Jamie. I'm so tired, but I'm begging you to be my voice, to tell Annie everything I've told you.'

And so the story began again; Joey's disappearance, the wrecked and empty boat. My anguished walks along the cliff that I'd obliterated from my memory. Our return to Cornwall after five years, and my reluctance to come back. My strange dreams since we got here, and my compulsion to visit Jamaica Inn, where I saw a foul vision of such evil that it unhinged me. My conviction that I must discover what had happened to my son, that I was being guided along a path. My move to Hope's little house so I could be alone to concentrate on him; and finally our walk today, my behaviour when I saw the gate, and my odd drowsy demeanour inside the gardens.

Annie listened intently. When Jamie had finished she asked me to tell her exactly what I'd seen at Jamaica Inn that had so terrified me. I told her. She sat back in her chair and nodded to herself. She poured us all another cup of tea, and then began to talk:

'Molly, the reason I know who you are is that I first saw you on your walks five years ago, the ones you have forgotten. Everyone in the village understood your terrible grief, and why you were so silent and self-absorbed. No one could get through to you. You wouldn't talk to anyone.

'I watched you walk past my house every day; then, one day, I was just coming out of the allotments, and the gate was wide open as you were passing. You stopped, and started to walk towards it. I was pleased, actually. I thought you wanted to speak to me at last. I thought you'd let me show you around the allotments and talk about the stuff we grow there. I thought a chat might do you good, take your mind off things for a moment.'

Annie sighed. 'That was very silly of me, but I had no idea how deeply you were wrapped in grief. I held the gate open for you, and you walked right in past me. But you took absolutely no notice of me and began to walk through the gardens towards the sea. I followed you; I was frightened by your silence. You walked as if you were in a dream, straight on through the allotment strips. You were quite a bit ahead of me by then; I kept back because I didn't want to intrude. Then, to my horror, I saw that you were making for the fence sealing off the headland. Someone had left the gate open, and you walked straight through it, and on towards the cliff edge. You got right up to it, and then you stood and swayed, backwards and forwards. I was petrified, convinced you were about to throw yourself off. I walked very quietly up behind you. I thought if I startled you, you might jump. And then, just before I could grab you, you turned round. I'll never forget your face. You looked straight through me – I'm convinced you never even saw me – but you certainly saw something, and your eyes were full of terror. I swung round to find what had scared you so much, and I realised you were staring at the Ancient Mariner. I suppose he looked a bit more threatening in those days. We used to have annual competitions every Hallowe'en for the most terrifying scarecrow, and the previous year the local kids had gone to town; they gave him a really nasty mouth, and new eyes – pearlised silver buttons that reflected the light of the sky and sea, so they changed constantly. They were quite eerie. And you were walking late that day, it was early evening and the light was strange; the Mariner's eyes looked like they were moving. I jumped myself when I saw them. And it was quite windy, and his arms were blowing about; I could hear the twigs snapping. Suddenly there was a big gust of wind and it pushed him forward. He sort of lunged towards us. I could have sworn he'd moved but it was only the wind. And I looked back at you and you'd gone white with terror. I thought you might faint, and that would have been so dangerous, you were so close to the edge. I managed to grab your shoulders, and I tried to get you to snap out of the state you were in. You looked like my little brother used to when he was sleepwalking. I spoke to you gently so as not to scare you, and I said something like: 'It's all right, it's only a scarecrow, it's only the Ancient Mariner.' And you looked at me as if I was mad and pushed me away. And then you were sick; you vomited on the grass and before I could get to you, you started running. I chased after you but you ran so fast I couldn't catch up. By the time I got to the main gate you were a long way up the path, still running, going back to where you were staying in the village I presumed. I didn't go after you; I just went home. I'm an old lady, not used to running and scarecrows that look as if they're moving.'

I stared at her. So that was it. I'd felt compelled to go to Jamaica Inn because I had subconsciously remembered the name of Annie's house, opposite the allotments where I'd been so scared. And I had internalised the sight of the scarecrow I saw there, an experience that frightened me badly when I was in a hallucinatory state of mind. I'd remembered Annie calling him the Ancient Mariner, and that was why, when I thought I saw it again at Jamaica Inn, the words from Coleridge's nightmare-like poem, already in my mind because I'd been teaching it to sixth formers, had sprung into my mind. My evil, doom-laden vision had been a chimera, nothing more than a half-remembered vivid dream of horror.

Chapter Thirty-Nine

A couple of hours later I was back at Hope Cottage with Jamie. We sat down in the living room; Jamie kept asking me if I was all right. 'I'm OK, I suppose,' I replied shakily.

He looked thoughtful. 'You know, Molly, Annie's explanation about the scarecrow is actually the best thing that could have happened today. You say Len was telling you to go to the allotments. He meant you to realise just how the fright you had at Jamaica Inn came about. There was nothing supernatural about it; it was simply a repressed memory of what you saw at the allotments when you were in shock after Joey's accident. You're waking up, Molly. You're beginning to remember what happened when you were so traumatised.'

I supposed Jamie was right. At least now I had a rational explanation for what I thought I'd seen at the Inn. But what about my walks to the island? Was there anything rational about that?

I felt exhausted. And very alone. Jamie was with me, but it was Adam I wanted.

The tears started again. I apologised to Jamie. He moved onto the sofa next to me and touched my hand. 'Don't apologise. Of course you're upset, you've had a very emotional day. I don't think you should go to the island today. Just rest for the time being, and perhaps Adam will take you there tomorrow.'

Would Adam do that? Would he even come back to Cornwall again?

Jamie got up and went over to his medicine bag. 'Why don't you go upstairs now. Get into bed and I'll give you something to make you sleep. No, really,' he insisted as I began to protest. 'You must sleep, and I'm worried that if you don't you'll go haring off to the island by yourself and see something . . . ' He trailed off.

He was right. After he'd gone I knew I'd start obsessing again. I'd seen what Len wanted me to at the allotments. Convinced something else awaited me on Looe Island I would go there, impatient to get Len's predictions over with. And, tired and upset as I was, God knows what I might have experienced there, with no one to help me.

'You're right, Jamie. I will go to bed.'

He took a small bottle of pills out of his bag, and shook a few into a small brown envelope. 'Temazepam. Just take one. I've given you five in case you can't sleep for a couple of days.' He hesitated. 'Do you want me to call Adam?'

I shook my head. 'No, thanks. I'll call him myself when I've had a nap.'

Jamie walked to the front door and opened it. 'Don't get up,' he said as I rose from the sofa. But I joined him at the door, clutching the brown envelope he'd given me.

He put a hand on my shoulder, and smiled at me. 'Don't give up, Molly,' he said seriously. 'Honestly, I do think you're getting better. After what Annie told you, at least you know you're not going mad.'

I smiled back at him. 'Yes, that's true. But . . . there's still Joey.' I suddenly felt desperately bereft. 'Will I find him, Jamie? Will I ever know what happened to him?' I bowed my head, unable to bear the prospect of living with this torment for the rest of my life. Jamie put his hand under my chin and lifted my face up to his. He was looking at me with enormous kindness.

'I don't know, Molly. But I will say that, whatever happens, you will get better. We will get you through this, I promise.'

I felt overwhelmed by his warmth. He put his arms around me. I leant my head on his shoulder, and he patted my back. All I could feel was his solid strength, his masculine protectiveness. Adam, I thought. I want you. I looked up at Jamie and suddenly I was kissing him. My lips found his with no thought, just a desperate instinct to feel love.

Jamie stiffened. His protective arms were rigid on my back. He pulled back from my kiss. I was covered in confusion. 'Jamie, I'm sorry. I don't know what I was thinking . . . '

He shushed me, taking hold of both my shoulders. 'Molly, it's all right. You need affection and strength.

Don't apologise to me, I quite understand; but you really should call Adam and ask him to come back. You need him, and he very much needs you.' He pecked the top of my head. 'Go to bed now and take a sleeping pill. I'll call round tomorrow. If you need me, you've got my number.'

And with a reassuring squeeze of my shoulder, he walked down to the path and turned right towards the village.

Chapter Forty

Late in the evening, I was awakened from a deep induced nap by the telephone. Befuddled, I groped for the handset on my bedside table. 'Hello?' I croaked.

'Molly?' It was Adam. 'I had a missed call from you.'

'Oh yes. I remember,' I said dopily.

'Are you all right? You sound half asleep.'

'Sorry, Adam. I was having a nap. I just woke up.'

'Well, did you want to speak to me?'

'Yes. I didn't realise you'd gone back to Manchester.'

'Yes. I had some things to do. Actually I've been making some enquiries. About Ben.'

'Ben? Really?'

'I should have done it a long time ago. I'm sorry I didn't.'

'What do you mean, Adam? What have you found out?'

He was quiet for a minute. 'Look, I don't want to discuss this over the phone, especially given the way you've been lately.'

'Hysterical, you mean? Yes, I know I have.'

'Molly, I need to speak to you. I'm coming back to Cornwall tomorrow. I don't really want to intrude on your precious solitude in Polperro, so I'll meet you at Coombe.'

I sighed. Adam was right to be cross with me.

He went on. 'One of the things I've found out about Ben I'll tell you straightaway. Would you believe he lives in Cornwall now? In Polperro, for Christ's sake? He kept that quiet, didn't he?'

He paused, obviously expecting an astonished reply from me. He didn't get one. I simply couldn't find it in myself to pretend I hadn't known where Ben lived. I stayed silent.

'Jesus Christ,' he said quietly. 'You knew, didn't you? How could you know and not tell me?'

'Because you wouldn't let me contact him. I told you I needed to speak to Ben again. You more or less forbade me. So I did it anyway. I called his old number, and he picked up. And told me where he's living.'

'Have you met him?'

I hesitated, then decided it would be pointless to prevaricate. 'Yes. I saw him in the Blue Peter.'

'Oh God, so everyone knows – everyone saw you with him.'

'What do you mean "everyone knows"? What on earth does it matter? Anyway, only Queenie was in that day, she's the only person I recognised.'

'What did he say?'

'Ben? Nothing.' I gave a bitter laugh. 'Absolutely bloody nothing. He said he couldn't remember anything he hadn't told us already. He got quite angry; in fact I'd only been talking to him for a few minutes and he practically ran away.'

'Right. I'm coming back to Coombe tomorrow. Will you meet me there? I'll call you once I'm on my way.'

'Yes, I will. Adam . . . ?'

'What?'

'Can we be calm about all this when we see each other? I can't stand the thought of another row.'

'You're not the only one.'

I sighed again. 'OK. I'm sorry to be snappy. I'll see you tomorrow and we'll have a proper talk. Try and sort everything out.'

He sounded slightly mollified. 'Yes. I've got quite a lot to tell you, I'm afraid. I hope you won't be too upset.'

'I'll try not to be. I'll try to be a bit stronger. I really will, Adam.'

His voice softened. 'OK. Take care, Molly. See you tomorrow.' He rang off.

I sank back into sleep straightaway. And I dreamed about Adam, and Joey and Danny. When they were children. It was a happy dream. The boys were playing in our garden at home. Adam and I were in each other's arms.

Chapter Forty-One

Eating my breakfast next morning, I felt warmly happy about seeing Adam later. I was looking forward to having my husband to lean on again. I felt excruciatingly embarrassed about kissing Jamie yesterday, but I rationalised that I'd been emotional and upset, and Jamie's tall strength had made me think of Adam, and how much I needed his love. I felt quite different about Adam suddenly. I realised that my body was waking up from its long slumber. I wanted my husband; I wanted to feel his arms round me again. And I needed to know what Adam had found out about Ben. My stomach knotted when I thought of him; I dreaded finding out. I sensed that I was getting closer to finding out what had happened to Joey. I wasn't sure I was ready for it.

The doorbell rang. It no longer chimed the American national anthem. Apparently Hope had insisted on a doorbell app that changed its tune every few days, so I was serenaded by the ethereal tones of *The Little Mermaid*'s signature tune, Ariel trilling breathlessly: 'Aah-aah-aah, Aah-aah-aah, Aah-aah-aah, Aah-aah-aah-aah-aah.' I smiled at the thought of Hope's passion for Disney and things American.

I opened the door and the smile vanished from my face. Josie stood on the porch, her face puffy, her eyes red. She gave me a tremulous nod. I held the door open and she walked in.

'What is it, Josie?' I asked as I fetched another mug from the kitchen and poured her a cup of tea.

'Hope.' She said briefly. Her throat sounded sore. She took the tea from me, drank a long gulp and said, 'She's going into hospital today. I came here because I didn't want her to see me crying. Sorry.' And she bent her head and sobbed.

I remembered what Jamie had told me yesterday. I

put my arms round Josie and we both sank onto the sofa.

'Tell me, Josie. Is it bad?'

She nodded. 'Yes. This time it's very bad. Her consultant says . . . her heart's deteriorated. They're not sure she'll . . . well, they're operating but they're not hopeful it will work this time. Oh, Molly, she looks so ill. She can't breathe properly, and she looks blue. I just can't bear it.' She rested her head on my shoulder and wept with an abandonment that broke my heart.

'Oh, Josie, I'm so sorry.' I kissed her forehead, and mopped her face with a napkin I'd picked up from the table. 'Tell me exactly what's going to happen.'

Josie took a deep breath and blew her nose on the napkin. 'The ambulance will be here in an hour. They'll take her to Derriford and probably operate this afternoon. She had a check-up last week. They decided to admit her today for observation, but yesterday she got so ill. Dr Torrance wanted her to go in then, but she begged to stay at home another day. She was so upset, so Tony and I said she could. But she had a really bad night, and when I rang the hospital first thing they said they'd send an ambulance.' She looked at me, her eyes streaming. 'Oh, Molly, I think this is it. This is what I've always dreaded.'

I recalled what I'd been thinking just before Josie arrived: that I was close to finding out what had happened to Joey. And that may involve facing up to the very worst possibility I had ever imagined. Like Josie, this was what I'd always dreaded.

I hugged my friend tight. 'You don't know yet, Josie. It may be all right. They may be wrong about the outcome. They don't know for sure that the op won't work, do they? If they thought it was hopeless, then they wouldn't put her through it, would they?'

Josie nodded, unable to speak, trying to signal she hoped I was right.

'Listen, Josie. I'll tell you something a friend said to me before I came down here. He's a clergyman, a sweet kind person. He told me, "Molly, don't pay interest on your troubles." He got through to me. You and I, we have troubles enough. We shouldn't imagine the worst while there's still hope. Josie, I'll help you not to pay interest.'

She gave me a ghostly smile. 'I'll help you too, Molly. God bless you.' She stood up. 'I've got to go.

Tony's sitting with Hope. They both need me. Thank you for listening. I just needed to escape for a minute.'

'Call me or come round anytime, Josie. If you want me I'll come right over, it doesn't matter if it's day or night.'

She kissed my cheek. 'Thank you. That means such a lot.'

I watched her go. As she reached the path and turned left towards Emerald Point I saw her lift her head and square her shoulders. There she goes again, I thought. There goes Josie, strong capable Josie, loving mother and tower of strength, whose heart is breaking inside.

I went back to the kitchen and made more tea. I thought about the sadness, the heartache surrounding us. We don't see most of it. People put on brave faces. People like Josie, finding joy with a daughter she has known since birth could be taken from her at any moment. People like me, teaching my girls, loving their enthusiasm, taking pride in their success, adoring my baby granddaughter, keeping calm and carrying on even though my dreams are wracked with terror and my grief is absolute. Even if Joey were still alive . . . and here I caught myself. My pattern of thought was changing.

I never used to think 'if' before we came on this holiday. I always said 'when'; when I see Joey again, not 'if'. Something had changed my subconscious. Josie's visit had made me think of the inevitability of death.

My phone rang. It was Danny. He said Adam had called him to say he was about to leave Manchester, and he expected to arrive in the late afternoon, depending on traffic. Danny asked me to lunch at Coombe, and said he'd pick me up at the big car park at midday.

I looked at my watch. It was only 9.30. I washed up the breakfast dishes, went upstairs and ran a bath.

At midday, I was waiting for my son. I'd picked up a few groceries on the way, and some treats for Edie; strawberries, cream and ice cream, which she loved and couldn't get enough of. Danny's car honked at me from the entrance. I got in and he enveloped me in an enormous hug. I found myself smiling with pleasure as we drove to Coombe. I was going back, back to be with my family. How I'd missed them.

Edie and Lola were waiting on the porch as we drove into the little courtyard. I rushed to take the baby in my arms, irrationally afraid she would no longer recognise me. I'd said as much to Danny in the car, and he laughed at me. ''Course she will, Mum. It's not even been a week.' Had it? To me it felt I'd been away for months. Edie gave me a great big gummy grin and tried to pull my necklace off. I smothered her face with kisses and she chuckled with joy. Deeply happy, I followed Lola inside.

Lunch was a picnic on a rug in the garden. Edie was in seventh heaven; she could now eat and crawl at the same time. During the time I'd been away, she'd begun to pull herself up and totter along while holding onto something – today it was a bench. She pulled herself along, little bare toes squidging the grass, her face full of fierce concentration. When she got to the end, she turned her face to us and crowed with triumph and laughter. I'd never seen a child so excited. She knew she'd achieved something momentous.

'Oh, come on, Edie,' said Danny. 'Just be a bit braver. You can walk, you know, little one. Come on, walk to me.' Edie looked round at us all, obviously full of self-importance. She couldn't stop grinning, and suddenly she fixed me with a determined look. I felt giddy with pride. 'Edie,' I crooned softly. 'Come to Nanamoll; walk to Nanamoll. Come on, baby. You know you can do it.'

Lola moved behind Edie and put her hands on her

waist. 'Go on, darling,' she said softly. 'Go on. Just walk, baby.'

Edie gave a little wriggle. Her face was serious, completely solemn. Suddenly she launched herself out of her mother's arms and her stubby little legs propelled her forwards. She managed about ten shaky steps and threw her arms around my shoulder, laughing hysterically at her own success. I grabbed and kissed her, and Lola and Danny yelled with the massive happiness that all parents feel when their child achieves something enormous. No matter that every baby starts to walk eventually. For each mother and father, watching their little one make that first tremulous journey is a miracle. And for grandmothers, of course. I was beside myself with joy at witnessing such an ordinary but wonderful feat: a baby girl taking her first steps, not unusual, but so momentous for those who love and treasure her.

Edie's little triumph permeated the rest of the afternoon. I felt so close to Danny and Lola. These family moments are deeply precious; they bind us together. I wished Adam had been here to see it. Edie was thrilled at her triumph, and she responded by walking as if she'd been up on her two feet for years. She trundled round the garden, flopping down onto her bottom every few yards, but always with a beatific smile on her face, looking at us as if our only function in her tiny universe was to be her ecstatic audience. We duly fulfilled our familial duty. By the time Adam arrived, we were all rolling about the garden, consumed with delirious happiness.

Adam stood and looked at us all benignly. 'Good heavens, what on earth's going on?' he asked. Danny jumped up and threw his arms round his dad. 'Edie's just started walking,' he shouted. Adam gave him a fatherly look, congratulatory and full of affection. 'Well, of course she has,' he said in a proud voice. 'Hooray. She's been on the verge for a while now.'

Adam beamed as he swept Edie up into his arms. 'Kiss your Gramps, gorgeous,' he said. And she did, showering his face with slurpy caresses. 'Well done, kid. I always knew you'd be a genius.'

And so the day crept happily by, as we sat in the garden eating smoked salmon and strawberries; the sun shone bright, crowning our happiness, and Edie crawled, tottered and chortled, beside herself with glee.

When at last Lola took her inside for her bath, milk and bed, silence fell. Still wreathed in contentment,

Adam and I were both aware that our talk about Ben could not be put off much longer. Neither of us wanted to discuss Joey's best friend in front of Danny, so Adam suggested we should go out, maybe to Fowey for dinner. I'd dressed with some care earlier in the day, admitting to myself that I wanted to look good for Adam. I understood, shamefacedly, that this was because I'd kissed Jamie last night. I wanted a repeat of that kiss, but this time with the man I was married to. So I wore a pretty pink sundress that made the most of my figure, and my shoulder-length blonde hair was behaving itself for once. I popped up to the bathroom to repair my make-up, and then we were both in the Volvo, heading towards Bodinnick.

'You look nice,' Adam said appreciatively, glancing at me as he drove.

'Thanks,' I murmured, pleased. Adam looked good, too, I thought. He'd had a quick shower before we left; relaxed in a crisp white open-neck shirt, his aftershave, Eau Sauvage by Christian Dior, smelled alluring. I'd always loved that fragrance on him, light and lemony and, to me, deeply sexy, reminding me of holiday nights when a romantic dinner was always infused with the promise of passion to follow. Sitting beside him in the car, I felt my heart quicken and my stomach lurch.

Confused, I wondered why I suddenly felt so attracted to Adam, after the years of sexual drought that had plagued us since Joey's accident. It was as if the kiss I had so nakedly desired from Jamie the previous night had kick-started something in my body. Jamie was an incredibly attractive man. I felt guilty. If Adam and I did have sex, would I be fantasising about Jamie while we made love? This thought made me feel deliciously depraved, and I realised I was relishing my own naughtiness. *Molly, my girl*, I admonished myself, *you are in a very skittish mood.*

How strange. Nothing had changed – Joey was still missing. But somehow, my body, my thoughts, seemed different. The grief was still there; I felt the tears rise even as I thought of my son, and yet I didn't feel … what? *I don't feel dead any more,* I thought suddenly. *I no longer feel as if I died when Joey did.*

My heart thudded. What had I just let myself think? I had actually used the word 'died' about my beloved son. I had never, ever allowed myself to do that before.

This, of course, was what Adam had been trying to

get me to acknowledge all along. Knowing that my husband thought Joey was no longer alive had been at the root of my coldness towards him. So what did it mean that I had now allowed this previously forbidden thought into my mind? Jamie had said something to me yesterday, after I'd seen the scarecrow at the allotments, after Annie had explained what had happened to me there five years ago when, catatonic with grief and shock, I'd been frightened by the effigy's scary appearance after its leftover Hallowe'en makeover. Now I knew that my experience at Jamaica Inn was not supernatural, but an understandable trick of my memory prompted by anxiety and trauma.

Jamie had told me that I was, at last, waking up.

Waking up from the long nightmare of grief and denial that had set me apart from everyone, even my family, since my boy went missing. Waking up. Was that why my body now felt so alive? Was that why I suddenly felt so physically drawn to my husband? Passion suddenly felt for another man had jolted me into renewed desire for my husband.

Sort of the opposite of what happened to Lady Chatterley, I said to myself ruefully, and then I giggled. I started humming to myself. Adam looked over at me, amused. 'Why are you humming "I Feel Pretty" to yourself?' he asked. 'You do though; you look really lovely tonight.'

I smiled at him; he smiled back, and I saw his surprise, his quickening interest. He realises I feel sexy, I thought. I refuse to feel guilty about kissing Jamie. Maybe that brief embrace had been just what I needed.

And as we boarded the ferry at Bodinnick, we looked at each other with pleasure. Nothing had been said, but we had turned a corner during that drive. I think we'd made a promise.

We sat opposite each other across a candlelit table at the Old Quay House, an old and pretty hotel in Fowey. We ordered dinner, happily flirting with each other, knowing there was a serious conversation to be had but, for the moment, putting it off and relaxing into our new awareness of each other, which was of course simply a well-trodden memory of how things always used to be.

Who knows how that evening might have ended? Might we have booked a room at the hotel and stayed the night? I think we would, but as we started eating, before we'd even mentioned Ben, my phone rang.

It was Josie. She was weeping as she spoke, weeping as if she would never stop.

'Molly? She's gone, Molly. Hope has gone.'

Poor Josie, poor Tony – Hope, as well as her name-sake emotion, had gone. The hope they had lived with ever since their beloved daughter was born: all gone now. My throat ached but I made myself sound calm. 'Josie, my love. I am so, so sorry. Do you want me to come to the hospital?'

'No. We're just sitting here, Tony and I. They've taken her away for a while, but they're bringing her back soon. We're making some calls.' Josie continued to sob as she talked, quite calmly, as if this were the only way of speaking left to her, as if from now on she would always weep, it would be her natural state. 'We need to be on our own with her for a while. But I wanted you to know. We'll be coming back to Polperro later on tonight. Would you like to come and see her tomorrow? They're going to put her in a spe-cial room, before . . . and then when the undertakers have done what . . . they need to do, she's going to come back to Emerald Point. We want her with us until the funeral.

'So will you come to Derriford tomorrow? At, say, ten o'clock?'

'Yes, of course I will. Josie, you sound very strong.'

'I'm not, believe me. But Tony and I, we've talked about this for so long. I just want to do the best for her; I want to be strong for her. I have to go now, Molly. They need to . . . talk to us. I'll see you tomorrow.'

And she rang off, leaving her tears behind to stain my soul. I told Adam what had happened. He'd never met Hope, or Josie, but of course he too knew what it was like to lose a child, and he immediately sank into sadness. 'Can I take you to the hospital tomorrow, Molly? You haven't got a car; I'd like to help.'

I gratefully said yes. The mood between us had changed, no longer sexually charged, but tender. I couldn't eat. Another child, another tragedy. Of course Hope and Joey were grown-up, but to us, their mothers, they would always be our children. When you have a baby, what joy they bring, and how little you know of the sorrow that lurks at the edges of motherhood; if you're lucky, it will stay outside the charmed circle of your family – if you're not, you will know a grief that seems too much to bear.

We talked, and I apologised finally for blaming Adam for Joey's death. I told him I knew it wasn't his fault, it never had been, and the things I convinced myself of then had come from the depth of my grief, which had driven me almost mad. He said he understood, although it had hurt him deeply, but we could find a way forward now.

And we talked about Ben. Adam said he had tried to trace him through the university, not knowing, of course, that he now lived in Cornwall. But although the administration office couldn't tell Adam Ben's address, they did say he hadn't completed his degree course. He hadn't returned to the university in the summer term after Joey went missing. His tutors accepted that he was too upset to come back so soon, but he did resume his course again the following September. Adam said no one at the university would tell him much, but he got the impression Ben had had a difficult time when he tried to get back to his studies. At any rate, he had left for good at Christmas, and seemed to have disappeared.

Adam had the phone numbers of a few of Joey's friends at the English and Drama Department, and two of them – a boy called Seb and a girl named Nina – agreed to meet him at the Red Lion, a student pub near our house in Didsbury. They were affable and pleasant, now in their mid-twenties and anxious to be helpful in any way about Joey. They reminisced for a while and then Adam asked them what they remembered about Ben.

'Not much, really,' said Nina. 'I was always closer to Joey than Ben. And when Ben came back to Uni for the Christmas term he was very withdrawn. He hardly spoke to anyone, especially about Joey and the accident in Cornwall.'

Seb agreed. 'He became a bit of a hermit. Wouldn't talk about Joey. I remember a party near the end of term when some bloke, pretty drunk of course, started baiting him about the boat wreck. He wanted to know exactly what happened, and why Joe had gone out in the boat on his own. He sort of implied Ben had been negligent and had let Joe down. I remember Ben really tensed up and asked this guy if he was saying the accident had been his fault. The bloke backed down – he looked scared. Ben's a big bloke, and could be aggressive if he'd had too much to drink. I honestly thought he was going to deck the other guy, but in the end he just walked out, left the party looking thunderous.'

Nina grew thoughtful. 'I always thought Ben looked incredibly sad that term,' she said. 'Obviously he was missing Joey – they were always very close.'

'Yes,' said Adam. 'Best friends since primary school. Do either of you know where Ben is now? Is he still in Manchester?'

'Don't think so,' said Seb, 'Haven't seen him since that party years ago. I'd know if he was still up here.'

'But, hang on,' Nina joined in. 'I did hear something about him not too long ago; something about film. What was it? You know, of course, he was incredibly talented? Easily the best in his year at directing. We all used to think he was going to be really famous. Then he disappeared without finishing his degree, but someone mentioned a while ago that he had a job with an agency, directing ads or something. Sorry, can't remember who told me, but if it's true it's pretty jammy. Most of us would give our eye-teeth to get a filming job with a kosher agency at our age.'

Adam thanked them and said that gave him something to go on at least, bought them another round of drinks and left the pub.

As he neared the door, Seb caught up with him. He

looked slightly embarrassed, but determined. 'Mr Gabriel, I don't know if I should mention this. It may be just gossip, but the fact is there were a lot of rumours that Ben had got back into drugs that last term.' Adam asked him to go on. 'Well, everyone knew Ben used to do quite a lot of heavy stuff, but Joey never gave up on him. I mean, none of us were prudes; smoking weed was part of the university experience for most of us, but for Ben it went deeper than that. He was very cool, was Ben; a lot of us were in awe of him, so a lot of legends sprang up around him, the kind of guys he was hanging out with and stuff. There were always a few heavy types loitering around the student union then. They weren't students, but they were always there, hanging out with the coolest kids on campus. We knew they were pushing drugs. They were local gangsters; everyone knew that. Anyway, Joey would have nothing to do with them, like most of us, but Ben was definitely involved. They were quite aggressive, swaggered around as if they owned the place, and Ben seemed to enjoy feeling part of all that.'

Seb looked slightly stricken now.

'Look, Mr Gabriel, I'm not saying Ben was dealing

or anything like that. And Joey kept well out of it, but he was definitely concerned about Ben.'

This was what Adam told me that sad night when little Hope lost her life. We sat in that attractive seaside restaurant, watching the smiling faces of couples all around us enjoying a sophisticated holiday dinner, all of them beautifully dressed, sipping wine and looking as if they hadn't a care in the world, and I thought about Hope and Josie, Joey and Ben.

I felt like a bad fairy at a christening, spreading gloom like a curse because inside I was coiled up with grief and anxiety and couldn't bear any other parent to be lucky, to be blessed with children in perfect health, who didn't disappear never to be seen again.

I gave up pretending to eat and asked Adam to take me home. He paid the bill without demur, and we walked to the little car park up the road. Inside the Volvo he asked me if I would come back with him to Coombe. I was tempted, but I realised I needed to get back to Hope's house. I wanted to be in the little cottage she had loved so much, with all its sweet Americanisms, all the Disney charms that had enchanted her. She was still alive for me there; the place was full of her girlish enchantment.

Adam stopped the car at the top of Polperro and insisted on walking me home. We were both quiet, but relaxed together. He held my hand, and when we reached Hope Cottage he kissed me gently and said he'd see me tomorrow morning at nine fifteen, to take me to the hospital in Plymouth.

I let myself in. I sat in Hope's sitting room, furnished by Josie but with devoted attention to her daughter's wishes. It was full of good taste, polished floor, high-quality rugs, beautifully upholstered furniture. And yet there were tiny Mickey and Minnie Mouse ceramic ornaments dotted around the room. Tinkerbell hovered over the fireplace. A glittering rendition of the Sleeping Beauty Castle was tucked into a corner on a blond-wood pedestal. Photographs of Hope and her parents were everywhere in silver frames. In all of them she looked happy, full of beans. Tony looked strong, capable and in charge. Josie looked beautiful, delicate, and love blazed from her face as she hugged her daughter.

I sighed, said a prayer and went up to bed. Undressing, I remembered that Adam hadn't had the chance to tell me how he discovered that Ben was in Cornwall. No matter. At the moment my head was full of Hope and Josie. Nothing else was important right now. Adam would no doubt tell me everything he knew tomorrow. I took a sleeping pill. Tonight I didn't want to dream. Or if I did, I hoped for peaceful visions of Hope: walking on the beach with Josie, watching her dad building her dream cottage. How lucky and lovely for Hope to have a grown-up doll's house designed especially for her. How many little girls would covet that? Darling Hope had enjoyed hers; she had adored her parents. She had known nothing but love her whole life.

What more can any of us ask for?

Chapter Forty-Two

Adam drove me to the hospital next morning. He insisted on staying in the car when we arrived. He didn't know Josie and Tony, had never met Hope, and thought his place was solely to stay on the periphery and offer as much practical help as he could.

I was guided to a small room next to the hospital chapel. It was cold inside, heavily refrigerated. Josie sat bent over a small hospital cot. She looked like Mary tending to the infant Jesus in his crib. Hope lay on the little bed, her beautiful red hair vivid on the pillow. Tony wasn't there. I moved over to the cot. Josie looked up at me and half-smiled. 'She looks peaceful, doesn't she?' she said. Her face was drowsy. She bent her head down to Hope again and her face nuzzled her daughter's cheek.

I turned away and walked to a chair at the side of the room. It was a pretty, restful place, gently decorated in shades of soft rose pink. Candles burned on small tables at either side of Hope's bed, behind her head and at her feet. The cloth that covered her was blue and yellow, reminding me of her little cottage, the sunny doll's house which had become my sanctuary as well as hers.

Josie kissed her daughter one more time, then crossed the room and sat down in a chair next to mine. I held out my hand and she clasped it, squeezed it and began to talk.

'She didn't survive the operation,' she said softly, still weeping, speaking as if she was unaware of the constant tears rolling slowly down her cheeks. To me she looked noble, full of dignity. 'Her heart stopped on the operating table; a cardiac arrest. I think the team half expected it. They knew the odds on her pulling through this time were slight. They tried very hard to get her back. They wouldn't give up. They did everything they could. I'm grateful for that. I know they did their best.'

I gently let go of her hand, stood up and asked, 'May I?' She nodded. I walked to Hope's bed, and looked down at her sweet, childish face. I remembered her huge smile, her happiness when she played with younger children at Emerald Point, her confidence when she showed toddlers round the farmyard, their little faces lighting up when she told them stories about the animals. Hope had loved children. She had wanted her own baby to look after, entirely sure that with her parents' help she could have given it a happy life. I remembered the graciousness Hope had shown; the constant love that shone upon her. Her life had been short but blessed. Grace and kindness flowed around her in a benevolent loving stream. I could sense that goodness even now, surrounding her as she lay still, at the end of her life.

I bent to kiss her clear brow, and whispered goodbye. Josie waited for me at the door of the room. Holding my hand, she thanked me for being there. I kissed her and told her seeing Hope, knowing Hope, had been a privilege and a gift.

I left the hospital. Adam was waiting for me in the car. He saw my stricken face and squeezed my shoulder, but said nothing. As we drove away I knew we were both thinking the same thing. Would we ever see Joey in death? And would we be able to bear it?

Chapter Forty-Three

Seeing Hope at peace, all her trials over, made me long for a resolution to our own tragedy. I told Adam I wanted to go to the island. I was anxious to drive there straightaway. He was quiet; he clearly didn't think it was a good idea. He thought I was too emotional after seeing Hope; and of course I was, still weeping for her and Josie. But I yearned for peace. And I knew that to find it I had to face the island. Len had told me that on his deathbed. He said it was my next step, and although I might not understand to begin with, this first visit was essential. He also told me I should see it with Adam.

The time, I felt, had come. For better or worse I was going to look upon Lammana today.

Adam saw I was determined, and drove out of Plymouth without a word. He headed towards Looe, rather than Polperro or Talland Bay. The Estuary appeared on our right as we headed closer to the fishing town, the little railway track running along the riverbank, quiet and deserted. We drove past the small medical centre, where Danny and Lola had taken Edie when she was feverish the other evening. At the bridge over the river we turned right, and then immediately left into West Looe and carried on up the road.

As we neared the sea, the road swept round to the right, now running parallel with the waves. I tensed. Although I'd often shopped in Looe, I'd never come so far before. Staring at the ocean I could see nothing except boats; there was no land in sight, no island, nothing but water.

Adam drove up a hill, crested it and came down the other side. He stopped the car in a grassy area where the road came to an end; after this there was only the footpath, leading back along the coast to Talland Bay, and on from there to Polperro. This was the section of the cliff path I'd walked along every day after Joey disappeared; the walk of which I had absolutely no memory, and here the spot at which I stopped each time, where I stood for hours, according to Jamie Torrance and Annie Trelawney. It was a place about which I had no recollection. As far as I was concerned, I'd never been here before.

Adam got out of the car, walked round to my side and opened the passenger door. In a daze I stepped out onto the grass. I raised my eyes, and there it was. The island. This place I'd been mysteriously drawn to, this quiet teardrop of land that so compelled me, my daily goal after I lost Joey.

But why – why had I spent so much time, so much energy walking to this place? I stared at the small green outcrop, watching the waves crashing against its rocky sandy beach, its forbidding cliff face. I could see no one, and no sign of habitation; and I felt nothing. Not a shiver of recognition, not the slightest sense of why it had meant so much to me. *Joey,* I said silently to myself. *Joey? Why here? What is it? What do you want to tell me?*

There was no answer. The wind was fresh and strong here, the waves no longer smooth and friendly but vigorous, purposeful, as if they were holding their true force back, scuttled briskly between the shore and the rocky island. I suddenly had a sense of how difficult sailing conditions could be here, how treacherous. I glanced to my right. Joey's boat had found wrecked just yards up the coast from here, trapped in a small inlet wreathed in sharp jutting spears of rock. I couldn't even remember seeing what remained of it, although I surely must have been taken there. Adam had talked about the wreck; I would have been with him when the harbourmaster retrieved the small vessel, towing it back to the boatyard to be broken up. I closed my eyes and tried desperately hard to visualise Joey's boat, lonely and shattered after it had abandoned my son. That's how I thought of that wretched hired vessel, a rented pleasureboat to entertain two boys on a jolly Easter holiday; a boat that brought no pleasure, only tragedy. But, although I knew I'd seen photographs, I couldn't remember what it looked like.

Everything had fled my mind; everything except my beloved child's face. I could see that in front of me now. I would never forget him. Or would I? Would this creeping memory loss eventually encompass my boy's face too? Would there come a time when I could no longer conjure up his smile, his voice?

I clasped Adam's arm; this visit was a terrible disappointment. I had expected so much, but there was nothing for me here; there was no sense of terror, no strange fearsome apparition like the scarecrow in the allotments that could explain my forgotten obsession with this place. And I remembered what Len had told me: that I wouldn't understand at first, but this trip here with Adam was a necessary first step to discovering what had happened to my son.

I looked at Adam. He was staring at me, his face pensive. 'Do you remember anything, Molly?' he asked gently. 'Do you want me to see if I can get someone to take us out there?' I shook my head and turned back towards the car. Adam followed me; we strapped ourselves in, he did a three-point turn and we drove back into Looe. I had no idea what to do next. I stared at the road ahead. I no longer looked at Adam, but it seemed to me he was both relieved and disappointed by my lack of reaction. I was simply baffled. No, not just that. I felt empty, hollow, like a wandering soul trapped in a wasteland.

Chapter Forty-Four

We drove back to Coombe, stopping on the way to pick up fish and chips for lunch. We ate them sitting at the picnic table in the farmhouse garden. Danny, Lola and Edie were out, for which I was grateful. The conversation Adam and I had to have was going to be sombre.

I asked Adam why he hadn't stopped me from wandering trance-like down the cliff path every day five years ago. He sighed. 'Dear God, Molly, don't you think I tried? I came with you at first, of course I did, but you fought me off. You screamed at me, you actually hit me, telling me to leave you alone, that what you were doing was solitary, a journey for you and Joey alone. You said I had no place beside you, that Joey's disappearance was all my fault anyway.'

I winced. It was as I had thought, but hearing from my husband about the sheer cruelty of my behaviour towards him, the way I had used him as a scapegoat for my agony was still a shock.

'I followed you,' Adam continued. 'I wanted to make sure you were safe. Jamie Torrance came with me; we watched you staring at Looe Island, day after day. There was no point asking you why you did it. You behaved as if I didn't exist; you wouldn't speak to me. Eventually Torrance advised me to leave you to it. He said you were obviously not going to harm yourself; you were just in shock. You'd come round in your own time, he said, and I shouldn't make you more anxious by questioning you all the time. Well, I had my doubts about that, but he was the doctor, so I took his advice. But you didn't stop walking the cliff path until the day we left Cornwall. Then, when we got back home to Manchester, you were very vague and drowsy. I rang Geoff at the surgery. He came and gave you some sleeping pills. After that you slept for a couple of days, and then you seemed back to normal. Except you weren't, of course,' he said, looking at me meaningfully.

He meant I started to function again. I went shopping, cooked. I arranged a meeting with the new Head at my school and explained why I would have to miss a few weeks, because I intended to spend quite a lot of time in Cornwall to keep in touch with the investigation. I was very cool and collected. I could tell she was astonished at how 'normal' I seemed. She asked me if I was absolutely sure I was OK, if I didn't think I should have some counselling. God, that word 'counselling'. Geoff and Jamie Torrance, my doctors in Manchester and Cornwall, had kept asking me the same thing. I didn't want to talk to anyone about Joey. He was locked in my heart, and I was not going to let him out. Ever. No one else was going to see him, or know just what he meant to me. He was mine. He wasn't even Adam's, or Danny's. Just mine.

So the months and years crept on, and nothing changed. Now, all this time later, eating fish and chips at the holiday home we'd spent so much time in with the boys, we were both aware that something had happened, something significant had added to our knowledge of Joey's last day. And that something was Ben.

I began. 'How did you find out Ben lives down here in Polperro?' I asked.

'I traced his mother. She told me. She's a pitiful soul really; she's got mental health problems and she lives in sheltered accommodation now. Very lonely, I think, but she told me, quite proudly, that Ben is doing very well now as a freelance film director, mostly working on commercials. He sends her money. Good of him when you think how badly she treated him, kicking him out when he was only sixteen.'

'They were a really dysfunctional family,' I said. 'It wasn't just her, his dad was a swine. He was such a self-ish sod, marrying a younger woman who didn't want Ben around. I heard he's had a couple of other kids with her now. I hope to God he treats them better than he treated Ben. He was an awful father; he abandoned his own son because he found a new woman.'

Adam sighed. 'Yes, you're right, but let's not forget Ben was no picnic either. He was incredibly difficult, into drugs even then.'

'OK,' I agreed, 'but can you really blame him? He

was only a kid and his home life was beyond terrible. He needed guidance and love, and he got neither.' As we talked about Ben, I decided to phone him. I went inside to the landline.

When it was answered, by the same girlish voice I'd heard when I first rang Ben, the young woman told me he was away from home. I asked her when he would be back.

'I'm not sure. Possibly tomorrow, or maybe the day after.'

'It's Molly Gabriel here,' I said. 'I spoke to Ben a few days ago.'

There was a slight hesitance in her tone. 'Oh . . . yes, of course. Well, as I said, Ben's away working. I'm not sure when he'll be back. Shall I tell him you called?'

'Yes, please. Tell him we're still in Cornwall and we need to speak to him. I think he's got my number.'

The girl said she'd pass on the message, and then rang off. I went back outside to report to Adam.

Later, I got Adam to drive me back to Hope Cottage. I had half intended to stay at Coombe. Now Hope had died, her little house would soon be filled with sadness.

And I thought Josie and Tony would want it back; they would want to sit in it together, thinking of her, the life they had given her, even though, much as they loved her, they had not been able to save her from her fate. There was a lesson there for me, I thought. Something I needed to think about.

But although I longed to see the baby, I had to finish my quest to find Joey. The thought of Edie filled my stomach with love and hope. The idea that she was new, untainted, that she was the future, comforted me even though I felt wretched.

Adam was a bit put out with me wanting to go back. When we got to Polperro he dropped me off, gruffly saying that he would stay in Cornwall until Ben came back. He was determined to have it out with him. I nodded. It was the obvious next step. Then he drove away, back to the family life I had to leave right now because of my determination to find Joey.

I walked down to the Blue Peter, hoping to find Queenie there. Clouds were gathering as I walked. It looked like we were in for rain, which suited my mood. As I reached the pub, heavy, slow drops began to fall, dimpling the water in the harbour, and cooling my head with soft damp insistence. I welcomed it. I needed the weather to change, to underline my broken dreams, the dreariness of the future that awaited me.

I pushed open the heavy blue door. It was only four in the afternoon, but the place was more than half full. Queenie saw me immediately. I gave her a disconsolate wave and found a comfortable seat by a window. I saw her whisper to a lanky youth lounging against the bar. She gave him a drink and nodded in my direction. He came over and put a gin and tonic in front of me, grinning. 'Cheer up. It may never happen,' he said. I felt seriously cross for a minute, but then I looked up at him, and his tanned lively face, bursting with health and good humour, made me unable to resist smiling back. He laughed.

'That's better,' he said, in a strong Cornish accent. 'The G and T's from Queenie. She'll be over in a minute.' I looked over at my friend behind the bar. She was busy taking food orders from a man with a wife and three children in tow. She looked, for Queenie, a tad harassed.

My tall new friend plonked himself down next to me and said, 'Go on. Get it down you.'

I took a sip, feeling amused but faintly annoyed at his cheek. When I looked at him, his smile had disappeared. 'Sorry, I don't mean to bother you. Queenie told me you've been up at Derriford to see little Hope. You look sad, but then we all are. She was a gorgeous girl; her dad used to bring her in here sometimes. She was a treasure, that kid, the happiest girl I knew. It's a terrible shame.'

I felt grateful to him for normalising my bad mood. Yes, of course I was desperately sad for Hope, or more truthfully, for Josie. Hope, I thought, was peaceful. No more spells in hospital, no more operations. For Josie everything was different. She'd stopped being a mother. She couldn't help her baby now.

But, to be absolutely honest, my wretched sadness was for Joey, and for myself. I was glad this young man had mistaken the real reason for my unhappiness.

Queenie materialised at my side. 'Thanks, Wren,' she said to the boy sitting at my side. 'Off you go now.'

He grinned and got up. 'Ever polite, Queenie. I thought you promised me a drink?'

'It's on the bar. Make sure your friends don't pinch it.'

With a huge smile on his face, he moved back to the

bar, joining a small coterie of friends who clapped him on the back and immediately enveloped him in warmth.

'Wren?' I asked Queenie, raising a quizzical eyebrow.

'It's an old Cornish name. Especially here in Looe and Polperro. Didn't you ever read that book by the Atkins sisters, *We Bought an Island*?'

I shook my head.

'Well, Babs and Evelyn Atkins were two sisters who bought Looe Island and lived virtually alone on it for years. They needed a lot of practical help from people who lived on the mainland, because it was so difficult to get across to the place. When the spring tides were running, it was cut off for weeks. Wren is the grandson of the Looe boatman who helped them most. Wren's named after him. As I said, it's an old Cornish name.'

'Are the Atkins sisters still there?' I asked.

'No. They're both dead now, although Babs is buried on the island.'

'Looe Island? We're talking about St Michael of Lammana?'

'The very same,' said Queenie. 'It's had a lot of names.'

I sighed. My mind was full of Hope's death, and my

row with Adam about Ben. The island, which I'd contemplated in reality for the first time that morning, seemed completely irrelevant. I simply could not understand why it had fixated me for so long.

'Queenie. Can you tell me about Ben?' I asked the question suddenly, unsure where it had come from, except that I remembered Queenie's reservations about him the first time I'd been to the Blue Peter, when I told her I was going to meet Ben there.

She looked uncomfortable. 'I'm not sure what you mean, Molly. What is it that you want to know?'

'Was he taking drugs?' I blurted it out. 'When he and Joey were down here that Easter? Tell me, Queenie. I have to know.'

She was quiet for a moment. Then she said, 'I'm not sure I can tell you much, Molly. All I know is that there was a lot of bad stuff going on down here around that time.'

'What, here at the Blue Peter?'

'And in Polperro generally. It wasn't a time most of us want to remember. There were people . . . strangers; men we'd never seen before. They were rough. We knew they were up to no good.'

'And did they know Joey and Ben?'

'Ben, certainly. Not Joey, I think. There was something wrong between Ben and Joey; I noticed it. But we didn't know what the problem was.'

'And . . . was Joey taking drugs?'

'No, Molly. I'm sure he wasn't. I've known that boy since he was a toddler. He wasn't part of that crowd that used to meet up here. I hated them, so did Pete, the landlord. But it was hard to bar them when we had no proof. I mean, we suspected they were dealing, they were so rough, but we never caught them doing anything here.'

'And Ben?'

'I don't know. But he was certainly thick with them; in here every night, drinking, laughing. It was all, well, they were all, quite aggressive. Not violent, but very standoffish. Kept themselves to themselves. They were a tight circle, and Ben was certainly part of it.'

'Joey, too?'

'No. Not Joey. Although he did turn up here a couple of times, very late, looking for Ben. They'd have a bit of a row; I think Joey wanted Ben to leave, and Ben would be pissed off, but eventually he always gave in, and Joey took him home.'

Queenie raised her hand, and waved at Wren, who was now sitting down with his mates, drinking a half of bitter. She beckoned him across. 'Molly,' she said quietly. 'I'm going to ask Wren to talk to you; he'll remember much more about that time because of his age – he was eighteen when Ben and Joey were on that holiday. He often used to have a drink with them here. I remember he particularly looked up to Joey.'

Wren arrived at our table, and raised an eyebrow at Queenie. 'Wren, I don't know if you remember Molly Gabriel. She's . . . well was, Joey's mother.'

I tried not to flinch. Even if he'd gone, even if I never saw him again, even if, God help me, he was dead, I would always be Joey's mother; always and for ever. I made myself smile at Wren. He smiled back, his eyes softening in sympathy.

'Molly needs to talk about the last time Joey was here, before his boat was wrecked,' Queenie continued. 'I remember you and Joey used to talk for hours.'

Wren sat down at the table. 'Yes, that's right. He was a great bloke, Joey. I was a bit wild and miserable in those days, knowing I was never going to amount to much. I mean, the men in my family have been fishermen for generations. No one's ever done anything else. And obviously that's what was on the cards for me too. I've always helped my dad on his boat, and I enjoyed it all right, but back then I was feeling rebellious. I wanted to get away, move upcountry, see life. I really wanted to go to university.' Wren laughed. 'Ideas beyond my station, you see. I was useless at school, never worked. Well, why bother when you know your life's been mapped out since you were born? So there's no way I was bright enough to go to Uni, but I totally resented it back then. I spent hours asking Joey what it was like; we talked for ages.'

He gave me a guilty look. 'I'm sorry, Mrs Gabriel. This must be very upsetting for you.'

'Molly,' I said immediately. 'Please call me Molly. And it's not upsetting me. I need to know as much as I can about Joey's last days. Thank you for talking to me.'

Wren looked thoughtful. 'He was very understanding, was Joey. He did tell me about Uni, and he said he enjoyed it, but that it wasn't for everyone. He said that with his mum and dad being teachers and all, he was always expected to go, just like I'd always been told I was going to be a fisherman. He said he loved sailing, and that in some ways he envied me. Exams and stuff were stressful, and he thought he might prefer a quieter life. He made me feel a lot better about myself; he was clever that way. I told him he should have been a shrink, and he laughed. Oh, and he also said that if I really wanted to go to university, I could always go later. Try fishing first, he told me, and if you still want to study, you can always do A levels at night school and then go on to university as a mature student. He said he'd help me, gave me his phone number, and said if I fancied a trip to Manchester he'd put me up and show me round.' Wren looked at me shyly. 'He was a good lad. Very kind.'

I smiled. Wren's memories of Joey made me feel happy. 'Yes,' I said. 'He was a smashing boy.' My eyes filled up, and I turned my head apologetically. Queenie swiftly stepped in.

'Molly was asking about Ben, too. You weren't quite as close to him, were you?'

The lanky young man frowned slightly. 'Well, not in those days, but of course he lives here now and he's completely changed. We're friends now.'

'But not then?' I asked quickly.

'No. He used to be kind of strange. Standoffish, a bit of a loner. Didn't want to talk much to anyone, except those pricks who used to hang around here back then.' Wren blushed. 'Sorry for the language, but they really were arseholes.' He blushed again.

'What was wrong with them?' I asked.

'Well, they were gangsters, weren't they? Manchester gangsters, up to their necks in very shady stuff. Drugs, was what everyone said.'

'How did you know?'

'We didn't, not for sure. It was just a rumour that was going round. Anyway, they were certainly up to something, and it wasn't anything good.' Wren looked at Queenie.

'Yes,' she continued. 'There was something very threatening about them, but like I said, Moll, nobody ever caught them out.'

'You didn't call the police,' I said.

'What for? They never put a foot wrong. And anyway, we've got a couple of local coppers who drink in here. They used to keep an eye out, but you can't arrest people for being ugly. They did look like brutes, though. In their thirties or forties, shaved heads, very big. Not fat, broad. And the way they stood; they were so intimidating.'

'How many of them?'

'Three usually, but sometimes another two would turn up, God knows where from.'

'And you say Ben used to talk to them?'

'Oh, yes,' said Queenie. 'Thick as thieves, they were. They'd drink and mutter together for hours.'

'Ben knew them,' said Wren suddenly. 'He knew their names and everything, right from the first night they came in. I assumed it was because they were all from Manchester.'

'What about Joey? Did he seem to know them?'

'No.' Wren shook his head. 'At least, I don't think so. He didn't like them, I could tell. He never drank with them, and he hated it when Ben did. He kept trying to pull him away. They had quite a few rows, but I never heard what they said to each other. There was a pretty bad atmosphere in the Blue Peter then.'

'In the whole of Polperro, really,' added Queenie. 'There was a lot of tension around, as if people were waiting for something bad to happen.'

'And it did,' I said grimly. 'Joey vanished.'

Wren looked shocked. 'Oh, I don't think Queenie meant that. She meant ... we all thought they were building up to something criminal. Some kind of big scam. But it never happened.'

'What *did* happen? When Joey's boat was found, what happened to these ... gangsters?'

Wren shrugged. 'They hung around for a while, then they just disappeared. It was odd. They were very unsettled about Joey. Almost as if they'd had something to do with it.'

'I bet they did,' I said bitterly.

Queenie looked at me sharply. 'Molly, what are you thinking? Wren's wrong. They couldn't have had anything to do with Joey's accident.'

'Why not?' I asked.

'Because they were all in here the morning it happened. Joey had set off alone that morning – we saw him leave the harbour. We thought it was a bit strange because he and Ben always sailed together, but Joey was definitely on his own, and those gangster types were all here in the pub. They played cards all morning. Then Ben came in at lunchtime. Normally he'd have had a drink with them, but this time he ignored them and sat on his own. I remember the big bruiser went over and had a word with him, but Ben just looked miserable and refused to talk.'

Wren chimed in. 'And soon after that Ben started to look worried. There was a squall outside then; it blew up halfway through the morning. After a bit, Ben came up to me and said he was bothered because he was supposed to meet Joey here and he was more than an hour late. Well, I told him not to worry, but to be honest I was concerned. It'd got pretty rough out there. I wouldn't have wanted to go out on a boat myself. We waited for another hour, and Ben was white as a sheet. I took him to see the harbourmaster, Dave, and he started the alert. The lads did a search and they eventually found Joe's boat wrecked and stranded in an inlet just off Looe.' He looked at me sorrowfully.

'And when they found the boat there was no sign of Joey,' I said heavily.

'No. I'm sorry. They did a huge search though. They did look for him Mrs Gab— Molly. They were searching and trawling for days. But . . . '

I knew the rest. They never found him. And they never found a body.

I sighed and stood up. I thanked them both for their patience and said I was going home. Queenie looked worried. 'I'll come down later, shall I?' she said. 'You shouldn't be on your own.'

I said I was going to see Josie, and told Queenie I'd be fine. Then, with a heavy heart, I left the Blue Peter and walked home to Hope Cottage. Hopeless cottage. For both Josie and me.

Chapter Forty-Five

I went to bed that night feeling guilty about not visiting Josie at Emerald Point. But I also thought I needed a rest from sorrow, whether mine or someone else's. There was a stack of DVDs on a shelf next to the widescreen television in the living room. Predictably, this being Hope's private collection, there was a surfeit of Disney animations: *Beauty and the Beast, Finding Nemo, The Little Mermaid*. Lots of earlier archive stuff as well: *Snow White, Sleeping Beauty, Fantasia*. But because Josie and Tony rented the cottage out to grown-ups from time to time, there were movies like *Mamma Mia,*

Shakespeare in Love, Sleepless in Seattle, and, striking a bizarrely dark note, *The Shawshank Redemption.* I settled for *Mamma Mia.* I wanted ABBA to remind me of my youth, when life was all about guilty cigarettes and parties. And boyfriends, too. Just fun, really. I'd forgotten how to have fun.

When I finally settled in my bed, I tried to keep that gorgeous, bouncy ABBA music in my head. Eventually I drifted off.

In my dream, Len walked beside me. The sky was dark, but poised to take on the colour of the day. Dawn hid itself away, only revealing an early promise of light in the east, a hint of dusky blue. I could see well enough, though; I was aware we were treading on rough grass and I could smell the salt of the sea. We walked up a steep track, although our motion was effortless. We glided along the ground; to the left I saw a rocky cliff carving down to a jagged foreshore. The sea lay calm, still, as if waiting for something, reflecting occasional diamond glints of light as the dawn grew brighter. To our right, nestling in woods, was a small dwelling. This was Smugglers Cottage, I gathered from Len, but although his benign presence by my side felt companionable, I never heard him speak. I seemed to absorb his thoughts by osmosis.

After we passed through the trees, glimpsing Looe Bay and the mainland to the left, we wandered through fields, flat and cultivated. Len murmured, and although I couldn't hear him, my mind filled with daffodils, bright, glorious and nodding in the early dawn light. Ahead of us there was a large and pleasant building, and I learned wordlessly again from Len that this was Island House, the main dwelling on Lammana. I was here at last, walking in the place to which I had been mysteriously called, day after day, after Joey disappeared.

Keeping the sea to our left, Len guided me uphill on a path that led past the house towards the island summit. Just before we reached the top I saw a seat and sank down upon it, Len, as always, by my side. I gazed out to sea, and watched the sun rise.

And in my dream I saw the gathering light coalesce, throb, take shimmering shape and cohesion. A grotto of golden beauty formed before me, an iridescent cave bathed in translucent light. The radiance beckoned me. I felt a longing to walk into its brilliance and warmth; it was as if a candle flame drew me into the heart of its heat.

I stood up and looked at Len. He knew I wanted to move into the grotto. He smiled and walked with me. We entered together, into a place of intense and joyous rapture. I felt strong, whole, reborn.

Again Len spoke to me soundlessly, and I knew he was telling me about a divine presence. The infant Jesus had walked on Lammana, brought by his uncle, Joseph of Arimathea, a merchant who traded silks and spices from Phoenicia for Cornish tin. I had heard this legend already, but in this golden holy grotto, I felt its truth, and how it had touched the imagination of poets such as William Blake; the story of Christ's sojourn on the island was said to have been the inspiration for his beautiful hymn *Jerusalem*:

> And did those feet in ancient time
> Walk upon England's mountains green?
> And was the Holy Lamb of God
> On England's pleasant pastures seen?

I closed my eyes, revelling in the calmness of my heart. Len's spirit prompted me to open them, and when I did I saw a lovely and familiar face. Her eyes smiled, her red hair streamed behind her, her sea-green robe rippled softly round her small body. Hope looked steadfastly at my face; she floated like the little mermaid she loved so much, she radiated joy. I heard her voice in my head: 'It's all right, Molly. Tell Mummy I'm happy. Tell her I'm happy, here. It's nice; everyone is so kind.'

There was a pause, a silence in my mind. I felt joy for Hope and an urgent wish to share this bliss with Josie. And then I heard Hope's voice again, soft and encouraging.

'Molly, look.'

And Len's face was suddenly before me, benign and happy. I felt his ghostly hands brush mine. 'Yes, Molly, look. Look my dear, and you will see that all is well.'

I lifted my head. Joey, ringed with brilliance, stood before me, his eyes wide with welcome. He was beautiful, perfect, untouched by the sea and the savage creatures of my nightmares. He looked as he did when I last saw him in my kitchen, healthy, happy and full of love. He held my gaze. My voice broke.

'Joey, oh Joey, my Joey. I've finally found you, my love. Please stay, please stay with me. If I lose you again my heart will shatter.'

And I moved towards him, my arms open wide, desperate to hold him at last. He let me fold my body around him. He felt insubstantial, but oh, I could smell him. That robust young man's smell, the scent that had survived his absence. My soul feasted on the essence of my son. He stepped back and smiled at me. 'Mother . . . Mum,' he said softly, and it filled me with joy.

'You'll find me now,' he breathed. 'And all will be well. Now you've found me, you too will be well again, Mother. You'll be healed, and I'll always be with you. I will never leave you. I am at peace. I am happy. Don't fret about me any more. Keep me in your heart. I love you.'

And I thought he'd fade away, that the golden grotto would shrink and disappear, that the dawn light would sink into the inkiness of night, and I would find myself alone on Lammana, without Len, without Hope and without my dear beloved son. But none of that happened. Instead I awoke and felt myself still bathed in shimmering brightness. All around the room white moonbeams darted, shining on my coverlet, glinting off the walls. Silvery starlight gathered at the undraped window and flew across the dark bedroom, touching my face, my hands, stroking me, coaxing me to be happy. And as I let the stars and moonbeams caress me, I felt again the peace and stillness I had found in Talland churchyard. I glimpsed the journey's end, the rest granted to weary bodies, the gladness to be found in bowing one's head, accepting one's fate; and most of all the joy of knowing that I had found my son, and he was at peace, and all would be well.

Chapter Forty-Six

When I woke up again the sun was high in the sky. I stretched, completely relaxed, feeling as if I'd slept for days. The happiness of the night had stayed with me. I felt as if I'd completed a long quest; that I'd successfully reached the finishing line after an interminable marathon that had nearly killed me. I luxuriated in bed, allowing peaceful waves of pleasure to wash over me.

Something, a strong instinct, was telling me my dream of the island was significant, that it was more than an attractive and restful fantasy. What had Len told me while he lay dying in his hospital bed? That I would first see the island when I was with Adam, and that it would mean nothing to me at the time. I would understand only later the place's true purpose, what it really signified for me. And now he had sent me the dream. He meant me to understand something momentous. And was that something that Joey was dead? My son's spirit had appeared to me and told me all was well, he was happy. Was that all that my dream had told me? Should I now give up the search, find Adam and go back home to a new life?

But why, then, was Len's ghost so eager to take me to Lammana? Why had I met my son in a dream on the very island that had compelled me to walk for miles to look at it?

And why had I made that same daily journey, in some kind of trance, just after Joey's empty boat was found wrecked? What was my subconscious trying to tell me?

I leapt out of bed. I had to get back to the island straightaway. I had to walk on it once more, this time awake and aware. Because something was missing from my interpretation of last night's dream. Where was my son, his physical remains? I had to find Joey.

I dressed hurriedly and was rushing out of the front door when my mobile rang. I looked in my bag; it wasn't there. Damn. What had I done with it? I ran upstairs to the bedroom, and there it was on the little lamp table under the window. I picked it up and answered without looking at the caller ID.

It was Adam. His voice was urgent. 'Molly? Ben's back in Polperro. I want to see him.'

'How do you know he's back?' I asked.

'I saw him,' said Adam grimly. 'I was coming to see you, and as I pulled into the top car park I saw him coming out of the Crumplehorn. I ran after him but by the time I reached the lane he'd disappeared. I don't know where he lives, but I'm going to find him.'

'Where are you now?'

'Still at the car park. I was thinking of going into the Crumplehorn and asking if anyone knows where he lives.'

'No, Adam. Don't do that. We need to call him first.'

'Why? You said he ran away from you when you met him at the Blue Peter. Why give him the chance to refuse to see us? He's obviously got something to hide. We need to confront him.'

I remembered Ben's scared face as we walked through the village that day. If we surprised him, 'confronted' him as Adam wanted to, Ben would see it as aggressive. I felt sure this was not the way to talk to Ben. He would respond best to gentleness – he would only open up if he felt we were not going to blame him for whatever had happened to Joey. And at the moment, Adam was looking to blame him.

'No, Adam. Please listen to me. Can you and I meet and talk first? We need to plan this. I'll walk up to the Crumplehorn now, and I'll see you inside in about ten minutes.'

Adam grumpily acquiesced, and I finally left the cottage to meet him. As I walked up through the village, I worried about my husband's fury; not just with Ben, but also me. I dreaded a row, and it wouldn't get us anywhere. I prayed that Adam would listen to me and accept we had to tread carefully with Ben. I was also frustrated at not being able to go back to the island straightaway, and wondered if Adam, not content with simply antagonising Ben, would stop me from doing that as well. He was in an uncompromising mood, my husband, a familiar stubborn cussedness I recognised from the occasions when things were not going well at his school. For a moment I thought of not going to the Crumplehorn. I could ring Adam and make some excuse, tell him I had a headache and needed to lie down. Then I could get a taxi to Looe harbour and find a boatman to take me to the island.

I sighed. It was no good. If I didn't meet Adam, he'd only go storming off on his own, find Ben and no doubt start a humungous row. Ben would shut the door in his face, and probably disappear to avoid talking to us. It was best I was there to keep things calm. And I suddenly remembered that Len had said something else on his last day. He said I must talk to Ben; he said the boy was important. Ben was next. The old man's mysterious messages had all made sense so far. Perhaps I should talk to Ben before I went back to the island. Perhaps that was the right order; the Charmer knew what he was talking about.

I walked into the Crumplehorn. It was a big pub, full of dark brown tables and banquettes, and I couldn't see Adam at first. Eventually I found him in a small side room, an airy red-carpeted snug containing just two tables, one of which was empty. At the other Adam sat nursing a half of cider. He looked very serious and I was glad that we had the room to ourselves.

He stood up when he saw me. I raised my eyebrows at his cider, and he looked at his watch. 'It's nearly midday. Do you want a drink?' he asked.

'Nothing alcoholic, not yet. I'll have a Diet Coke, please.' Adam stuck his head into a hatch dividing the snug from the bar, and moments later my Coke stood on the ledge. He passed it to me and sat down.

'Right,' he said. 'How are we going to go about this?'

'Adam,' I began. 'Of course we must talk to Ben, about everything that was going on between him and Joey that Easter. But we must tread carefully; if we don't, I think he'll bolt. Let me fill you in on what I heard last night at the Blue Peter.'

I told him what Queenie and Wren had said about Ben's strange behaviour at that time, about what Wren called the 'Manchester gangsters' and Ben's involvement with them. Adam listened eagerly. 'Can I meet this Wren?' he asked. 'It seems like he could be the missing link.'

'Yes, you can talk to him later,' I said. 'But first we've got to find Ben. Please, Adam, when we talk to him, let me take the lead. If you get angry, he'll just walk out.'

Adam looked belligerent, then he flung his head back and gave a great sigh. 'Yes, OK, Molly. That makes sense. You always were closer to him. He saw you as a substitute mother, I think.'

I was grateful for Adam's obvious effort to be conciliatory. 'Yes,' I replied. 'I was always very fond of him, and I think he trusted me. It's been a long time, and something terrible happened to Joey, but I agree with you that Ben knows more than he's ever said. We must get it out of him, but, Adam, I beg you, be gentle. He's still young, and whatever it was, he's probably traumatised by it.'

Adam nodded in agreement. I got my phone out of my bag and pressed Ben's number.

He answered immediately.

Chapter Forty-Seven

We sat in the garden at Coombe. Ben had agreed to talk to us, but not at the pub. I suggested the old farmhouse, because Adam had told me Danny and Lola had taken Edie out for the day. I also knew Ben had fond memories of the place, having joined us there on so many family holidays as Joey's best friend.

So we picked him up at the car park, and drove back to Treworgey. Ben was bashful, shy, and Adam was as good as his word. He talked to Ben in a fatherly way, asking about his work and his life, and by the time we got to Coombe the atmosphere in the car was as cordial as it could be, given the circumstances.

When we arrived at the house, I realised Adam was wrong about Danny and Lola. It turned out that they had gone to the beach earlier, but it was crowded and Edie was playing up, so they'd come home. When we walked into the garden Edie was in the middle of a marathon hike, chubby legs stomping over the grass, an enormous grin on her face, and her parents were dutifully clapping her progress. Ben saw them all before they noticed him, and stopped short. His eyes widened with a kind of wonder as he looked at the baby; at that moment Danny looked up and saw his little brother's best mate. He got to his feet with a whoop, and engulfed Ben in a strong embrace. Edie stopped in the middle of her power-toddle, staring at the stranger wrapped in her daddy's arms. Then she tottered across to them and flung her own little limbs around their legs. Danny picked her up and thrust her towards Ben. He took her and she immediately gave him a great big sloppy kiss. Ben laughed with delight, twirled her around and all three of them collapsed on the grass next to Lola.

I watched this happy tableau with tears of happiness. It was almost as if Joey were here too. I could sense his presence in the garden, see him smiling at his friend, his brother and his niece. Danny had had no idea that Ben was in Cornwall, and was astonished to see him. They chattered and laughed, touching each other on the shoulder, their eyes shining with pleasure at the sight of each other.

Adam and I left them to it and retired to the kitchen. We had a brief discussion and decided that it was a good thing Danny and his little family was here. Ben would be more relaxed, and we could all have a calm talk about Joey, rather than an awkward exchange dominated by two tense and anxious parents.

Adam took cider and wine out to the garden; I followed with a tray of glasses, crisps and olives. We set it out on the small picnic table, and Edie immediately started demolishing the crisps. When everyone had a drink I looked at Adam. He nodded, and I began.

I asked Ben to tell us again what had happened on that Easter day five years ago. Danny looked startled and started to protest. He didn't want to talk about something so dark on a sunny day with his wife and baby by his side, but Lola calmly stroked his arm, and Danny subsided.

Ben was silent for a minute, looking down at the grass. Then he raised his eyes and looked straight at me. 'I'm sorry for running off when you tried to talk to me the other day, Molly. I couldn't talk to you then. I've been thinking hard since. I can't tell you any more than I know, and you must understand, both of you, Adam and Molly, that I really don't know where Joey is.' He looked pleadingly at us, his handsome hawk-like face with its prominent nose and sharp intelligent eyes restlessly sweeping from Adam's face to mine.

'What happened, Ben? Why did Joey take the boat out on his own?' My voice was gentle.

Ben stood up and walked to the end of the garden. Edie watched him with interest. He stood next to the fence and faced us all with a desperate dignity.

'This isn't easy,' he said quietly. 'I've behaved like a shit. I've been trying to forget what happened for five years now. But I'll tell you. You'll probably hate me. I actually hate myself. But you must believe that I didn't mean to harm Joey. I would never have done that in a million years. I loved him, you see.' Ben looked at each of us in turn, fastening his gaze at last on Danny. He kept his eyes on Joey's brother as he began to tell us his story.

'You know all about the drugs I took when I was a teenager; I was pretty wild then, completely out of control. That's why Mum threw me out – I used to fill the house with some real dross, dealers, and she couldn't take it. She had ME as well; some days she couldn't get out of bed. Dad was useless as far as I was concerned, and his new wife couldn't stand me. I don't blame any of them now; I was really obnoxious. But at the time I hated them, I was so angry. I used to come to your house with Joey for Sunday lunch, and I wanted what he had so much: a normal, loving family.

'It wasn't until I went to university that I began to calm down. I started to feel more normal. I was no longer a sixteen-year-old freak with no home and parents who detested me. I was an ordinary student, living in a Hall of Residence, and doing well on my course. I discovered I had a talent for film-making. I had a future at last and I was ambitious. I virtually stopped the drugs; I calmed down. And then, in my second year, something happened. I faced up to the idea that I was gay.'

Danny's eyes widened with surprise. He glanced at

me but I was just as astonished as my son. I had had no idea of Ben's sexuality. He saw that we were both startled and smiled ruefully.

'I'm not surprised you didn't guess,' he went on. 'I went to great lengths to conceal it. I never came out at school. I had girlfriends like everyone else. Joey had no idea, nobody did. I never told a soul. But it was soul destroying, and in my second year I started to crack up. I went to gay clubs, got picked up by older men, but I hated myself. I started to drink a lot, and I got back into drugs big time; not only weed, but cocaine, ecstasy, ketamine. Eventually heroin. I wasn't an addict, but I was getting there fast. Joey couldn't understand it. He'd thought I was clean, and suddenly I was worse, more obnoxious than I'd ever been.

'We'd planned the boating holiday in Polperro for a long time, but Joey got cold feet when I fell off the wagon. He wanted to cancel it, but I was desperate to get away from Manchester, so I promised him I wouldn't do anything stupid while we were away. Joey wasn't happy, but I think he felt responsible for me.

'So off we went, and I was ecstatic at first. It couldn't last, though. Joey hadn't a clue about my sexuality –

I was still pretending to fancy girls. But I started to unravel in Polperro. You see, being gay wasn't my only secret. It wasn't even the biggest, and there was no way I could confide in Joe. The fact was . . . I was in love with him. Had been for years.

'When we'd been at our cottage for a couple of days, I got very drunk one night. Like a fool I made a pass at Joey; I climbed into his bed. He was shocked, of course. He pushed me out and we had a fight. It ended with me in tears, hysterically telling him I was in love with him.'

'He never told us about any of this,' said Adam, looking bewildered. I reached for his hand.

'He never had the chance,' I said softly. 'He disappeared soon after.'

'The next day,' continued Ben, 'I apologised and tried to explain. Joey was sympathetic, but I could tell he was deeply uncomfortable. He wanted to call time on the holiday and go back to Manchester, but I begged him to stay. I promised I wouldn't do anything stupid again. I couldn't bear the thought of us both going home, knowing that Joey would probably drift away from me out of sheer embarrassment. I'd known him since I was four, and I'd loved him for so long. The thought of losing him as a friend was horrible. Anyway, Joey agreed we should stay in Polperro, but he started going out for long walks on his own. Just to get away from me. I was miserable and heartbroken, and spent most of my time in the Blue Peter. I was drinking heavily again and one night some guys I knew from Manchester suddenly arrived. I had no idea why they were there at first. They were pretty much the scum of the earth, I knew that, but I was feeling like scum myself, full of self-loathing. I knew them well from my drug-dealing days.'

'These were the same men Seb and Nina told me about in Manchester,' said Adam to me. I squeezed his hand.

'I was just a mixed-up kid when I got to know them, but they were the real deal. Big-shot dealers and push-ers, very dangerous. I had no idea what they were doing in Polperro, but bizarrely they seemed glad to see me. They bought me endless drinks and they slipped me free cocaine. They told me they'd left Manchester for a while because it had got too hot for them; a lot of increased attention was coming their way from Manchester CID, and they decided to chill out in

Cornwall for a while. They told me it was great to see a friendly face, and they kept flattering me, saying they'd heard how talented I was, and how I was obviously heading for the big time. They were convinced I was going to be discovered and become a shit-hot Hollywood film director. Of course half of me knew it was bullshit, but my self-esteem was on the floor, especially as Joey had rejected me. I let them flatter me, and allowed myself to feel bitter about Joey. Maybe he'd feel differently about me if I was a famous director. Maybe he'd be sorry he'd turned me down.'

I felt desperately sorry for Ben. To have loved my son so much, to have wanted to impress him so he would love Ben back. I knew Joey loved Ben anyway; just not in the way he craved.

'Of course, it was ridiculous,' Ben went on. 'Joey was straight, he was never going to fancy me. But I was only twenty and, what with all the alcohol and the coke, their flattery turned my head. At that stage I had no idea what these guys were really planning, why they were in Cornwall, or why they were being so nice to me.

'One night in the pub, they told me about a "sweet

little deal" they'd done. They'd organised a massive haul of cannabis, cocaine and heroin to be shipped over from Holland. They needed to hide it for a while, and the boss decided to do that in Cornwall. It's always been a smugglers' paradise, the guys said. A record haul of marijuana, worth millions, had been smuggled ashore at Talland Bay in the seventies, and hidden in a secret compartment under the counter at the local beach café, appropriately known, even now, as The Smuggler's Rest.

'But what they were planning was a lot more audacious. The launch carrying the drugs would pull up on the southern shore of Looe Island.'

I stiffened. The island. Where my dream had taken me last night.

'That beach is completely hidden from the mainland, so it would be a perfect place to unload the cargo, but it was also a dangerous place to land, rocky and treacherous. Still, assuming it could be done, the island would make a great hiding place for the drugs, because underneath the surface it's supposed to be honeycombed with ancient caves. They could stash the stuff there; no one would ever find it except them. They told me if I helped them, they'd pay me enough to go to film school in New York. I'd already told them that it was my life's dream, but I knew I'd never be able to afford it.

'I was drunk, of course, when they told me all this, and it struck me as quite exciting. But the promise of the money had me salivating. It would mean the biggest break of my lifetime. I said I'd do it, and then asked – a bit late, of course – what they wanted me to do.

'Actually, it sounded easy. They just wanted me to go on a recce for them before the boat set off from Holland. They needed to make sure that the southern shore of the island was still accessible as a landing stage; smugglers and wreckers had used it in the past, but that was a long time ago. It was all the stuff of lore and legend, there was nobody around these days who could confirm the shore was viable for boats, but my guys needed to make sure their Dutch crew could get the stuff ashore when they landed. They wanted me to do it because everyone in the area knew who I was; I'd been coming to Polperro with Joey and his family since I was a kid, and everyone knew I was mad about sailing. Nobody would even blink if I went off in my boat to do some exploring. If these Manchester bruisers did it themselves, they'd have to charter a boat, and the skipper would have asked a lot of questions.

'So I agreed to do their recce. We shook hands on it and the deal was done.'

Chapter Forty-Eight

'Where did Joey fit in?' I asked him. 'What happened next?'

Ben began to look upset. 'That night, Joey came into the Blue Peter while I was going over the plan. He knew who those guys were of course, vicious gangsters from the Manchester underworld, and he hated me talking to them. He came straight over and asked me to leave with him. I refused, but Joe was adamant. We started to row, and one of these guys, the biggest bruiser, stood up and told Joey to leave me alone. Joe went over to the other side of the bar and started talking to Wren. Queenie was staring at us. I was sure she knew something was up. Joey threw me a filthy look and left the pub. I wanted to go after him, but the big guy wouldn't let me. They kept on buying me drinks. When I eventually got away, he followed me to the door. He swore me to secrecy. He said if I told anyone about their plans then not only was our deal off, and I could whistle for the money, but that he personally would make sure my arms were broken so badly I'd never pick up a film camera again. I got the message, and went back to our cottage.'

'Was Joey there?' I asked.

'Yes. We had a really bad fight. Joey was furious with me. He said he knew I'd got thick with that scum, as he called them, and he assumed they were giving me drugs. Eventually I broke down. I was beside myself; I was sobbing and telling Joey how much I loved him and how he'd broken my heart. And then, in a pathetic attempt to make myself look better in his eyes, I started boasting about going to film school in New York. Joe just looked at me sadly and went to his bedroom; I heard him turn the key in the lock. That made me even more upset, that he wanted to lock me out. He'd never done that before.'

'Was that the night before Joey went out in the boat on his own?' Adam looked grim but determined.

Ben nodded. His eyes glistened with tears. 'I woke late the next day, very hungover. Joey had already gone. He'd left a note on the kitchen table.'

This sad, confused young man stood up, and pulled something out of his trouser pocket. He walked over to me. He held the note out. 'Read it, Molly. I've kept it all this time. I brought it to show you today because I decided I had to tell you.'

He looked around at Adam, Danny, Lola and Edie, who was sitting open-mouthed, staring at Ben as if she'd understood every word he'd said. 'I had to tell you everything that happened.' He looked shamefaced. 'I didn't dare show you Joey's letter before. I was wrong to keep it from you. I'm sorry.'

I took the piece of paper. Ben walked back across the lawn and sat down next to Danny, whose poor face looked old before its time. Joey's letter was scrawled on a piece of A4 ripped out of an exercise book. I breathed deeply and read it:

Ben,

I'm leaving you to sleep. Last night was
bad and I guess you need to sleep it off.

I've been thinking about everything, trying
to decide what to do. I'm going out in the boat
for a bit. It always helps me to see things
clearly. All the stuff you told me last night
about those appalling shits planning a drugs
deal in the Blue Peter has horrified me.
There's no way I'm going to stand by and
watch those evil bastards involve you in
something so utterly vile. Anyway, I think the
whole idea of landing drugs on Looe Island is
absurd. There are no bloody caves there. This
isn't Treasure Island, you know. I'm going to
take the boat out there and find out if, as I
suspect, the whole scheme is a load of old
bollocks. I don't want you going out there and
risking your life for those bastards. I'm going
to prove once and for all they are a bunch of
brainless idiots way out of their depth.

I'll meet you in the Blue Peter at
lunchtime. If those sods are there, we'll leave

immediately. I think we should probably tell the police, but we'll talk about it later.

Ben, you are my oldest friend. I care about you deeply. I'm sorry it's not the way you care about me; I had no idea, and it's been a shock. But we'll get over it. You'll always be my best mate. Don't worry about anything, and look after yourself. See you later.

Joey

Adam reached out to take the letter from me, but I wouldn't let it go. I turned away from him, trying to keep myself under control, but I was hyperventilating. I thought I'd faint. My son's last letter; the last words my beautiful, kind-hearted son ever wrote. Seeing the anguish on my husband's face, I reluctantly passed the note to him.

Ben was openly weeping now.

'For him to care about me,' he muttered brokenly, 'for him to tell me to look after myself after I'd been such a fool, was so typical of Joe. I realised he was right about the drugs deal. I couldn't get in any deeper with these guys, but because they knew me and were from my home town I was scared they'd beat me up, or worse, if I went to the police. I didn't know what to do. I turned up at the Blue Peter at lunchtime, and waited for Joey. But he ... he never came back.'

Adam finished reading our son's last note and stood up.

'Right,' he said tersely. 'We're going to ring the police right now.'

I stood up too. 'No, Adam. Don't you see? There never was a drug deal. It didn't happen, did it Ben?'

He shrugged. 'I doubt it. Once I'd told the harbour-master that Joey was missing, all hell broke loose. There were coastguards and lifeboat dinghies everywhere, and local fishermen, all searching for his boat. When they found it, wrecked on the rocks near Looe, it turned into a hunt for Joey. You must remember, it went on for days. I never did that recce, and I never saw those men again either. They just disappeared.'

'Wren told me they hung around, on and off, for most of the summer,' I said.

'Well, I never saw them. But of course I went back to Manchester when you both did. I suppose they might have hung around for a while to see if they could save the deal, but the coast was heaving with searchers for weeks. I'm sure they called it off. They wouldn't have taken the risk when there was so much activity around the island.'

I stiffened. 'Ben, Joey's note said he was going to the island. I think he wanted to show you how dangerous this deal could be. He said he didn't want you risking your life. Joey may have got to Lammana.'

'Lammana?' Ben was confused.

'Looe Island. It used to be called Lammana years ago. Joey may be there. I know his boat wasn't anywhere near, but maybe Joey swam there or something.'

Adam looked at me pityingly. 'Molly, don't you remember they searched the island? Fishermen, coast-guards and police swarmed all over it. Joey wasn't there, love.'

'Yes, they combed Looe Island, the searchers,' added Ben. 'That's why I'm sure those Manchester guys wouldn't have closed their deal. They must have known it would look very suspicious if they were spotted hanging around there after Joey disappeared.' Ben looked at me sadly. 'I'm sorry, Molly. If Joey had somehow made it to the island, he would have been found. The

Wildlife Trust has people there, only a few, but Joey would have reached them. It's a really small place; and anyway, he would have wanted to be found. He must have been pretty traumatised if he'd lost his boat.'

'How would he lose his boat?' I asked.

It was Adam who replied. 'He must have been knocked overboard. It happens. He could have been caught by the boom and it knocked him in. Or maybe he lost his balance when the storm blew up. A really big wave could have thrown him over. And if the boat was on automatic pilot, it would just have gone on without him. There was no way he could have caught up with it.'

'So?' I said. 'He could have swum to the island.'

Adam shook his head. 'Molly, they searched the island,' he repeated patiently. 'He wasn't there. It's not a desert island, Moll. People, not many, but a few, work on it every day, for the Wildlife Trust. They would have found him.'

'Not if he was injured,' I said.

'Yes, Molly. Even if he was injured they would have found him. They combed every inch.'

'What about the caves?'

There was silence. I repeated my question: 'What about the caves? Did anyone search them?'

Ben said hesitantly, 'I'm not sure they even exist.'

'And yet those drug dealers wanted to use them?'

'Well, yeah; but that's why they wanted me to do a recce, to make sure they actually exist. It's all folklore. Nobody really knows.'

Adam interceded. 'But people work on the island every day. Surely these men would have been seen if they'd tried to land drugs there?'

Ben shook his head. 'That's just it. They were going to land on the southern side of the island. There's no proper foreshore there and it's very dangerous, but that's where smugglers used to get onto the island in the old days. It's completely invisible from the mainland. And then they'd hide the stuff in the caves – if they exist.'

'And you never did the recce, but Joey said he was going to, didn't he? Well, suppose he did. Suppose he found the caves, and then he ... ' I couldn't finish the sentence. I made a supreme effort and carried on. 'Suppose he found the caves but was injured somehow? Suppose he couldn't come back? Suppose he's still ... there?'

Adam and Ben sat down suddenly. Poor Danny; he had been pacing round the garden since Ben finished his account of Joe's last evening. Now he was reading his brother's letter, running his hands through his hair, tears pouring down his cheeks. Lola had taken Edie inside; the poor mite had looked worried enough when Ben started crying. She would have been terrified if she'd seen her daddy's tears as well.

Now Danny looked up, and stared at his father. 'I think Mum's right,' he said. 'I think we need to search the island caves. We should talk to the coastguard and the police. Now.'

Chapter Forty-Nine

Afterwards I remembered standing on Hannafore Point, the island sparkling and sunny before us. I can still see in my mind the three orange dinghies speeding towards Lammana, bearing Lifeboat volunteers and coastguards. Behind them were half a dozen fishing boats. Wren and his friends had joined their fathers in the search for my son. I remember feeling anxious, but also terribly grateful. None of them had laughed at me when I told them that I knew where Joey was. They had looked thoughtful and serious, and now, as I watched, they were on their way to find him.

I remember Adam beckoning me to follow him back to Looe Harbour. That's where the boats had set off from, and that's where they would return with whatever news they had gathered from their subterranean search.

I remember we bought tea at the harbour and sat on a bench. Adam, Ben and Danny had wanted to go with the searchers, but accepted that their lack of knowledge of the terrain might hinder the others. Lola and Edie had stayed behind at Coombe.

I remember the long wait, the hours we sat there with hope and dread in our hearts. I remember Adam's start when he saw the dinghies coming back.

I remember he told me to stay on the bench while he walked over to greet the boats as they reached harbour. I remember Danny squeezing my hand so hard it hurt. I was glad of the crunching pain. It took my mind off the agony in my heart.

I remember the look on Adam's face as he turned back to me after talking to the grave-faced coastguards. I remember Wren jumping off his father's boat and walking slowly towards me.

I knew they'd found him.

Chapter Fifty

They'd found Joey in a cave not far from the foreshore of the island. Later, after I'd recovered from the horror caused by the sight of the body bag on the leading dinghy, after Adam and Danny had taken me back to Coombe, they told me he must have managed to swim ashore after he was knocked out of the boat. How he had stumbled into the cave no one knew, but his body had been hidden. They found him at the bottom of a crevasse, his pelvis shattered. He had fallen into a deep ditch, probably stumbling around in the dark, disorientated and soaked to the skin after he fell off the boat.

They brought him back to the mainland. There was little left of him except for his lovely bones. They found his watch, engraved with a message from us on his eighteenth birthday, and a signet ring etched with his initials, a Christmas present I gave him after his first term at university. They found his sailing jacket, still wrapped around his body. And they found, zipped in a pocket and wrapped tightly in a waterproof sealed plastic bag, a copy of the *Tide Times*, and an old biro.

He had written on the little yellow book, the bible of Cornish sailors. He had scrawled a message across the tide tables, barely legible. But I could decipher it. He wrote it for me.

Mum, it began.

Mum, I don't know how long I've been here but I'm very weak. I fell into this crevasse, and my leg's broken. There's a small amount of fresh water seeping through into this hole, there must be a spring nearby. I keep licking the walls, and I've been taking some paracetamol I found in my jacket pocket, but the pain is awful. Please find me soon, Mum.

The next few lines, the last he wrote, were heart-breaking.

Mum, I keep passing out. I'm falling asleep and I want to. The pain's not so bad when I'm sleeping. Soon I don't think I'll wake up again, and I hope for that. Mum, I love you and Dad so much. I hope you find me here, because I can't imagine what it will be like for you if you never see me again. Please give my watch to Danny and my signet ring to Rowan.

Mum, Mum, find me. Please find me. I want to feel your arms around me. I love you. Please find me and hold me.

That was it. I heard his voice again, the voice which had reached after his death as I sat in the garden at Coombe, the voice that had pulled me to the island again and again after he disappeared. 'Mother, please find me. Please hold me.'

Chapter Fifty-One

Some time after we arrived back at Coombe, while Adam was on the phone arranging Joey's funeral at Talland church, Lola brought a cup of tea up to my bedroom and gently asked if I was up to seeing visitors. I shook my head, but Lola said she thought I would like to see one of them, who had introduced herself to my daughter-in-law as Hope's mother. She had brought my things back from the cottage. I hadn't been back there since they found Joey; I had come straight to Coombe.

Josie told Lola she wanted to help me as I had helped her. I went down to the living room. Josie stood by the fireside, another, older, woman beside her. My friend walked over immediately and embraced me. I cried on her shoulder as she had cried on mine. The other woman stood patiently by.

Eventually I got myself under some kind of control, and Josie beckoned to the older woman.

'Molly, this is Thelma Brookes. She's a bereavement counsellor.'

Thelma. The woman Jamie Torrance had suggested I see when I was ill at Coombe.

Thelma Brookes nodded at me and said slowly, 'Molly, do forgive me if I'm intruding. I've been working with Josie about Hope's death. She asked me if I'd come and see you. I understand about losing children, you see. I've lost one myself.'

Josie squeezed my shoulder. 'I thought you might like to talk. Thelma has made such a difference to me, made me feel stronger. I just wanted you to meet her, so you can decide if you want to see her again, perhaps later, if not now.'

Thelma had a kind face; but even so, I knew I didn't want to talk to a therapist. Not now. Joey had been my therapist. He had come to me when I most needed him.

I remembered my dream when I went to Lammana with Len, when I saw first Hope and then Joey in that golden grotto of soft warm light. I remembered they had both looked serene, radiant, had said they were at peace. Hope said I should tell Josie that. Joey said I should always remember it; his spirit intended me to take comfort from his words. Suffering and death are inevitable, but afterwards comes peace.

And, as if she read my mind, Thelma said, 'You must embrace your release from suffering, Molly. It's been five years. Enough now. Enough.'

There was a slight noise from the French window behind me. I turned. Edie stumbled in from the garden, her wide eyes huge and curious. She looked around, saw me and immediately ran towards me with her arms outstretched, chortling happily. 'Nanamoll,' she laughed. I scooped her up, held her close and closed my eyes. 'When we first got here,' I said to Thelma, 'I thought she was the key to my future. I thought she would point me towards finding Joey. I was so wrong.' I kissed Edie and rocked her in my arms.

'What makes you think you were wrong?' asked Thelma.

'Because she wasn't the key at all. I didn't find Joey through her. I found him through Ben, and all I found was his dead body. I seemed to see a false dawn when I looked at my grandchild. I suppose I was a fool to think so much rested on her tiny shoulders.' I nuzzled Edie, loving the feel of her soft cheeks against my face.

'But of course she's the key. She is absolutely the key to your future, your happiness. What you saw in Edie is your path back to love. You've found Joey now, and naturally you're grief-stricken; but you will walk forward, and you will have Edie's hand to hold. Believe me, Molly. I know.'

I held the baby. As if she sensed my need, she didn't wriggle. Instead she rested her little curly head on my shoulder, and crooned softly to herself.

Adam came in. He looked at me gravely and told me the funeral would be in two days' time at Talland. 'The vicar said that could be arranged, and I didn't think it was sensible to wait any longer,' he said. 'We've waited long enough, Molly. So has Joey. Let's get him into the ground where he will be safe.'

I nodded. Yes, that was the right thing to do.

Chapter Fifty-Two

Joey's casket lay in front of the altar at Talland church. The ancient building was packed, but I was too focused with grief and pride to look at anything but the coffin, only half aware of the crowds of people who had flocked here to say a final farewell to my son. I was, though, deeply conscious of Adam, Danny and Lola by my side. We'd left Edie in the care of the deeply kind owners of the Talland Bay Hotel, playing happily among the elves and fairies, scrambling up to sit on the giant snail and the winged horse.

I listened to the prayers and hymns with rapt

attention, but taking little in. All I knew was that I was at an event too momentous even to describe. I focused on the coffin before me, and what it contained. I stroked the soft silk pouch on my lap, feeling the small objects inside, Joey's watch and his signet ring. The pouch was where I kept all my most precious things: the hospital identity bracelets both my babies wore when they were born; tiny, fluffy locks of hair clipped from their heads when they were only weeks old; the first milk teeth they had lost, hidden away by the maternal tooth fairy so she could treasure them for ever more.

As we left the church to lay Joey in his freshly dug grave, I was overcome by the memory of the graveyard dream I had had in the night garden at Coombe. Just as in my vision, the priest led the procession, Joey's casket carried by Adam, Danny, Ben and Wren. I watched in wonderment, remembering how in my prescient fantasy I'd seen Len, whom I'd never met at that point; the man and woman holding hands with the grown girl with red hair.

The moonlit memories of that strange night filled my head with gauze; hazy thoughts as I watched the actual funeral of my son. This was real; what I'd seen while I slept in the garden of our rented farmhouse was a haunted dream, but extraordinarily emotionally accurate. All the tremulous signs I'd seen engulfing the principal figures of my vision had come to pass.

Len, now but not then dead, surrounded by twinkling golden rays which touched his face as if to cheer him up. Josie and Tony, holding onto flame-haired Hope, about to succumb to the fate that had dogged her all her life, but nevertheless caressed by the same teasing, playful shimmering dots, bidding her welcome to the light.

I forced myself to come back, to watch the ceremony unfolding before me. I had no further need of visions. This was my son's burial; this was truly the end, and yet I had my child at last. Here in Talland churchyard, Joey at last existed for me. I had his body to bury. I would have his headstone to mark his passing; a place to sit and talk with my poor dead boy.

I threw my single red rose tenderly into Joey's grave, and stood back to watch his friends cast their white ones after mine. Only two days' notice, yet so many of those who knew and loved him at school and university had come to his funeral to witness his burial at last, to see him found and loved, and laid into sacred ground.

I looked fondly at all of them; but all I could think about was the children who played among them; always, always, the children.

Chapter Fifty-Three

We held the wake at the Talland Bay Hotel; wine and sandwiches for the throngs who had come to say good-bye to our son.

After a while we drifted down from the terrace to the sweeping lawn leading down to the bay. We stood at the cliff edge, Adam, Danny and I, watching the sea, the sea I should hate for its claim on my son, but whose beauty I would always love. The sight of the ocean, gleaming with otherworldly promise, filled me with tenderness for my lost boy. Lola joined us, Edie riding on her hip. We formed a small family circle, our arms wrapped loosely round each other; we wept and prayed for Joey, and then, together, raised our glasses of red wine to the sea. We toasted our beloved Joe and his everlasting memory.

Behind us came Ben's gentle voice. We turned; beside him stood a young woman. I remembered her too from my graveyard vision, but I had no idea who she was. Ben took her hand, looked at all of us, and said, quite formally: 'I'd like you all to meet Rowan.'

She smiled at us, small, dark, sweet and unmistakably Cornish. She looked shy, but spoke quite steadily in a quiet determined voice. 'I'm sorry, I know you are all very sad. So am I, but at least I know now what happened to Joey. Ben said you've got something for me, I think.'

Astonished, I looked at this sweet-faced girl. 'Rowan?' I asked. She nodded. I took the silk pouch of precious things from my bag. I put my hand inside and brushed through the contents until I touched what I needed.

'Joey wrote a note,' I said. 'He said I was to give his signet ring to Rowan. That's you?'

'Yes, that's me.'

I held out the initialled ring. She took it, and slid it onto her wedding finger.

Ben spoke, almost proudly. 'Joey and Rowan met in Polperro the summer before he died. It was a complete love-match. Before I idiotically told Joe how I felt about him, he'd already told me he wanted to marry Rowan. He was planning to bring her home to meet you as soon as our holiday ended.'

'But why didn't you say? Why didn't you find us?' I asked, unable to grasp this sudden turn of events.

Rowan looked nervous. She glanced up at Ben, who nodded encouragingly. 'Go on, Rowan, tell them,' he said. 'It's all right. They're good people. Tell them why you didn't want to find them.'

'It was difficult,' she said in her soft Cornish accent. 'You see, I have no one in the world. I was brought up in care. I was working as a hotel chambermaid when I met Joey, living at the hotel, the only home I had. We were so happy we had found each other. He was wonderful to me; he said he would take me with him when he went back to university. He said his parents would love me. He told me he wanted to marry me. I thought I was in a dream. I was so excited to meet his family.

And then ... they found his boat, but no trace of him. I never saw him again. I thought I'd die of grief.'

'But, Rowan,' I said again. 'Why didn't you get in touch with us? Why didn't you tell us? We could have helped you.'

'I didn't think you'd believe me,' she said softly. 'I never knew my parents. My mother gave me up at birth. Until Joey, I'd never trusted anyone. I just moved from foster home to foster home. I had nobody to vouch for me. I thought you'd think I was lying; that I was an opportunist.'

'Opportunist?' asked Adam, puzzled. 'But how could you be?'

Ben looked at me. 'You remember I told you I'd moved to Cornwall because I'd fallen in love with someone?' he asked.

I nodded. 'So it was Rowan?' I asked.

He smiled. 'No, Molly. Hardly. My sexuality hasn't changed. No, I love Rowan as a friend, but it was someone else I moved to Cornwall for.'

He looked behind him towards the top of the meadow. Wren was standing at the edge of the terrace, watching us. Ben nodded and waved at him. Suddenly a small boy whirled down the slope, whooping and shrieking as he ran. He reached Ben and Rowan and hurled himself at them. Rowan shushed him and he stood giggling at us, his eyes alight with mischief.

'Molly and Adam,' said Ben in the same formal way he had introduced Rowan. 'I want you to meet Joseph. He's four years old and an absolute terror.'

I stared at this excited, full-of-life child. I knew exactly what I was looking at: his dark hair, his shining brown eyes, his nose, his mouth; God, his mouth.

I saw my boy, my son; I saw my grandson.

I looked at Adam. He, too, looked amazed but over-joyed. Like me, he recognised this child; he knew immediately the man who had fathered him. He was looking at the son of the lost boy we loved so much.

I looked at Edie, who was wriggling with impatience to get down from Lola's hip and meet this strange new playmate. I looked at Adam, and then at Danny. Both of them stood in shocked astonishment, their faces wreathed in delighted happiness.

'No one knows,' said Ben. 'Here, he's just another kid.'

The boy clocked Edie, and started to tickle her bare feet. She crowed with laughter.

'I've looked after Rowan and Joseph ever since he was born,' said Ben. He looked away at the sea. 'I wanted to make amends. I … I hoped Joey would know somehow, would understand what I was doing.

'I know I should have let you know about the baby. Rowan didn't want me to – she thought you wouldn't believe her. I don't blame her though; I blame myself. I was too scared to talk to you again, to bring it all back. I felt so guilty about Joey … in the end, it was easier just to block it out. I thought if I looked after the baby it might somehow be enough.'

Ben looked at the little boy. Joseph, still hanging on to Edie's little toe, glanced at each of us in turn, his eyes sparkling with curiosity.

'Introduce yourself, Joseph,' said his mother. 'Introduce yourself to your family.'

He straightened up and marched towards us, his small face now serious. He held out his hand, shook Adam's first and then mine. And then, looking deep into my eyes, he said with all the polite formality of a well-mannered young man four times his age:

'How do you do? My name is Joseph Gabriel Tremain.'

Acknowledgements

Everyone says writing a second novel is tough, and how right they are. For their fortitude in putting up with my hesitations, and their constant encouragement, I would like to thank the following vital people:

First, my editor at Sphere, Cath Burke, who despite producing a far more important creation of her own, her first baby, Felix, while I was writing, nevertheless found the time and energy to talk me through this book.

Second, huge thanks to my Agent, Luigi Bonomi, for, among many other helpful suggestions, encouraging and supporting my belief in the title of this book, from the immensely moving bereavement poem by Mary Elizabeth Frye. And for all the laughs Luigi and

I had at the Emirates Literary Festival in Dubai with his witty wife, Alison.

Thirdly, many thanks to the wonderful team at Sphere who have been so kind and helpful while I struggled to produce this second book: Rebecca, Thalia and Kirsteen.

I'm so grateful to all of you – Cath, Luigi, Alison, Rebecca, Thalia and Kirsteen; your support, warmth and, above all, senses of humour and proportion, have been essential in stopping me tearing my hair out on more than one occasion.

Two very special thanks are due. Firstly to our first grandchild, Ivy Florence, who was born on October 16th 2012, just days after my first novel, *Eloise*, was published, and who throughout this second book has been the gorgeous, chubby and chatty inspiration for Molly's granddaughter Edie.

And, as always, enormous love and thanks to my husband, Richard, who has spent many a patient hour giving me feedback and ideas. We may no longer work together on the telly, but are still adroitly enmeshed behind the scenes.

Many, many thanks, and as Bella Emberg used to say at the end of Morecambe and Wise: 'I love you all'.

Author Note

I've obviously taken some artistic liberties with Looe Island in Cornwall – once, many centuries ago, known more romantically as the Island of St Michael of Lammana. In Celtic times, the name Lammana was derived from the Cornish word 'Lan', meaning a Celtic religious enclosure and, 'managh', meaning 'monk'; so Lammana roughly translates as 'a holy place where monks dwell'. I am indebted for this knowledge and many other invaluable facts about the island's history to Mike Dunn, whose fascinating little book *The Looe Island Story, An illustrated History of St George's Island* helped me enormously with the island's past and in particular with its rich religious significance and smuggling history. 'St George's Island' is yet another name for this intriguing little place, first surfacing in 1579, a fact again documented by Mike Dunn.

I am also indebted to two more beguiling booklets by Rose Mullins: *The Inn on the Moor, A History of Jamaica Inn* and *White Witches, a study of Charmers*. Rose Mullins is an enticing chronicler of old Cornish legends, lore and people. I thoroughly recommend you read her little books if you are as entranced by the powerful mystery of Cornwall as I am.

And finally I would like to pay tribute to the legendary Atkins sisters, Babs and Evelyn, two brave and intrepid women from the comfortable and safe Epsom Downs in the Home Counties who bought the island in 1964. They fell in love with it, despite the extraordinary challenges they faced in bringing a small measure of civilisation to this windswept, storm-tossed place, on which they were often stranded for weeks at a time by the raging seas. Their life there is chronicled in Evelyn Atkins's entrancing book, *We Bought an Island*. I can't recommend it enough, both for the vividness in which she writes about island life, and for the wonderful way it shows just what these suburban sisters from Surrey were capable of. Talk about the empowerment of women! These two strong ladies were, without knowing or boasting about it, the embodiment of the burgeoning early Women's Liberation movement.

They also loved a good party with their neighbours in Looe, and their legendary recipe for homemade Elderflower 'Champagne' is included at the back of Mike Dunn's book, *The Looe Island Story*. It's delicious, so thanks, Mike, and cheers.

Questions for your Book Club

1 *I Do Not Sleep* deals with the devastating subject of losing a child. Five years on from Joey's disappearance, Adam accepts that he is dead and is trying to move on but Molly won't give up until he is found. Why do you think they have such different approaches to the situation?

2 Adam wants their family to visit Cornwall again for a holiday. Do you think this was a wise decision? Do you think you would want to go back there?

3 Molly declares she'll 'do everything in [her] power, move heaven and earth, to find him.' Put yourself in Molly's position. What do you think you would do in her situation?

4 What do you think about the way Adam copes with what is happening to Molly?

5 In the novel, a variety of characters set out to help Molly with her grief. Why do you think she is so determined to find her son alone?

6 When Molly moves into the cottage by herself she strikes up a close friendship with Josie, whose daughter has Downs syndrome. Why do you think this relationship is important?

7 There are very complex relationships in the novel – husband and wife, mother and child, siblings and childhood friends. How does the author portray these relationships?

8 Adam and Molly's marriage suffers greatly under the weight of their grief. Discuss what the novel tells us about the complexities of marriage and relationships in the hardest of times.

9 This novel has a very strong sense of place. How do you think that the distinctive setting contributes to the story?

10 Discuss the ending of the novel – do you feel that everything is resolved?

Cornish Charmers

As *The Wizard of Oz* lays claim to the Wicked Witch of the East, so Cornwall proudly presents the county's White Witches of the West.

The origins of these practitioners of the ancient Wicca craft are shrouded in time, and by no means confined to Cornwall. Throughout the world shamanism, the rituals of healing involving incantations, charms, talismen, amulets and sacrifice, date back to the Stone Age. Long ago, healing, using herbal remedies, was the province of women. Priestesses held secret cures close to their breast, but during Druidic times men of magic, like the legendary wizard Merlin, replaced the women. By the time Christianity had reached Britain, brought by St Augustine (in AD 597), Druidic lore had mostly dissipated. In its place, Wicca, or the 'wise craft', flourished throughout the towns and villages of the British Isles, conducted mostly by Wise Women who handed down their powers from mother to daughter, and used plants, animals and even human parts to make ointments, pills and potions.

Over the years, these witches became shunned, and practiced their art in hidden places. They were subject to terrible persecution, particularly in the sixteenth and seventeenth centuries, but for some reason in Cornwall these Wise Ones continued to flourish, probably because this part of the west country was so remote. Roads were rare, and when they did exist were scarcely fit to travel, so the county's inaccessibility protected its healers from punishment.

But since those days, Cornish Charmers have become completely part of the Christian faith. They still exist, and would hate to be associated with witchcraft and paganism. They believe their powers are a gift from God, and recite their charms like prayers, ending with the words 'In the Name of the Father, Son and Holy Ghost'. In the far west, the wisdom of Charmers is still sought by farmers and villagers.

Charmers specialise in different ways of healing. Some can stop bleeding; others can cure warts, shingles, excema, ringworm and adder bites. Others can set bones, curing animals and humans. Many can douse successfully for water far underground.

Holy wells are common, even rife in Cornwall. These natural pure springs bubbling up from underground are used, together with strips of cloth from the person to be healed, for charms. Sometimes a lock of hair or nail clippings are placed in a charm bag and hung around the well. Charmers believe that this means that the spirit of the afflicted person will continue to absorb the magic properties of the sacred water.

Nowadays, Charmers believe their powers are passed from mother to son and father to daughter. Some have the gift of second sight and use crystal balls. Some are clairvoyant and can predict the future, including death.

All of them, like Len in *I Do Not Sleep*, believe that their powers are gifts from God. They have a simple faith and a genuine desire to do good and help people. Even today tales of Charmers' uncanny abilities abound in rural Cornwall. One of my oldest friends used to visit an old man who gave uncannily accurate forecasts for her family. She told me that with him she always felt in the company of extraordinary insight and benign, almost supernatural wisdom. His name was Len. I never met him, but I like to think he would have approved of the Len in my book, whose last mission in life was to bring peace to Molly Gabriel.

With grateful thanks to Rose Mullins for her book *White Witches – A Study of Charmers*, to which I owe my knowledge of these fascinating men and women who are still such an intriguing part of rural Cornish life.

A Q&A with Judy Finnigan

I Do Not Sleep **encompasses some quite serious themes. Where did the idea for the book come from?**
There are many drowning tragedies in Cornwall; fishermen perish at sea, holidaymakers mistake the tides or can be caught off guard by sudden squalls. I've been aware of these real-life stories, and I wondered how a mother would cope if her grown-up child were to be lost at sea while on holiday in Cornwall. Molly's passion to find Joey after he disappears in a boating accident is, I think, elemental to motherhood. She needs to find him, and if he is not alive, she needs his body to bury and mourn over. Molly's love for her son and her journey to peace and reconciliation are the central themes of the book.

How carefully did you plan the novel in advance?
I didn't really plan it beyond the initial accident in which Joey disappears. Molly's grief and her quest to discover what happened to him unfolded as I wrote.

When and where did you write the book?
I started it in Cornwall but I also wrote at home in London, and even on holiday in France. Deadlines loom, and even though in an ideal world I would have completed *I Do Not Sleep* in Cornwall, needs must; actually, I found I could write almost anywhere this time, to my amazement.

You are so well-known for championing books and reading, especially through the Richard and Judy Book Club with WHSmith. How do you think reading so many books affected your writing?
We both love working on the Richard and Judy Book Club with WHSmith. Supporting so many excellent novels for the club inevitably

means it's more than daunting for us to write our own. We are always aware that we are both taking a risk. But I love reading and I think evaluating so many inspiring books for the club has added enormously to my knowledge, and my ability to write. I do feel that if you want to be an author, you absolutely must love reading. It's wonderful when someone else's novel opens up your mind and imagination.

There are some quite mysterious and supernatural elements in the book, particularly with Len, the Cornish Charmer; do you, personally, believe in such things?

The supernatural elements in *I Do Not Sleep* (and also in my first novel, *Eloise*) are very important to me. I'm never sure exactly where I stand on, say, believing in ghosts, or the strange psychic awareness of Cornish Charmers like Len, but I do believe that in this life we are surrounded by membranes through which we may not see, but can occasionally perceive worlds and truths other than those we know. I believe deep love, such as that felt for a mother for her child, can allow us sometimes to cross so-called psychic barriers. And I think love and grief can propel us into places we never knew existed.

Which characters in *I Do Not Sleep* did you most enjoy writing?

I always love my main female characters; Cathy in *Eloise*, and Molly in *I Do Not Sleep* both contain elements of myself. And I love their husbands, Chris and Adam, both baffled by their wives' strange ideas and often irritated – even frightened – by the women's behaviour, but ultimately loyal and loving.

Have you any plans for your next novel?

No idea, I'm afraid. I've got the kind of brain which exhausts itself by the end of writing a book, and needs, like soil, to lie fallow for a while before recovering its fertility. I hope and pray I get another idea soon!